AQUARIUS

AQUARIUS

AQUARIUS

AQUARIUS

Catcher

一如《麥田捕手》的主角，
我們站在危險的崖邊，
抓住每一個跑向懸崖的孩子。
Catcher，是對孩子的一生守護。

聯合報策劃・編譯／感謝AIT協助
取材自President Barack Obama In His Own Words，並感謝美國在台協會協助提供文稿

敢於大膽希望

歐巴馬七篇關鍵演說

　　本書是認識新任美國總統歐巴馬非常重要的資料。通過翻譯，中文讀者可以了解他的思想和願景。藉由書中系列詞彙與語法解析，讀者可以直接體會歐巴馬總統簡潔流暢、鏗鏘有力的英語演說。

　　This book provides very important material for understanding America's new president, Barack Obama. Through the Chinese translation, Chinese-language readers can come to know America's new president's thoughts and hopes. Those readers who wish to experience President Obama's eloquent English directly can use this book's helpful glossaries and grammatical explanations.

——Stephen M. Young, Director, Taipei Office, American institute in Taiwan

【前言】

敢於大膽希望

——歐巴馬七篇關鍵演說

聯合報策劃・編譯／感謝AIT協助

取材自 President Barack Obama in His Own Words，並感謝美國在台協會協助提供文稿

◎ 陸以正（無任所大使）

美國第四十四任總統歐巴馬（Barack Hussein Obama），本來就是雄辯滔滔的演說家。從華盛頓一七八九年在紐約市就任第一屆總統算起，迄今兩百二十年裡，歐巴馬既是第二位最年輕的白宮主人，更是第一位黑人坐上總統寶座。

僅就本書第一篇他的就職演說而言，報載全世界聆聽的人達十億之眾，超過美國人口三倍有餘。台灣也有不少人犧牲睡眠，在一月二十日午夜打開電視聆聽轉播。

總統日理萬機，白宮設有演說撰稿人（speechwriter）代筆，最負盛名的是替甘迺迪（John F. Kennedy）捉刀的索倫生（Theodore Sorenson）。

一九六一年甘迺迪就職演說的名句：Don't ask what your country can do for you; ask what you can do for your country，膾炙人口，就出於索倫生筆下。

美國歷史上出於總統之口的名言，還有不少。其中只有林肯在蓋茲堡演說（Gettysburg Address）裡的of the people, by the people, and for the people，中文譯作「民有、民治、民享」是他自己寫的。其餘如小羅斯福（Franklin D. Roosevelt）的We have nothing to fear but fear itself，譯成「我們唯一需要害怕的，就是害怕本身」，也常被後人引用。這句話是他自己或任職國務院的Sumner Welles寫的，至今尚無定論。

黑人民權運動領袖馬丁·路德·金恩牧師（Martin Luther King）的「我有一個夢」（I Have a Dream）演說，不但激勵了五千餘萬黑人，也感動了許多白人。他也是歐巴馬崇拜的偶像；今年一月十五日是金恩牧師八十歲冥誕日，五天後歐氏的就職講稿自然要提到這位先驅。

本書共選譯歐巴馬七篇演說，從二〇〇四年在民主黨推舉總統候選人大會上的主題演講（keynote address）起，到二〇〇九年就職，橫跨五年時間，讀後能把握他一生重要關鍵。

部分媒體把歐巴馬的演說，歸功於他幕僚中負責撰寫演講稿、年僅二十七歲的法福如（Jon Favreau），我不完全同意。歐巴馬能在哥倫比亞大學和哈佛法學院畢業，做過《哈佛法學評論》（*Harvard Law Review*）主編，才華優越無庸置疑，他的英文寫作能力更是有目共睹，令人讚不絕口。

他從前年春天開始，和希拉蕊（*Hillary Rodman Clinton*）競爭民主黨提名，激戰一年半之久。無論何時、在何種場合，歐巴馬起立演說，總是滔滔不絕，口若懸河，證明他是天生的演說家。合理的判斷，應該說這許多篇演講，都是他和法福如兩人合作的果實。

　　本書中譯文由聯合報編譯組執筆，以對原文忠實為第一要件。中英對
照，並排刊印，希望對學習英文的人能有幫助。

目錄

專文推薦／楊甦棣（美國在台協會台北辦事處處長）   009

前言／陸以正   011

The Remaking of America
再造美國——歐巴馬就職演說

2009年1月20日於華府--017

Change Has Come to America
改變終於來到了美國——歐巴馬當選演說

2008年11月4日於芝加哥--045

A World That Stands As One
四海一家——歐巴馬參議員演說

2008年7月24日於德國柏林市--073

A New Strategy for a New World
重建我們的盟友關係：新世界的新戰略

2008年7月15日於華府--111

A More Perfect Union
一個更完美的聯邦——歐巴馬參議員演說
2008年3月18日於賓州費城---157

Our Past, Future & Vision for America
我們的過去、未來和美國的願景
——宣布競選總統　2007年2月10日於伊利諾州春田市------------------------199

231 The Audacity of Hope
無畏的希望——2004年民主黨全國代表大會主題演講
2004年7月27日於麻州波士頓---231

Washington D.C., January 20, 2009

The Remaking of America

——Barack Obama's Inauguration Speech

2009年1月20日於華府

再造美國

——歐巴馬就職演說

◎ 深度導讀：陸以正（無任所大使）

◎ 單字、文句解析：李振清（世新大學英語系客座教授、世新大學前人文社會學院院長、前教育部國際文教處處長）

◎ 翻譯：聯合報國際新聞中心編譯組

◎ 審訂：彭鏡禧（國立臺灣大學外文系及戲劇系特聘教授）

第一部分 深度導讀

讓我們重建美國

二〇〇九年一月二十日歐巴馬的就職演說

◎陸以正（無任所大使）

美國第四十四任總統歐巴馬本來就是雄辯滔滔的演說家。從華盛頓一七八九年在紐約就任第一屆總統算起，迄今兩百二十年裡，歐巴馬既是第二位最年輕的白宮主人，更是第一位黑人坐上總統寶座。他這篇就職演說，據說全世界聆聽人數達十億之眾，超過美國人口三倍有餘。

部分媒體把這篇演說歸功於他幕僚中負責撰寫講稿，年僅二十七歲的法福如（Jon Favreau），恐怕不盡可靠。歐巴馬在哥倫比亞大學和哈佛法學院畢業，做過《哈佛法學評論》（Harvard Law Review）社長亦即總編輯，才華過人，無庸置疑。媒體又說，法福如是在一家「星巴克」咖啡館裡，用手提電腦寫出初稿。合理的說法應該是，這篇演講是他們兩人的共同創作。

歐巴馬站在國會大廈（The Capitol）南面安全玻璃圍繞的講台上，向現場萬餘聽眾，以及全球電視觀眾發表就職演說時，手中並沒有拿這篇經過千錘百鍊的講稿，他的姿勢自然，語氣堅定，聲音激昂，照例說一些感謝話後，直接進入主題。

歐巴馬也坦承美國在過去「未能作出困難的決定，為新時代預作準備」。其後果是民眾喪失信心，認為美國勢將步入逐漸衰退之途。但他說：美國不會退縮，重建美國的工作即將開始。

　　其次是鼓舞民眾的勇氣。歐巴馬引用了獨立宣言人人生而平等、自由、並有權追求福祉的詞句。但他緊接著就說：偉大不會從天而降，必須付出代價，用血汗去換來。懦弱、投機取巧、耽於安樂的人不會成功。美國必須倚賴不問出身高低、不畏艱險困難、肯拚命苦幹的男女們，肩負起重建一個富強社會的責任。

　　再次是灌輸有志者事竟成的觀念。歐巴馬提醒聽眾說：美國仍是世界上最繁榮、最強大的國家，美國商品仍受各國歡迎，生產力也並未減退。美國人只消振作精神，捲起袖子打拚，該做的事多得數不清：從道路到供電網，從發展科技到建立全民健保制，從尋找替代能源到提高教育水準，這些都是迫不及待的課題。他要檢討政府所有施政計畫，以贏得百姓的信任。

　　然後他把眼光擴大到美國國境以外，以國防為主題。歐巴馬說：美國的法治與人權觀念是照亮世界的明燈。美國並非僅靠飛彈和坦克，才擊敗法西斯主義和共產主義，所倚賴的是與盟邦對民主自由的共同信念。他要負責地把伊拉克交還給伊人自主，也要摧毀阿富汗的恐怖集團。美國不會為自己的生活方式道歉，更不會向敵人屈膝。

　　作為新任總統，他深知各國都急於知道他將如何處理對外關係。歐巴馬強調美國是個多民族、多文化的國家；從本身經驗，深知世界正在日益變小，必須營造一個嶄新的和平時代。他呼籲伊斯蘭教國家和他尋求共同利益，並互相尊重。對於獨裁殘暴的領袖，他說：你們站在歷史錯誤的那邊。他也希望富國對窮國伸出援手，因為世界在變遷中，各國都應隨著改變。

　　從各個戰場的美軍士兵，他想到在阿靈頓公墓（Arlington National Cemetery）裡長眠的陣亡將士，號召美國人學習他們無私的奉獻。他說：美國面臨的挑戰和武器或許前所未見，但忠誠和愛國心永遠都不會改變，這也就是為什麼他父親幾十年前還不能在白人餐館用餐，而他今天能站在這裡，宣誓就任美國最高職位的原因。

第二部分 主文/中譯

主文中譯◎聯合報國際新聞中心編譯組
單字解說◎李振清（世新大學英語系客座教授、世新大學前人文社會學院院長、前教育部國際文教處處長）

My fellow citizens:
I stand here today **humbled** by the task before us, grateful for the trust you have **bestowed, mindful** of the sacrifices borne by our ancestors. I thank President Bush for his service to our nation, as well as the generosity and cooperation he has shown throughout this **transition**.

Forty-four Americans have now taken the presidential **oath**. The words have been spoken during rising tides of **prosperity** and the still waters of peace. Yet, every so often, the oath is taken amidst gathering clouds and raging storms. At these moments, America has carried on not simply because of the skill or vision of those in high office, but because **We the People** have remained faithful to the ideals of our forebearers, and true to our **founding documents**.

So it has been. So it must be with this generation of Americans.

單 字 解 說

◎ humble（v.）原為形容詞「謙卑」，此處的humbled作動詞（過去分詞），意為「令人感到謙卑」。
◎ bestow（v.）賜予。
◎ mindful（adj.）"to be mindful of" 對於某事緬懷在心、銘記在心。
◎ transition（n.）過渡；交接——此指政權移轉。
◎ oath（n.）誓言。

各位同胞：

今天我站在這裡，為眼前的重責大任感到謙卑，對各位的信任心懷感激，對先賢的犧牲銘記在心。我要謝謝布希總統為這個國家的服務，也感謝他在政權轉移期間的寬厚和配合。

四十四位美國人發表過總統就職誓言，這些誓詞或是在繁榮富強及和平寧靜之際發表，或是在烏雲密布，時局動盪之時。在艱困的時候，美國能篳裘相繼，不僅因為居高位者有能力或願景，也因為人民持續對先人的抱負有信心，也忠於創建我國的法統。

過去如此。這一代美國人也必如此。

◎ prosperity（n.）繁榮。
◎ We the People（片語）「我們人民」——《美國憲法》序言的第一句。
◎ forebearer（n.）先人；祖宗。較通用的是forebear。
◎ founding documents（n.）立國的重要文件——指《美國憲法》、《獨立宣言》等重要文件。

That we are in the midst of crisis is now well understood. Our nation is at war, against a far-reaching network of violence and hatred. Our economy is badly weakened, a consequence of greed and irresponsibility on the part of some, but also our **collective** failure to make hard choices and prepare the nation for a new age. Homes have been lost; jobs **shed**; businesses **shuttered**. Our health care is too costly; our schools fail too many; and each day brings further evidence that the ways we use energy strengthen our **adversaries** and threaten our planet.

 These are the **indicators** of crisis, subject to data and statistics. Less measurable but no less **profound** is a **sapping** of confidence across our land a **nagging** fear that America's **decline** is inevitable, and that the next generation must **lower its sights**.

 Today I say to you that the challenges we face are real. They are serious and they are many. They will not be met easily or in a short span of time. But know this, America: They will be met.

 On this day, we gather because we have chosen hope over fear, **unity of purpose** over conflict and **discord**.

◎ collective（adj.）共同的。
◎ shed（v.）裁撤；去除。
◎ shutter（v.）關閉。
◎ adversary（n.）敵手；敵人。

◎ indicator（n.）指標。
◎ profound（adj.）（影響）深遠。
◎ sap（v.）使透支精力；使元氣大傷。
◎ nagging（adj.）揮之不去的；一直糾纏的。

現在大家都知道我們正置身危機之中。我國正處於對抗深遠暴力和憎恨的戰爭。我們的經濟元氣大傷，是某些人貪婪且不負責任的後果，也是大家未能作出艱難的選擇，為國家進入新時代作準備所致。許多人失去房子，許多人丟了工作，許多人生意垮了。我們的醫療照護太昂貴，學校教育辜負了許多人。每天都有更多證據顯示，我們利用能源的方式壯大我們的對敵，威脅我們的星球。

 這些都是得自資料和統計數據的危機指標。比較無法測量但影響同樣深遠的，是舉國信心盡失——持續擔心美國將無可避免地衰退，也害怕下一代必須放低眼界。

 今天我要告訴各位，我們面臨的挑戰是真的，挑戰非常嚴重，且不在少數。它們不是可以輕易，或在短時間內對付的。但是，美國要了解，這些挑戰會被對付的。

 今天，我們聚在一起，因為我們選擇希望而非恐懼，選擇追求共同目標而非紛爭與不合。

---

nag（v.）嘮叨、糾纏。
◎ decline（n.）衰退。
◎ lower one's sights（片語）將眼界調低；降低標準。

◎ unity of purpose（片語）目標的一致性；有共同的目標。
◎ discord（n.）不合；不和諧。

On this day, we come to **proclaim** an end to the petty **grievances** and false promises, the **recriminations** and worn-out **dogmas**, that for far too long have **strangled** our politics.

 We remain a young nation, but in the words of **Scripture**, the time has come to set aside childish things. The time has come to **reaffirm** our enduring spirit; to choose our better history; to carry forward that precious gift, that noble idea, passed on from generation to generation: the God-given promise that all are equal, all are free, and all deserve a chance to pursue their full measure of happiness.

 In reaffirming the greatness of our nation, we understand that greatness is never a **given**. It must be earned. Our journey has never been one of shortcuts or **settling for less**. It has not been the path for the **fainthearted**—for those who prefer leisure over work, or seek only the pleasures of riches and fame. Rather, it has been the risk-takers, the doers, the makers of things–some celebrated, but more often men and women **obscure** in their labor–who have carried us up the long, **rugged** path toward prosperity and freedom.

 For us, they packed up their few **worldly possessions** and traveled across oceans in search of a new life.

單 字 解 說

◎ proclaim（v.）宣稱。
◎ grievance（n.）埋怨；牢騷。petty grievances（n.）氣度狹小的牢騷；心胸狹隘的埋怨。
◎ recrimination（n.）指責；指控。
◎ dogma（n.）教條。
◎ strangle（v.）掐脖子；勒斃。
◎ scripture（n.）經文。大寫的Scripture指《聖經》。

今天,我們來此宣示,那些小心眼的抱怨和虛偽的承諾已終結,那些扭曲我們政治已久的相互指控和陳舊教條已終結。

我們仍是個年輕的國家,但借用《聖經》的話,擺脫幼稚事物的時刻到來了,重申我們堅忍精神的時刻到來了,選擇我們更好的歷史,實踐那種代代傳承的珍貴權利,那種高貴的理念:就是上帝的應許,我們每個人都是平等的,每個人都是自由的,每個人都應該有機會追求全然的幸福。

我們再次肯定我們國家的偉大,了解偉大絕非天生具備,而必須努力去求得。我們的旅程從來就不是抄捷徑或很容易就滿足。這條路一直都不是給不勇敢的人走的,那些偏好逸樂勝過工作,或者只想追求名利就滿足的人。恰恰相反,走這條路的始終是勇於冒險的人,做事的人,成事的人,其中有些人很出名,但更多的是在各自崗位上的男男女女無名英雄,在這條漫長崎嶇的道路上支撐我們,邁向繁榮與自由。

為了我們,他們攜帶很少的家當,遠渡重洋,追尋新生活。

◎ reaffirm(v.)重申;再次肯定。
◎ given(n.)理所當然的事。
◎ settle for less(片語)降低標準;輕易滿足。
◎ fainthearted(adj.)膽小的;懦弱的。
◎ obscure(adj.)隱晦的;不為人知的。

◎ rugged(adj.)粗獷的;崎嶇的。
◎ worldly possessions(n.)世俗的財物──指所擁有的物質面的東西(相對於精神內涵)。

For us, they toiled in **sweatshops** and settled the West; endured the **lash** of the **whip** and plowed the hard earth.

 For us, they fought and died, in places like **Concord** and **Gettysburg**; **Normandy** and **Khe Sahn**.

 Time and again, these men and women struggled and sacrificed and worked till their hands were **raw** so that we might live a better life. They saw America as bigger than the sum of our individual ambitions; greater than all the differences of birth or wealth or **faction**.

 This is the journey we continue today. We remain the most prosperous, powerful nation on Earth. Our workers are no less productive than when this crisis began. Our minds are no less inventive, our goods and services no less needed than they were last week or last month or last year. Our **capacity** remains **undiminished**. But our time of **standing pat**, of protecting narrow interests and putting off unpleasant decisions–that time has surely passed. Starting today, we must pick ourselves up, dust ourselves off, and begin again the work of remaking America.

◎ sweatshop（n.）「血汗工廠」，指剝削勞力的工作環境（工時長、環境差，雇用廉價勞工的工作場所）—— 早期美國的新移民往往必須在此種工作環境中謀生。
◎ lash（n./v.）鞭打；鞭策。
◎ whip（n.）鞭子。
◎ Concord（n.）（美國麻州）康科特——一七七五年美國獨立戰爭首役戰場。
◎ Gettysburg（n.）（美國賓州）蓋茲堡——一八六三年美國南北戰爭決定性戰役之主戰場。林肯總統（Abraham Lincoln）在此發表著名之「蓋茲堡演說」（Gettysburg Address），力倡解放黑奴。

12 為了我們，他們胼手胝足，在西部安頓下來；忍受風吹雨打，篳路藍縷。

13 為了我們，他們奮鬥不懈，在康科特和蓋茲堡，諾曼第和溪山等地葬身。

14 前人不斷的奮鬥與犧牲，直到雙手皮開肉綻，我們才能享有比較好的生活。他們將美國視為大於所有個人企圖心總和的整體，超越出身、財富或派系的分別。

15 這是我們今天繼續前進的旅程。我們仍舊是全球最繁榮強盛的國家。比起這場危機爆發之時，我們的勞工生產力並未減弱。我們的心智一樣創新，我們的產品和勞務和上週或上個月或去年相比，一樣是必需品。我們的能力並未減損。但是我們墨守成規、維護狹小利益、推遲引人不悅的決定，這段時期肯定已經過去。從今天起，我們必須重新出發，再次展開再造美國的工程。

◎ Normandy（n.）（法國）諾曼第——二次世界大戰聯軍登陸歐陸之地。
◎ Khe Sahn（n.）（越南）溪山——一九六八年越戰的主戰場之一。
◎ raw（adj.）皮開肉綻。
◎ faction（n.）派系；派別。
◎ capacity（n.）容量；產量；產能。
◎ undiminished（adj.）未減；未消退。diminished（adj.）減少；消減。
◎ stand pat（片語）守舊不肯嘗新；固執不肯變通。

For everywhere we look, there is work to be done. The state of the economy calls for action, bold and swift, and we will act–not only to create new jobs, but to lay a new foundation for growth. We will build the roads and bridges, the electric **grids** and digital lines that feed our commerce and bind us together. We will restore science to its rightful place, and **wield** technology's wonders to raise health care's quality and lower its cost. We will **harness** the sun and the winds and the soil to **fuel** our cars and run our factories. And we will transform our schools and colleges and universities to meet the demands of a new age. All this we can do. And all this we will do.

 Now, there are some who question the **scale** of our ambitions–who suggest that our system cannot **tolerate** too many big plans. Their memories are short. For they have forgotten what this country has already done; what free men and women can achieve when imagination is joined to common purpose, and necessity to courage.

 What the **cynics** fail to understand is that the ground has shifted beneath them–that the **stale** political arguments that have consumed us for so long no longer apply. The question we ask today is not whether our government is too big or too small, but whether it works–whether it helps families find jobs at a decent wage, care they can afford, a retirement that is **dignified**. Where the answer is yes, we intend to move forward. Where the answer is no, programs will end. And those of us who manage the public's dollars will be **held to account**–to spend wisely, reform bad habits, and do our business in the light of day–because only then can we restore the vital trust between a people and their government.

◎ grid（n.）網格；棋盤網路。electrical grids（n.）（棋盤網路式的）電力系統。
◎ wield（v.）揮舞；運用。
◎ harness（v.）駕馭；運用。

◎ fuel（v.）為……提供燃料；刺激……的成長。
◎ scale（n.）規模；大小。
◎ tolerate（v.）容忍；承受。
◎ cynic（n.）諷世者；不看好者。

我們無論朝何處望去,都有工作必須完成。經濟情勢需要大膽、迅速的行動,我們將有所行動,不光是創造新工作,更要奠定成長的新基礎。我們將造橋鋪路,為企業興建電力網格與數位線路,將我們聯繫在一起。我們將讓科學再度得到應有的重視,運用科技的奇蹟來提高醫療品質並降低費用。我們將利用太陽能、風力和土壤作為汽車的燃料和工廠的能源。我們將讓中小學及大專院校轉型,因應新時代的需要。這些我們可以做到。我們也將會做到。

---

17 有人質疑我們的企圖心規模,暗示說我們的體系無法承受太多的大計畫。這些人的記性不好。因為他們忘記了這個國家已有的成就,當創造力與共同目標結合時,當需求與勇氣結合時,不受約束的男男女女可以完成何等成就!

---

18 唱衰者無法理解的是他們的主張已經站不住腳,長期以來折磨我們的陳腐政治爭議已經行不通。我們今天的問題不是政府太大或太小,而是有無功效,是否能幫助家庭找到薪水不錯的工作,支付得起照顧費用,有尊嚴的退休。答案肯定的,我們就往前走。答案是否定的,計畫就會停止。所有我們這些管理大眾金錢的人都將負起責任,花錢要精明,改掉惡習,正大光明做事情,只有這樣,我們才能重建政府與人民間最重要的信任。

◎ stale(adj.)陳腐的;毫無新意的。
◎ dignified(adj.)有尊嚴的。
◎ hold to account(片語)亦作hold accountable;要求對所做的事情負責;要求對方承擔行為之後果。

Nor is the question before us whether the market is a force for good or ill. Its power to generate wealth and expand freedom is unmatched, but this crisis has reminded us that without a watchful eye, the market can spin out of control—and that a nation cannot prosper long when it favors only the prosperous. The success of our economy has always depended not just on the size of our **gross domestic product**, but on the reach of our prosperity; on our ability to extend opportunity to every willing heart—not out of **charity**, but because it is the **surest route** to our **common good**.

 As for our common defense, we reject as false the choice between our safety and our ideals. Our **Founding Fathers**, faced with **perils** we can scarcely imagine, drafted a **charter** to assure the rule of law and the rights of man, a charter expanded by the blood of generations. Those ideals still light the world, and we will not give them up for **expedience's** sake. And so to all other peoples and governments who are watching today, from the grandest capitals to the small village where my father was born: Know that America is a friend of each nation and every man, woman and child who seeks a future of peace and dignity, and that we are ready to lead once more.

 Recall that earlier generations **faced down fascism** and communism not just with missiles and tanks, but with sturdy **alliances** and enduring **convictions**. They understood that our power alone cannot protect us, nor does it **entitle** us to do as we please. Instead, they knew that our power grows through its **prudent** use; our security **emanates** from the justness of our **cause**, the force of our example, the **tempering** qualities of **humility** and **restraint**.

單 字 解 說

◎ gross domestic product（片語）國內生產毛額，縮寫成GDP。
◎ charity（n.）施捨。
◎ sure route（n.）；surest route（n.）不二法門；最穩當的途徑。
◎ common good（n.）共同利益；眾人的利益。

◎ Founding Fathers（片語）開國元老。
◎ peril（n.）危險；危機。
◎ charter（n.）憲章。
◎ expedience（n.）便利；方便。
　 for expedience's sake為了方便起見。
◎ face down（片語）在對峙中以聲勢壓倒對

我們眼前的問題也不在於市場的力量是善或惡。市場創造財富和增加自由的力量無與倫比,但是這場危機提醒我們,沒有監督時,市場發展將失控,當市場只偏愛有錢人時,國家無法永續繁榮。我們經濟成功的依據,不只是國內生產毛額的規模,還有繁榮可及的範圍,以及我們將機會拓展給每個願意打拚的人——不是出於施捨,而是因為這就是達到我們共同利益最穩健的途徑。

至於我們的共同防衛,有人說我們必須在我們的安全和理想之間作一抉擇——這是不確實的,我們拒絕接受。我們開國元老在我們難以想像的危難之中,擬具了確保法治和人權的憲章,被一代代以鮮血擴大充實的憲章。這些理想依然照亮這個世界,我們不會為了便宜行事而揚棄它。同樣地,今日在觀看此情此景的其他民族和政府,從最宏偉的都城到家父出生的小村莊,我要說:任何一個國家、男、女和孩童,只要你在追求一個和平且有尊嚴的未來,美國就是你的朋友,我們準備再次帶領大家。

回想先前的世代力抗法西斯主義和共產主義,靠的除了飛彈和戰車之外,還有強固的聯盟和持久的信念。他們知道單單力量本身不足以讓我們自保,也不能讓我們為所欲為。相反地,他們知道我們的力量因為謹慎使用而增強,我們的安全源自我們理想的正當性,我們的以身作則,以及謙遜和克制所具有的調和特質。

方,令對方退卻。
◎ fascism(n.)法西斯主義。
◎ alliance(n.)聯盟;結盟。
◎ conviction(n.)信念。
◎ entitle(v.)讓人享有某種權力;讓人有特權。
◎ prudent(adj.)謹慎;小心。

◎ emanate(v.)發源;散發。
◎ cause(n.)所支持的理念;所追求的理想。
◎ temper(v.)調和。tempering(adj.)有調和作用的。
◎ humility(n.)謙卑;謙遜。
◎ restraint(n.)克制;節制。

We are the keepers of this **legacy**. Guided by these principles once more, we can meet those new threats that demand even greater effort–even greater cooperation and understanding between nations. We will begin to responsibly leave Iraq to its people, and **forge** a hard-earned peace in Afghanistan. With old friends and former foes, we will work tirelessly to lessen the nuclear threat, and **roll back** the **specter** of a warming planet. We will not apologize for our way of life, nor will we **waver** in its defense, and for those who seek to **advance their aims** by **inducing** terror and slaughtering innocents, we say to you now that our spirit is stronger and cannot be broken; you cannot outlast us, and we will defeat you.

 For we know that our **patchwork heritage** is a strength, not a weakness. We are a nation of Christians and Muslims, Jews and Hindus–and nonbelievers. We are shaped by every language and culture, drawn from every end of this Earth; and because we have tasted the bitter **swill** of **civil war** and **segregation**, and emerged from that dark chapter stronger and more united, we cannot help but believe that the old hatreds shall someday pass; that the lines of tribe shall soon **dissolve**; that as the world grows smaller, our **common humanity** shall reveal itself; and that America must play its role in **ushering in** a new era of peace.

單 字 解 說

◎ legacy（n.）所遺留下來的使命；所遺留下來的傳統。
◎ forge（v.）鑄造。
◎ roll back（片語）使退卻；使後退。
◎ specter（n.）原意為「幽靈」，此引申為「恐懼」、「隱憂」。

◎ waver（v.）信心動搖；意志動搖。
◎ advance one's aim（片語）；又作advance one's agenda——求己利；達到自己私人的目的。
◎ induce（v.）引起；產生。
◎ patchwork heritage（n.）由各民族拼湊而成

我們是這些遺產的保存者。在這些原則的再次指引下，我們可以面對那些新的威脅，這些威脅有賴國與國間更大的合作與諒解方能因應。我們將開始以負責任的方式把伊拉克還給它的人民，並在阿富汗建立贏來不易的和平。我們會努力不懈地與老朋友和昔日的敵人合作，以減輕核子威脅，和地球的暖化。我們不會為我們的生活方式而道歉，也會毫不動搖地保護它，對那些想要藉由帶來恐怖與殺害無辜以遂其目的者，我們現在告訴你們，我們的精神強過你們，無法摧折，你們不可能比我們長久，我們必定打敗你們。

因為我們知道，我們由各族群揉合而成的血統是我們的強處，而非弱點。我們是由基督徒和穆斯林，猶太教徒和印度教徒，以及非信徒組成的國家。我們由取自世界四面八方的各種語文和文化所形塑。而且由於我們曾嘗過內戰和種族隔離的苦果，並且在走出那黑暗時期之後變得更堅強和團結，這讓我們不得不相信舊日的仇恨終究會過去，族群之間的界線很快就會泯滅。隨著世界越來越小，我們共通的人性也會彰顯，而美國必須扮演引進新和平時代的角色。

的血統（指美國種族大熔爐的特性）。
◎ swill（n.）苦酒。
◎ civil war（n.）內戰（此指一八六一——一八六五年美國南北戰爭）。
◎ segregation（n.）種族隔離。
◎ dissolve（v.）消散；溶解。

◎ common humanity（n.）（人類所共有的）人性、良知。
◎ usher in（片語）領進；引進。

034 ▶▶▶ 敢於大膽希望──歐巴馬七篇關鍵演說

 To the Muslim world, we seek a new way forward, based on mutual interest and mutual respect. To those leaders around the globe who seek to sow conflict, or blame their society's ills on the West: Know that your people will judge you on what you can build, not what you destroy. To those who **cling to** power through **corruption** and **deceit** and the silencing of **dissent**, know that you are on the wrong side of history; but that we will extend a hand if you are willing to **unclench** your fist.

 To the people of poor nations, we pledge to work alongside you to make your farms **flourish** and let clean waters flow; to **nourish** starved bodies and feed hungry minds. And to those nations like ours that enjoy relative plenty, we say we can no longer afford **indifference** to suffering outside our borders; nor can we consume the world's resources without regard to effect. For the world has changed, and we must change with it.

 As we consider the road that unfolds before us, we remember with humble **gratitude** those brave Americans who, at this very hour, **patrol** far-off deserts and distant mountains. They have something to tell us today, just as the fallen heroes who lie in **Arlington** whisper through the ages. We honor them not only because they are guardians of our liberty, but because they **embody** the spirit of service; a willingness to find meaning in something greater than themselves. And yet, at this moment−a moment that will define a generation-it is precisely this spirit that must **inhabit** us all.

◎ cling to（v.）緊抓住；緊抓不放。
◎ corruption（n.）貪污。
◎ deceit（n.）欺騙。
◎ dissent（n.）不同意見；異議。to silence dissent箝制異己；壓制不同意見。

◎ unclench（v.）放鬆；放開。clench（v.）緊握拳頭。
◎ flourish（v.）繁榮；興旺。
◎ nourish（v.）滋養；養育。
◎ indifference（n.）漠不關心；冷漠。

24 對穆斯林世界，我們尋求一種新的前進方式，以共同的利益和尊重為基礎。那些想播植衝突並把自己社會的問題怪罪於西方的領袖，須知你的國民藉以判斷你的，是你能建立什麼，而非你能毀壞什麼。那些靠著貪腐欺騙和箝制異己保住權勢的人，須知你們站在歷史錯誤的一邊，而只要你願意鬆手，我們就會幫忙。

25 窮國的人民，我們保證會和你們合作，讓你們的農場豐收，讓清流湧入，滋補餓壞的身體，餵養飢餓的心靈。而對那些和我們一樣比較富裕的國家，我要說，我們不能再對國界以外的苦痛視而不見，也不能再消耗世上的資源而不計後果。因為世界已經變了，我們也要跟著改變。

26 在我們思索眼前道路的此際，我們以謙虛感激的心想到，有些勇敢的美國同胞正在遙遠的沙漠和山嶺上巡邏。今天他們有話要對我們說，就和躺在阿靈頓國家公墓的英雄們世世代代輕聲訴說的一樣。我們尊榮他們，不只因為他們捍衛我們的自由，更因為他們代表著服務的精神；願意在比自己更大的事物上找尋意義。而在此刻，能夠界定一個世代的此刻，必須常駐你我心中的，正是這種精神。

◎ gratitude（n.）感激；感謝。
◎ patrol（v.）巡邏。
◎ Arlington（n.）
　指美國維吉尼亞州（Virginia）的阿靈頓國家公墓（Arlington National Cemetery）。

其中埋葬著美國歷代名人，以及兩次世界大戰、韓戰和越戰的美軍陣亡將士。
◎ embody（v.）體現；呈現。
◎ inhabit（v.）存在於中；深植其中。

For as much as government can do and must do, it is ultimately the faith and determination of the American people upon which this nation relies. It is the kindness to take in a stranger when the **levees** break, the selflessness of workers who would rather cut their hours than see a friend lose their job which sees us through our darkest hours. It is the firefighter's courage to storm a stairway filled with smoke, but also a parent's willingness to nurture a child, that finally decides our fate.

 Our challenges may be new. The instruments with which we meet them may be new. But those values upon which our success depends—hard work and honesty, courage and fair play, tolerance and curiosity, loyalty and patriotism—these things are old. These things are true. They have been the quiet force of progress throughout our history. What is demanded then is a return to these truths. What is required of us now is a new era of responsibility—a recognition, on the part of every American, that we have duties to ourselves, our nation and the world; duties that we do not **grudgingly accept** but rather seize gladly, firm in the knowledge that there is nothing so satisfying to the spirit, so defining of our character, than **giving our all** to a difficult task.

 This is the price and the promise of citizenship.

 This is the source of our confidence—the knowledge that God calls on us to shape an uncertain destiny.

◎ levee（n.）堤壩；堤岸。
◎ grudgingly accept（片語）很不情願地接受。

即使政府能做也必須做,這個國家最終仍得靠美國人民的信念與決心。是堤防決堤時,善心人士敞開大門招待陌生人的精神;是工人們寧可減工時,也不願看到朋友失業的精神——是這種精神,陪伴我們度過最黑暗時期。是消防員衝進滿是濃煙的樓梯間的那種勇氣,是父母培育孩子的心甘情願——是這種情懷,最終決定我們的命運。

 我們的挑戰也許是新的。我們迎接挑戰的工具也許是新的。但我們賴以成功的價值觀——辛勤工作和誠實、勇氣和公平競爭、容忍和好奇心、忠實和愛國心——這些都是固有的。這些價值是真實的,是我們歷史上進步的沈默力量。我們有必要找回這些真實價值。我們現在需要一個勇於負責的新時代,每一個美國人都體認到我們對自己、對國家、對世界負有責任,我們不是不情願地接受這些責任,而是欣然接受,堅信沒有什麼比全力以赴完成艱難的工作,更能得到精神上的滿足,更能顯示我們的品格。

 這是公民的代價和承諾。

這是我們信心的來源——體認上帝召喚我們在前途未卜之際塑造自己的命運。

◎ give one's all(片語)全力以赴;盡全力。

31 This is the meaning of our liberty and our **creed**—why men and women and children of every race and every faith can join in celebration across this magnificent **Mall**, and why a man whose father less than 60 years ago might not have been served at a local restaurant can now stand before you to take a most sacred oath.

32 So let us mark this day with **remembrance**, of who we are and how far we have traveled. In the year of America's birth, in the coldest of months, a small band of patriots **huddled** by dying campfires on the shores of an icy river. The capital was abandoned. The enemy was advancing. The snow was stained with blood. At a moment when the outcome of our revolution was most in doubt, the father of our nation ordered these words be read to the people:

33 "Let it be told to the future world that in the depth of winter, when nothing but hope and virtue could survive that the city and the country, alarmed at one common danger, came forth to meet [it]."

34 America. In the face of our common dangers, in this winter of our hardship, let us remember these timeless words. With hope and virtue, let us **brave** once more the icy **currents**, and endure what storms may come. Let it be said by our children's children that when we were tested, we refused to let this journey end, that we did not turn back, nor did we **falter**; and with eyes fixed on the horizon and **God's grace** upon us, we carried forth that great gift of freedom and delivered it safely to future generations.

單字解說

◎ creed（n.）信條；教條。
◎ Mall（n.）指華盛頓特區國會山莊前的國家廣場（National Mall），簡稱The Mall，實為長形大草坪；是華府重要集會遊行之場所。兩旁為美國各國家級博物館。

這是我們的自由和信條的真諦——為什麼不同種族和信仰的男女老幼能在這個大草坪上共同慶祝，為什麼一個六十年前也許還不能進當地餐廳用餐的人所生下的兒子，現在卻能站在你們面前做最神聖的宣誓。

32 此時此刻，讓我們緬懷過去，記住我們是誰、我們走了多遠。在美國誕生那一年，在最寒冷的幾個月，在結冰的河岸，在即將熄滅的營火旁，一群愛國人士正凍得蜷縮顫抖。首都棄守，敵人進逼，雪沾了血。在那時，我們革命能否成功尚在未定之天，我們的國父下令向人民宣讀這段話：

33 「讓這段話流傳後世：在深冬，只剩下希望和美德，這個城市和這個國家，驚覺共同危險，站起來迎向它。」

 美國。面對我們共同的危險，在這個艱困的冬天，讓我們記得這些永恆的話語。懷著希望和美德，讓我們再度衝破結冰的逆流，度過接下來可能來臨的任何暴風。讓我們子孫繼續傳講下去，說我們受到考驗時，我們拒絕讓旅程結束，我們不回頭，也不躊躇；眼睛注視著遠方，憑著上帝給我們的恩典，我們帶著自由這個偉大的禮物，安全送達未來的世世代代。

◎ remembrance（n.）回憶；懷念。
◎ huddle（v.）蜷縮；身體縮成一團。
◎ brave（v.）此作動詞，指勇敢地去面對。

◎ current（n.）水流；潮水。
◎ falter（v.）動搖；退縮；倒下。
◎ God's grace（片語）上帝的恩典。

第三部分 🏆 文句解析

◎李振清（世新大學英語系客座教授、世新大學前人文社會學院院長、前教育部國際文教處處長）

　　歐巴馬的就職演說精采處，不但在於突顯啟發性的多元內涵、精湛感人的詞彙與堅實的文章結構，更重要的是整篇演說貫穿著跨時代精神，和虔誠的人文意涵。字裡行間同時也處處展現出對美國古聖先賢的尊崇與感恩，尤其是分別在二〇〇〇與二〇〇九年透過歷史學者與C-SPAN電視台票選為「最佳總統」（2009 Historians Presidential Survey）的亞伯拉罕・林肯（Abraham Lincoln）。就職演說中處處流露真情與全方位的人文素養。這和他早年居住過印尼雅加達、在夏威夷接受高中教育，以及後來分別在哥倫比亞大學和哈佛大學的踏實歷練，有密切的關係。由此可見這篇文獻的珍貴、高度的文學價值與可讀性。

　　二〇〇八年九月二十八日出刊的「紐約時報」，曾在In Crisis, Glimpses of Candidates' Leadership（在經濟危機中──總統候選人的領導才能一瞥）文中，深入分析歐巴馬的特質：組織能力強、善於集思廣益、口才便給、分析力強，但態度冷靜、處世謙和審慎。這種謙和（humble）與謹記在心（mindful）的政治家人格特質，很明顯地反映於本就職演說的第1段：

　　I stand here today humbled by the task before us, grateful for the trust you have bestowed, mindful of the sacrifices borne by our ancestors. I thank President Bush for his service to our nation, as well as the generosity and cooperation he has shown throughout this transition.

　　同時，整篇就職演說的內涵中，也反映出歐巴馬充分肯定美國開國先賢（Founding Fathers）的無上功勳，以及對立國精神的堅定（第9段）。同

時，就職演說中明顯地充滿著林肯總統著名的「蓋茲堡演說」之人道精神與恢弘文氣。民權運動領袖金恩博士（Martin Luther King, Jr.）的 "I Have a Dream" 期許，也隱約地在這篇就職演說中呈現。

在這篇鏗鏘有聲的就職典禮演說中，歐巴馬一開始就參照林肯總統慣用的溫和，但堅定的語氣，暗示他所傳承自林肯的精神資產（legacy）。在全部34段的就職演說中，歐巴馬彷彿成為林肯的分身，並且藉由「蓋茲堡演說」的經典內涵、前瞻視野與修辭藝術，從頭到尾闡述著飲水思源、鑑往知來（1-2段）、因應挑戰、多難興邦（4-6段）、堅持革新、肯定自我（8-13段）、期許未來（15-16段）、替代能源、振興經濟（16-17段）、道德廉能（20, 28-30段）、同舟共濟、廣結善緣（21-27段）、繼往開來、求新求變（32-34段）等二十一世紀的新普世價值。

歐巴馬在本就職演說中，引經據典，扼要地點出歷史的典故。例如在第2段中所說的 "We the People have remained faithful to the ideals of our forebearers, and true to our founding documents."，係引自美國憲法（Constitution of the United States）之序言（Preamble）：

We the People of the United States, in order to form a more perfect Union, establish Justice, insure domestic Tranquility, provide for the common defence, promote the general Welfare, and secure the Blessings of Liberty to ourselves and our Posterity, do ordain and establish this Constitution for the United States of America.

中譯：

我們，美利堅合眾國的人民，為了組織一個更完善的聯邦，樹立正義，保障國內的安寧，建立共同的國防，增進全民福利和確保我們自己及我們後代能安享自由帶來的幸福，乃為美利堅合眾國制定和確立這一部憲法。（美

國國務院中譯）

「founding documents」指本演講中所提及之《美國憲法》（第2段）、美國《獨立宣言》（第9段）等重要文件。

第9段首句乃引用《聖經》哥林多前書13：11（Corinthinians 13:11）：

When I was a child, I spoke as a child, I understood as a child, I thought as a child: but when I became a man, I put away childish things. （以上引用《詹姆士王英譯本》〔King James Bible〕譯文）

中譯：「我作孩子的時候，話語像孩子、心思像孩子、意見像孩子，既成了人，就把孩子的事情棄掉。」（引自1878北京官話譯本《新約全書》）

第9段後半段內容是美國《獨立宣言》（Declaration of Independence）的口語轉述。茲比較如下：

歐巴馬（2009）第9段	美國《獨立宣言》（1776）第2段
The time has come…to carry forward that precious gift, that noble idea, passed on from generation to generation: the God-given promise that all are equal, all are free, and all deserve a chance to pursue their full measure of happiness.	We hold these Truths to be self-evident, that all Men are created equal, that they are endowed, by their CREATOR, with certain unalienable Rights, that among these are Life, Liberty, and the Pursuit of Happiness.

歐巴馬的這一句話，顯然也深受林肯總統著名的「蓋茲堡演說」之影響。「蓋茲堡演說」一開始就有這麼一句語意深遠、震撼人心、鏗鏘有聲的開場白：

Four score and seven years ago our fathers brought forth on this continent, a new nation, conceived in liberty, and dedicated to the proposition that all men are created equal.

歐巴馬和林肯的思維十分類似；核心用詞幾乎完全相同：「that all...are ...equal.」。

第33段：原文出自美國革命家潘恩（Thomas Paine, 1737-1809）一篇名為〈危機〉（The Crisis）之論述，在一七七六年冬被美國開國元首華盛頓用以鼓勵年輕人參加獨立革命，報效國家。潘恩為美國獨立革命期間之文宣大將，印有「常識報」（Common Sense）小報，藉之鼓吹革命。全長三千四百字之大作「危機」即出自「常識報」版面。

本文的另一特點是文法結構運用的簡潔有力。其中，現代英文句法最常使用的現在與過去分詞（present/past participial phrases）結構，以及從屬子句（subordinate clauses）的配合和轉換（transformation）等，正好是台灣的高中生可以學習、模仿，然後有效運用於英文寫作，或口語表達的基本範例。大學生更可進一步運用此種文類，作為英語文進階歷練的寶貴參考資料。例如第一段的第一句，就完全展現此種精簡語法結構的特色。而此一強有力的精簡句子，是由原來的五個簡單句經由語法轉換而形成的表層結構（surface structure）：

I stand here today humbled by the task before us, grateful for the trust you have bestowed, mindful of the sacrifices borne by our ancestors.

I stand here today.

I am humbled by the task before us.

I am grateful for the trust （that） you have bestowed.

I am mindful of the sacrifices.

The sacrifices were borne by our ancestors.

　　了解這個道理後，大家必然可以依此發現閱讀英文的奧祕，從而有效提升英語文學習的成效與興趣。無論是高中生、大學生，甚或英文老師們，這種閱讀經典英文，與提升英語文實用（讀、聽、寫、說、譯）能力的共識，應該及早藉此有效培養。

　　整體而言，歐巴馬總統的這一篇就職演說之精神、內涵、文采與影響力，堪與甘迺迪一九六一年的就職演說並列，同時也是一篇足以發人深省的絕佳好文。這種難得一見的精采實用性文類（genre），值得大家深入閱讀、分析、朗讀、模仿，以便作為提升英語文能力的參考。

Chicago, November 4, 2008

Change Has Come to America

——Barack Obama's Victory Speech

2008年11月4日於芝加哥

改變終於來到了美國

——歐巴馬當選演說

◎ 深度導讀：陸以正（無任所大使）

◎ 單字、文句解析：李文肇（美國舊金山州立大學外文系副教授、國立台灣師範大學翻譯研究所特約兼任副教授）

◎ 翻譯：聯合報國際新聞中心編譯組

◎ 審訂：彭鏡禧（國立臺灣大學外文系及戲劇系特聘教授）

第一部分 深度導讀

改變終於來到了美國

二〇〇八年十一月四日晚當選總統後的演說

◎陸以正（無任所大使）

　　不論民意調查的比數如何領先，也不論媒體預測對他如何有利，民主國家投票之夜，任何候選人總難免如坐針氈，忐忑不安。美國的總統候選人，常會準備兩篇講話稿，一篇是勝利演說，另一篇則備選敗之用，感謝支持群眾之外，還要向對手道賀，以表現風度。

　　二〇〇八年十一月四日夜晚，歐巴馬的「捉刀人（ghost writer）」有沒有替他準備兩篇演說稿，除競選總部之外，沒人知道。從說話的語氣判斷，我認為極可能是即興（impromptu）之作，一字一句出自肺腑。

　　儘管事前未曾備稿，歐巴馬講得氣勢如虹，一氣呵成，充分表現他的演說天才。開始那一段尤其動人，他問：還有人懷疑在美國，任何事情都有可能嗎？還有人敢不相信開國元老們的夢想，到今天仍然活著如新嗎？還有人質疑民主的力量嗎？如果仍有人不信，今晚就是最好的答案。

　　他以四日一整天全美各地投票所前排成長龍的隊伍為傲，稱讚那些耐心等待三、四個小時的選民；言外之意是，許多黑人為支持他，這輩子第一次出來投票。其實根據事後統計，投票人數共132,618,580人，佔全國年滿十八歲有投票權人數的56.8%，比二〇〇四年布希總統連任的投票率53.3%，只多了1.5%。

　　歐巴馬贏得選舉，有許多因素：第一，他打破了種族與膚色的藩籬，獲得不論

黑、白、紅、黃各族年輕一代人的擁護。第二，他的年齡和理想，恰與布希總統代表的傳統政治形成強烈對比，給美國帶來新希望。第三，他的競選總部善於運用新興的網路通訊，直接聯繫個人，把五元、十元或二十元的小額捐款積少成多，竟然募集七億四千四百萬美元，超過對手麥肯參議員所募的三億四千六百多萬元一倍有餘。

勝而不驕，歐巴馬顯露了他性格中謙遜的一面。先提競選對手麥肯來電話祝賀，承諾將與共和黨通力合作。他向當選副總統的拜登參議員、自己的太太蜜雪兒和兩個女兒、已故的祖母和兄弟姊妹、主持競選策略的David Plouffe和操盤手David Axelrod一一道謝。最後用手向台下聚集的上萬群眾說：「這是你們的勝利！」獲得如雷歡聲。

語氣一轉，他說：選贏了只是工作的開始；前途漫長，或許一任四年還無法完成。美國必須克服中東與南亞兩場戰爭、地球危機與金融風暴，但「我們會走完全程！」台下人齊聲回應："Yes, we can！"電視捕捉到不少人因興奮流淚的鏡頭。

因為出身貧賤，歐巴馬深知民間疾苦。他細數中下階級的父母，如何在子女入睡後，擔憂該付的到期房貸、醫生帳單，或怎樣籌措大學的學雜費用。他說：要做的事太多，選舉勝利並非就是人民渴望的改變，只是謀求改變機會的契機。

歐巴馬說：政府不能解決所有的問題，必須群策群力，不分黨派合作。他說這次大選會有許多故事流傳下去。但令他難忘的是在亞特蘭大市（Atlanta, Georgia）遇到的一位高齡一百零六歲的黑人婦女Ann Dixon Cooper，她只用手指碰觸一下電腦，就完成了投票。

這篇演說的地點是芝加哥，他抬出伊利諾州（Illinois）第一位共和黨總統林肯，作為榜樣。林肯當選時，國家分裂的情勢遠比今日嚴重，就職後就發生內戰。他引林肯的話說，我們彼此間不是仇敵，而是朋友，向他打敗的麥肯和共和黨遞出橄欖枝（an olive branch），謀求合作應付當前危機。

這的確是篇令人難忘的演說，值得細細品味咀嚼。

第二部分 主文/中譯

主文中譯◎聯合報國際新聞中心編譯組
單字解說◎李文肇（美國舊金山州立大學外文系副教授、國立台灣師範大學翻譯研究所特約兼任副教授）

 Hello, Chicago.
If there is anyone out there who still doubts that America is a place where all things are possible, who still wonders if the dream of our **founders** is alive in our time, who still questions the power of our democracy, tonight is your answer.

 It's the answer told by lines that stretched around schools and churches in numbers this nation has never seen, by people who waited three hours and four hours, many for the first time in their lives, because they believed that this time must be different, that their voices could be that difference.

 It's the answer spoken by young and old, rich and poor, **Democrat** and **Republican**, black, white, **Hispanic**, Asian, **Native American**, gay, **straight**, **disabled** and not disabled. Americans who sent a message to the world that we have never been just a collection of individuals or a collection of **red states** and **blue states**. We are, and always will be, the United States of America.

 單字解說

◎ founder（n.）創始人；此處指開國元老。見第19段found（v.）創立。
◎ Democrat（n.）指Democratic Party民主黨（見第19段）。
◎ Republican（n.）指Republican Party共和黨（見第19段）。
◎ Hispanic（n./adj.）西班牙裔；拉丁裔（指中、南美洲移民）。
◎ Native American（n./adj.）美國原住民（印地安人）。

哈囉，芝加哥！
如果外頭還有人懷疑，美國是否真的是任何事都可能發生的地方，懷疑我們開國先賢的夢想今天是否依然存在，懷疑我們民主的力量；今夜，就是你們要的答案。

 這是個用這個國家前所未見，環繞學校、教堂的無數人龍，所說出的答案。這些人，苦等三、四個小時，許多還是生平頭一次投票，因為他們相信，這次一定會不一樣，他們的一票也許就是勝負關鍵。

 這是個由不分老少、貧富、民主黨、共和黨；黑人、白人、西班牙裔、亞裔、美洲原住民；同性戀、異性戀人；肢障與四體健全者，大家共同訴說的答案。美國民眾向全世界發出訊息，我們絕非一盤散沙，也不是由紅州、藍州拼湊而成的集合體。我們現在是，未來也永遠是，美利堅合眾國。

◎ straight（adj.）異性戀者（非同性戀者──gay 的相反詞）。
◎ disabled（adj.）肢體殘障者；有身體缺陷者。
◎ red state（n.）支持共和黨的州（紅為共和黨的代表色）。
◎ blue state（n.）支持民主黨的州（藍為民主黨的代表色）。

It's the answer that led those who've been told for so long by so many to be **cynical** and fearful and **doubtful** about what we can achieve to put their hands on the **arc** of history and bend it once more toward the hope of a better day.

 It's been a long time coming, but tonight, because of what we did on this date in this election at this **defining moment**, change has come to America.

 A little bit earlier this evening, I received an extraordinarily **gracious** call from **Senator McCain**. Senator McCain fought long and hard in this campaign. And he's fought even longer and harder for the country that he loves. He has endured sacrifices for America that most of us cannot begin to imagine. We are better off for the service rendered by this brave and selfless leader. I congratulate him; I congratulate **Govenor Palin** for all that they've achieved. And I look forward to working with them to **renew** this nation's promise in the months ahead.

 I want to thank my partner in this journey, a man who campaigned from his heart, and spoke for the men and women he grew up with on the streets of **Scranton** and rode with on the train home to **Delaware**, the **vice president–elect** of the United States, **Joe Biden**.

單 字 解 說

◎ cynical（adj.）持嘲笑、諷刺態度的；不看好的；唱衰的。見第33段cynicism（n.）嘲諷的心態。
◎ doubtful（adj.）持懷疑態度的。
◎ arc（n.）圓弧。
◎ defining moment（n.）關鍵性時刻；決定性

時刻。
◎ gracious（adj.）落落大方的；很有風度的。extraordinarily gracious 非常有風度的。
◎ Senator McCain（n.）麥肯參議員（Senator John McCain），代表共和黨角逐二○○八總統選舉的候選人。

這個是引領國人把手放在歷史拱弧，再度讓它指向明天會更美好希望的答案。長久以來，這些國人一直被許多人灌輸，要嘲諷、害怕和懷疑我們自身的能力。

這個答案遲遲未出現，但是今晚，由於我們在這個投票日關鍵時刻的所作所為，改變終於降臨美國。

今晚稍早，我接到麥肯參議員打來，態度非常懇切的電話。麥肯參議員打了一場漫長艱苦的選戰。他為這個他所熱愛的國家所打的仗更久，更艱苦。他為美國的奉獻犧牲，是我們多數同胞難以想像的。因為有他這位勇敢無私的領袖的奉獻，我們才能過比較好的日子。我向他道賀；也向裴林州長道賀，為他們所成就的一切。在未來數月我期待和他們攜手合作，更新這個國家的許諾。

我要感謝我的選舉搭檔，這位先生全心全意競選，為與他在史克蘭頓街頭一起長大的男男女女代言，為與他在德拉瓦州一起搭火車通勤的男男女女代言，他就是副總統當選人，拜登先生。

◎ Governor Palin（n.）阿拉斯加州的裴林州長（Governor Sarah Palin），二〇〇八年共和黨副總統候選人，麥肯參議員的競選搭檔。
◎ renew（v.）復興；重建。
◎ Scranton（n.）美國賓州史克蘭頓市——歐

巴馬副手拜登（Joe Biden）的出生地。
◎ Delaware（n.）美國德拉瓦州——歐巴馬副手拜登（Joe Biden）後來移居德拉瓦州，當選德拉瓦州參議員。
◎ vice president－elect（n.）副總統當選人。
◎ Joe Biden（n.）喬・拜登（歐巴馬副手）。

And I would not be standing here tonight without the **unyielding** support of my best friend for the last 16 years, the rock of our family, the love of my life, the nation's next **first lady Michelle Obama**. **Sasha** and **Malia**, I love you both more than you can imagine. And you have earned the new puppy that's coming with us to the new White House. And while she's no longer with us, I know my grandmother's watching, along with the family that made me who I am. I miss them tonight. I know that my **debt** to them is **beyond measure**.

 To my sister **Maya**, my sister **Auma**, all my other brothers and sisters, thank you so much for all the support that you've given me. I am grateful to them.

 And to my **campaign manager**, **David Plouffe**, the **unsung hero** of this campaign, who built the best—the best political campaign, I think, in the history of the United States of America. To my **chief strategist David Axelrod** who's been a partner with me every step of the way. To the best campaign team ever **assembled** in the history of politics, you made this happen, and I am forever grateful for what you've sacrificed to get it done.

 But above all, I will never forget who this victory truly belongs to. It belongs to you. It belongs to you.

◎ unyielding（adj.）不退讓的；不鬆懈的。
◎ first lady（n.）第一夫人。
◎ Michelle Obama（n.）歐巴馬夫人蜜雪兒‧歐巴馬。
◎ Sasha（n.）歐巴馬七歲的小女兒——莎夏‧歐巴馬。
◎ Malia（n.）歐巴馬十歲的大女兒——瑪利

亞‧歐巴馬。
◎ debt（n.）虧欠。
◎ beyond measure（片語）多得無法衡量。
◎ Maya（n.）歐巴馬的母親與印尼籍繼父所生下的妹妹瑪亞‧蘇德洛（Maya Soetoro）。
◎ Auma（n.）歐巴馬的父親與其肯亞元配所生下的姊姊艾瑪‧歐巴馬（Auma Obama）。

如果沒有過去十六年來堅定支持的這位摯友，我今晚不可能站在這裡——
——她是我家庭的磐石，我一生的最愛，國家未來的第一夫人蜜雪兒·歐
巴馬。莎夏和瑪利亞。我對妳倆的愛遠超過妳們的想像。妳們已贏得即
將和我們一起到新白宮作伴的新小狗。還有，雖然她已不在我們身邊，
但是我知道我外婆，也和造就今日之我的家族一起在看。今晚，我想念
他們。我知道，我欠他們的，無法衡量。

 我妹妹瑪亞、艾瑪、我的其他兄弟姊妹們，非常感謝你們給我的所有支
持。我很感謝他們。

 還有，我的競選總幹事普羅費，這次競選的無名英雄，我認為他推動了
美國史上最佳的競選活動。感謝我的首席競選策士艾索洛，一路走來，
他一直是我的得力夥伴。感謝這個政治史上無出其右的最佳競選團隊，
你們造就了這項成果，我對你們的犧牲奉獻，永存感激。

 但最重要的，我絕不會忘記這個勝利真正屬於誰。它屬於各位。它屬於
各位。

◎ campaign manager（n.）競選總幹事。
campaign競選。
◎ David Plouffe（n.）歐巴馬競選總幹事大
衛·普羅費。
◎ unsung hero（片語）無名英雄；不為人
知、默默付出的關鍵性人物。
◎ chief strategist（n.）首席策略長。strategist
策略長；策略官。
◎ David Axelrod（n.）歐巴馬首席策略長大
衛·艾索洛。
◎ assemble（v.）集合；組織。

I was never the likeliest **candidate** for this **office**. We didn't start with much money or many **endorsements**. Our campaign was not hatched in the halls of Washington. It began in the backyards of **Des Moines** and the living rooms of **Concord** and the front porches of **Charleston**.

 It was built by working men and women who **dug into** what little **savings** they had to give–five dollars and ten dollars and twenty dollars–to the **cause**. It grew strength from the young people who **rejected** the **myth** of their generation's **apathy**, who left their homes and their families for jobs that offered little pay and less sleep. It drew strength from the not-so-young people who braved the bitter cold and **scorching heat** to knock on doors of **perfect strangers**, and from the millions of Americans who **volunteered** and organized and proved that more than two centuries later **a government of the people, by the people, and for the people has not perished from the Earth.** This is your victory.

◎ candidate（n.）候選人。likeliest candidate最被看好的候選人。
◎ office（n.）職位；此指總統職位。
◎ endorsement（n.）背書；支持。
◎ Des Moines（n.）愛荷華州（Iowa）首府第蒙市──二〇〇八年一月三日民主黨第一場初選所在地。
◎ Concord（n.）新罕布夏州（New Hampshire）首府康科特市──二〇〇八年一月八日民主黨第二場初選所在地。
◎ Charleston（n.）南卡羅萊納州（South Carolina）查爾斯敦市──二〇〇八年一月二十六日民主黨第四場初選所在地。美國南方莊園多有門廊，此處提及查爾斯敦的門廊（porches of Charleston）別具南方風味。

我從來就不是這個職位最被看好的候選人。剛開始,我沒什麼錢,也沒什麼後援。我們參選的念頭,並非始於華府大廳,而是來自第蒙市後院,康科特市客廳和查爾斯敦的門廊。

這次競選,是由眾多男女從他們有限的儲蓄中拿出五塊、十塊或二十塊美元相挺,共同打造出來的。經過那些拒絕承認他們是冷漠世代的迷思的年輕朋友加持,它成長茁壯。這些年輕人離開家,告別親人,投入待遇菲薄,永遠睡眠不足的工作。這次競選經過那些年紀不算輕的朋友加持,它成長茁壯——這些人冒著寒風酷暑,挨家挨戶向完全陌生的民眾敲門;這次競選經過數百萬民眾自發性的組織,證明這個民有、民治、民享的政府,在兩百多年之後,沒有從地球上消失,仍在成長茁壯。這是你們的勝利。

◎ dig into（v.）辛苦自……掘出。
◎ savings（n.）儲蓄;存款。
◎ cause（n.）所支持的理念;所追求的理想。
◎ reject（v.）拒絕;排除;摒棄。
◎ myth（n.）迷思;錯誤理解。
◎ apathy（n.）漠不關心;冷漠。
◎ scorching heat（n.）灼熱的暑氣。scorch（v.）灼燒。
◎ perfect stranger（n.）素未謀面的陌生人。

perfect完全的。
◎ volunteer（v.）當義工;自願幫忙。
◎「a government of the people, by the people, and for the people has not perished from the Earth」——引自林肯總統（Abraham Lincoln）著名的「蓋茲堡演說」（Gettysburg Address）末句（詳見導讀）。

And I know you didn't do this just to win an election. And I know you didn't do it for me. You did it because you understand the **enormity** of the task that lies ahead. For even as we celebrate tonight, we know the challenges that tomorrow will bring are the greatest of our lifetime－two wars, a planet in **peril**, the worst **financial crisis** in a century. Even as we stand here tonight, we know there are brave Americans waking up in the deserts of **Iraq** and the mountains of **Afghanistan** to risk their lives for us. There are mothers and fathers who will lie awake after the children fall asleep and wonder how they'll make the **mortgage** or pay their doctors' bills or save enough for their child's college education. There's new energy to **harness**, new jobs to be created, new schools to build, and **threats** to meet, **alliances** to **repair**.

 The road ahead will be long. Our climb will be **steep**. We may not get there in one year or even in one **term**. But, America, I have never been more hopeful than I am tonight that we will get there. I promise you, we as a people will get there.

 There will be **setbacks** and **false starts**. There are many who won't agree with every decision or **policy** I make as president. And we know the government can't solve every problem. But I will always be honest with you about the challenges we face. I will listen to you, especially when we disagree. And, above all, I will ask you to join in the work of **remaking** this nation, the only way it's been done in America for 221 years－**block by block, brick by brick, calloused** hand by calloused hand.

單 字 解 說

◎ enormity（n.）巨大；龐大。
◎ peril（n.）危險；危機。
◎ financial crisis（n.）金融危機；金融風暴。
◎ Iraq（n.）伊拉克。
◎ Afghanistan（n.）阿富汗。
◎ mortgage（n.）房屋貸款（註：二〇〇八年

的金融風暴乃是由次級房貸問題所引爆）。
◎ harness（v.）駕馭；運用。
◎ threat（n.）威脅。
◎ alliance（n.）聯盟；結盟關係。
◎ repair（v.）修復；重修舊好。
◎ steep（adj.）陡峭。

14 我知道，你們這麼做，不只是為了勝選。我也知道，你們這麼做，不是為了我。你們這麼做，是因為你們了解，橫在眼前的是千萬斤的重擔。因為正當我們今晚慶功的時候，我們也明白，明天所要面臨的是此生最大的挑戰：兩場戰爭，一個處於存亡之秋的地球，及百年僅見的金融危機。正當我們今晚站在此地的時候，我們也知道，為了我們，美國的勇士們正在伊拉克沙漠巡邏，在阿富汗山區出生入死。許多父母，在子女進入夢鄉後，仍輾轉難眠，擔心房貸、醫療帳單該怎麼付，或該怎麼存，才夠支應子女的大學教育費用。新的能源要研發，新的工作機會要創造，新學校要建，不少威脅要對付，既有盟邦關係要修補。

15 未來的路仍遙遠，要爬的坡仍陡峭，我們可能沒辦法在一年，或一任內抵達。但是，美國，我從來沒有像今晚的我，對我們的使命必達，更充滿希望。

16 一開始，挫折和失誤在所難免。有許多人不會同意我以總統身分所作的每一個決定或每一項政策。我們也知道政府無法解決所有問題。但我永遠會把我們面對的挑戰坦白告訴各位。我會傾聽各位，尤其是在我們看法不同的時候。最重要的是，我會邀請各位加入重塑這個國家的工作，以美國兩百二十一年來採用的唯一方法：一磚一瓦，胼手胝足。

◎ term（n.）任期。
◎ setback（n.）挫折；阻撓。
◎ false start（n.）（賽跑中的）起跑犯規；搶跑。比喻白費力氣；走錯方向。
◎ policy（n.）政策。
◎ remake（v.）重建。

◎ block by block（adv.）一磚接著一磚地（比喻腳踏實地一步步地）。
◎ brick by brick（adv.）一磚接著一磚地（比喻腳踏實地一步步地）。
◎ callous（n.）硬皮；老繭。calloused（adj.）被磨得長繭的。

What began 21 months ago in the depths of winter cannot end on this autumn night. This victory alone is not the change we seek. It is only the chance for us to make that change. And that cannot happen if we go back to the way things were. It can't happen without you, without a new spirit of service, a new spirit of sacrifice.

 So let us **summon** a new spirit of **patriotism**, of responsibility, where each of us **resolves** to **pitch in** and work harder and look after not only ourselves but each other. Let us remember that, if this financial crisis taught us anything, it's that we cannot have a **thriving Wall Street** while **Main Street** suffers. In this country, we rise or fall as one nation, as one people.

 Let's resist the **temptation** to **fall back on** the same **partisanship** and **pettiness** and **immaturity** that has poisoned our politics for so long. Let's remember that it was a man from this state who first carried the **banner** of the Republican Party to the White House, a party **founded** on the values of **self-reliance** and **individual liberty** and **national unity**. Those are values that we all share. And while the Democratic Party has won a great victory tonight, we do so with a measure of **humility** and determination to heal the **divides** that have **held back** our progress.

◎ summon（v.）喚起。
◎ patriotism（n.）愛國心；愛國主義。
◎ resolve（v.）下定決心。
◎ pitch in（v.）參與；參一腳。
◎ thriving（adj.）興旺的；繁榮的。
◎ Wall Street（n.）華爾街；美國紐約金融中心。此處藉街名比喻金融業者。

◎ Main Street（n.）小鎮的主要街道；此處藉街名比喻美國尋常百姓。
◎ temptation（n.）誘惑。
◎ fall back on（片語）以退而求其次的態度勉強接受；達不到理想而退到原來的位置。
◎ partisanship（n.）黨派偏見；忠於自己所屬黨派的心態。

17 二十一個月前發軔於隆冬的,不會就在這個秋夜結束。我們追求的改變,不僅僅是這個勝利。這個勝利只是給我們機會實現我們追求的改變。我們若走回頭路,改變便不會發生。少了你,少了新的服務精神,少了新的犧牲精神,改變就不會發生。

18 所以,且讓我們喚起新的愛國心、新的責任感,人人挽起衣袖,更加努力,照顧自己之外,更要彼此照顧。我們不要忘記,如果這次金融危機給了我們任何教訓,那就是在尋常百姓生活困頓下,華爾街也不可能獨自繁榮昌盛。在這個國度,不論興衰,都是全國與共,全民一體。

19 我們一定要抗拒誘惑,不再靠已毒害我國政治許久的黨派之私、褊狹和幼稚。我們不可忘記,第一個把共和黨旗幟帶進白宮的男士,正是來自本州。共和黨的建黨根基則是自立、個人自由及全國統一團結等價值觀。這些也是我們全體共享的價值觀。雖然民主黨今晚大勝,我們卻始終謙沖自持,並決心彌合阻撓我們進步的裂縫。

◎ pettiness(n.)小器;小心眼;心胸狹隘。
petty(adj.)小心眼的;心胸狹隘的。
◎ immaturity(n.)不成熟。mature(adj.)成熟。
◎ banner(n.)旗幟。
◎ found(v.)創立;創建。
◎ self-reliance(n.)自力更生;自立自強。

◎ individual liberty(n.)個人自由。
◎ national unity(n.)國家統一;全國一心。
◎ humility(n.)謙卑;謙虛。a measure of humility某種程度的謙卑;些許的謙卑。
◎ divide(n.)分隔;隔閡。
◎ hold back(v.)阻止前進;使人無法發揮。

As Lincoln said to a nation far more divided than ours, "We are not enemies but friends. Though **passion** may have **strained**, it must not break our **bonds of affection**."

 And to those Americans whose support I have yet to earn, I may not have won your vote tonight, but I hear your voices. I need your help. And I will be your president, too. And to all those watching tonight from beyond our **shores**, from **parliaments** and palaces, to those who are **huddled** around radios in the forgotten corners of the world, our stories are **singular**, but our destiny is shared, and a new dawn of American leadership is at hand. To those who would tear the world down: We will defeat you. To those who seek peace and security: We support you. And to all those who have wondered if America's **beacon** still burns as bright: Tonight we proved once more that the true strength of our nation comes not from the **might** of our **arms** or the **scale** of our wealth, but from the enduring power of our ideals: democracy, liberty, opportunity and **unyielding** hope.

 That's the true **genius** of America: that America can change. Our **union** can be perfected. What we've already achieved gives us hope for what we can and must achieve tomorrow.

◎ passion（n.）原指熱情、激情，此指堅強的友情。
◎ strain（v.）緊繃；緊張；出現僵局；受到考驗。
◎ bonds of affection（n.）感情的維繫；友情的維繫。
◎ shore（n.）海岸。beyond our shores國界之外（指外國的）。
◎ parliament（n.）議會（英式用法）。
◎ huddle（v.）蜷縮；身體縮成一團。

正如林肯向一個遠比今天更分歧的美國所說的,「我們不是敵人,是朋友。我們的友誼或曾出現僵局,卻不可影響彼此之間感情的維繫。」

 我要向那些我仍須努力爭取支持的美國同胞說,或許今晚我沒能贏得各位的選票,但是我聽到諸位的聲音,我需要你們協助,我也會是你們的總統。對那些今晚在海外、從各地國會和宮殿觀看美國選情的人士,在為世人遺忘的角落圍繞著收音機的人們,我要說我們的故事各不相同,命運卻是一體,美國新的領導就要出現了。對那些想撕裂這個世界的人,我要說:我們會打垮你。對那些追求和平安全的人,我要說:我們支持你。而對那些懷疑美國這燈塔是否依然明亮的人,今晚我們再度證實,美國真正的國力不是來自船堅砲利、富甲天下,而是來自發乎我們理想、歷久不衰的力量,這些理想是民主、自由、機會和堅持到底的希望。

 這正是真正的美國精神:也就是美國能夠改變。這個國家可以更完善。我們過去的成就,使我們企盼我們明天能夠做到,也必須做到的。

◎ singular(adj.)個別的;個人的。
◎ beacon(n.)烽火台;燈塔。
◎ might(n.)力量;威力。
◎ arms(n.)武器;兵力。
◎ scale(n.)規模;大小。
◎ unyielding(adj.)不退讓的;永不放棄的。

◎ genius(n.)特質;精神。
◎ union(n.)聯邦。United States的別稱。

This election had many firsts and many stories that will be told for generations. But one that's on my mind tonight's about a woman who cast her **ballot** in Atlanta. She's a lot like the millions of others who stood in line to make their voice heard in this election except for one thing: **Ann Nixon Cooper** is 106 years old.

She was born just a generation past **slavery**; a time when there were no cars on the road or planes in the sky; when someone like her couldn't vote for two reasons– because she was a woman and because of the color of her skin.

And tonight, I think about all that she's seen throughout her century in America–the **heartache** and the hope; the struggle and the progress; the times we were told that we can't, and the people who **pressed on** with that American **creed**: Yes we can.

At a time when women's voices were **silenced** and their hopes **dismissed**, she lived to see them stand up and speak out and reach for the ballot. Yes we can.

When there was **despair** in the **dust bowl** and **depression** across the land, she saw a nation **conquer** fear itself with a New Deal, new jobs, a new sense of common purpose. Yes we can.

◎ ballot（n.）選票；cast a ballot 投票。
◎ Ann Nixon Cooper（n.）安·庫柏——走過美國百年歷史，在二〇〇八年首度投票的一百零六歲黑人女人瑞。
◎ slavery（n.）奴隸制度；畜養黑奴的制度。
◎ heartache（n.）心碎；心痛。

◎ press on（v.）繼續推進；努力向前進。
◎ creed（n.）信條；信念。
◎ silence（v.）令其不敢出聲；壓抑反對意見。
◎ dismiss（v.）駁回；忽略；不予理會。
◎ despair（n.）絕望；完全放棄希望。

這次大選有許多創舉和故事足供世世代代傳頌。而今晚浮現在我腦海的,是在亞特蘭大投票的一位婦人。她和這次大選無數排隊投票以表達心聲的選民沒什麼差別,不同的只有一點,安·尼克森·庫柏已高齡一百零六。

 她出生於奴隸時代結束後那個世代;當時路上沒有汽車,天上不見飛機;而她這樣的人沒有資格投票,原因有二:其一,她是女人,其二,她的膚色不對。

 但就在今晚,我想到她在美國這百年人生的閱歷:心傷和希望;掙扎和進步;有人告訴我們我們不能的時候,和那些高舉著美國人「是的,我們做得到」的信念奮勇向前的人。

 身處女性聲音受壓制、希望被漠視的時代,她這一生親眼看到女性站起來,表達心聲,並爭取到投票權。是的,我們做得到。

就在塵盆地帶(指美國大草原的一部分,大致包括科羅拉多州東南部、堪薩斯州西南部、德州與奧克拉荷馬州鍋柄形突出地帶)陷入絕望,大蕭條席捲美國全境之際,她目睹一個國家以新政、新的工作機會、新的和衷共濟精神克服了恐懼本身。是的,我們做得到。

◎ dust bowl(n.)一九三〇年代美國中西部大平原出現的沙塵暴,嚴重影響中西部居民賴以維生的農業,使三〇年代的經濟大蕭條(Great Depression,一九二九──一九三九)雪上加霜。
◎ depression(n.)經濟蕭條。此處指the Great Depression,一九二九至一九三九年美國史上最嚴重的經濟大蕭條──當時股市崩盤、通貨緊縮、失業率高漲、消費者信心全失。
◎ conquer(v.)征服;克服。

When the bombs fell on our **harbor** and **tyranny threatened** the world, she was there to witness a generation rise to greatness and a democracy was saved. Yes we can.

 She was there for the **buses in Montgomery**, the **hoses in Birmingham**, a **bridge in Selma**, and a **preacher from Atlanta** who told a people that "**We Shall Overcome**." Yes we can.

 A man touched down on the moon, a wall came down in Berlin, a world was connected by our own science and imagination.

 And this year, in this election, she touched her finger to a screen, and cast her vote, because after 106 years in America, through the best of times and the darkest of hours, she knows how America can change. Yes we can.

◎ harbor（n.）海港；港灣；此處指美國夏威夷的珍珠港（Pearl Harbor）。（註：二次大戰期間，美國本未參戰，是在一九四一年日本派軍機轟炸美國海軍在夏威夷珍珠港的基地之後才全力投入戰局的。）
◎ tyranny（n.）暴政；專制的統治。
◎ threaten（v.）威脅。
◎ buses in Montgomery（n.）指一九五五至一九五六年的「蒙哥馬利公車罷乘運動」（Montgomery Bus Boycott）。當時美國實施種族隔離制（segregation），搭乘公共汽車時，黑人與白人座位必須隔開。一九五五年十二月一日，阿拉巴馬州蒙哥馬利郡的黑人女性羅莎‧帕克斯（Rosa Parks）因為拒絕讓位給白人而遭逮捕，引起黑人罷乘公車及一連串的後續抗議活動，拉開了黑人民權運動的序幕。
◎ hoses in Birmingham（n.）指美國黑人民權運動中的伯明罕示威（Birmingham Campaign）——一九六三年黑人民權領袖馬丁‧路德‧金恩博士（Dr. Martin Luther King Jr.）呼籲阿拉巴馬州伯明

28 當炸彈落在我們的港口，暴政威脅世界之際，她親眼看見一個世代巍然挺身而起，拯救了一個民主體制。是的，我們做得到。

29 在蒙哥馬利市（黑人）搭巴士抗爭，伯明罕市的水龍（警察以強力水龍對付抗議者），賽爾瑪城外的橋上（遭警察血腥鎮壓），來自亞特蘭大的一位牧師告訴一個民族「我們終必得勝」時，她都在場。是的，我們做得到。

30 有人登上了月球，柏林圍牆倒了，一個世界被我們自己的科學和想像連結了起來。

31 而今年，在這次選舉中，她用手指觸碰屏幕，投下她的一票，因為在美國生活了一百零六年，嘗遍酸甜苦辣之後，她知道美國能夠有什麼樣的改變。是的，我們做得到。

罕市的群眾上街示威，警察用消防水管（hose）的高壓水柱鎮壓。
◎ bridge in Selma（n.）指阿拉巴馬州賽爾瑪市愛德蒙・彼特可橋（Edmund Pettus Bridge）。一九六五年美國黑人民權運動正值巔峰，黑人走上街頭爭取投票權，原本計畫由賽爾瑪市遊行至蒙哥馬利，卻在賽爾瑪市的愛德蒙・彼特可橋遭警方以木棍、皮鞭和催淚瓦斯攻擊，爆發流血衝突。
◎ preacher from Atlanta（n.）亞特蘭大來的牧師──指生於亞特蘭大（Atlanta）的美國黑人民權運動之父──馬丁・路德・金恩博士（Dr. Martin Luther King Jr.）。他曾發動一九五五年的「蒙哥馬利公車罷乘運動」，更在一九六三年率二十萬人走上華盛頓街頭，發表著名的「我有一個夢」（I Have a Dream）演說，一九六四年成為有史以來最年輕的諾貝爾和平獎得主，一九六八年在田納西州遭人暗殺。
◎ We shall overcome.「我們一定贏」──美國黑人靈魂歌曲名稱──是一九五五至一九六八年美國黑人民權運動的主題曲，一九六三年華盛頓大遊行時由二十萬人同聲齊唱。

America, we have come so far. We have seen so much. But there is so much more to do. So tonight, let us ask ourselves–if our children should live to see the next century; if my daughters should be so lucky to live as long as Ann Nixon Cooper, what change will they see? What progress will we have made?

 This is our chance to answer that call. This is our moment. This is our time— to put our people back to work and open doors of opportunity for our kids; to **restore** prosperity and promote the cause of peace; to **reclaim** the American dream and **reaffirm** that fundamental truth, that, out of many, we are one; that while we breathe, we hope. And where we are met with **cynicism** and doubts and those who tell us that we can't, we will respond with that timeless creed that sums up the spirit of a people: Yes, we can.

 Thank you. God bless you. And may God bless the United States of America.

◎ restore（v.）恢復；使復原。
◎ reclaim（v.）（將失去的東西）收回；討回。

美國,我們已經走了這麼遠。閱歷了這麼多。眼前卻還有這麼多事要做。所以,今晚讓我們捫心自問,如果我們的子女能夠活到下個世紀;如果我女兒有幸如安·尼克森·庫柏般長壽,他們能看到什麼改變?我們又促成了什麼樣的進步?

此際正是我們回應那個召喚的機會,這是我們的時刻。就在此刻,我們大家要重新開始工作,為我們的孩子開啓希望之門;迎回繁榮並推展和平大業;重新擁抱美國夢並再次確立那基本的真理,也就是我們同舟一命,只要活著就懷抱希望。當旁人嘲諷、懷疑我們,告訴我們我們辦不到時,我們會回以那歷久不衰、總結一個民族精神的信念:是的,我們做得到。

謝謝大家。願上帝祝福你。願上帝祝福美國。

◎ reaffirm(v.)重申;再次確認。
◎ cynicism(n.)嘲諷的心態;犬儒主義。見第4段cynical持嘲笑、諷刺態度的。

第三部分 🏆 文句解析

◎李文肇（美國舊金山州立大學外文系副教授、國立台灣師範大學翻譯研究所特約兼任副教授）

二○○八年十一月四日，歐巴馬當選美國史上首位黑人總統，支持群眾為之瘋狂。四日晚間，歐巴馬來到家鄉芝加哥市區的葛蘭特公園（Grant Park），向二十四萬名支持者發表感性演說，演說中回顧美國歷史上的南北戰爭、經濟大蕭條、二次大戰、珍珠港事件，也回味黑人民權運動中的華府萬人大遊行、公車罷乘事件、警民流血衝突；援古證今，引述林肯與金恩博士，同時也提醒大家，過去再大的苦都撐過了，今日的困難也必能克服。這是一篇訴求改變（change），主打希望（hope）的經典演說，要民眾發揮美國人的樂觀天性，相信只要努力，什麼目標都達得到。

1-5段

歐巴馬利用演說的前兩段將本次總統選舉的特色數盡：第2段談到投票率四十年來首度突破六成，民眾排隊投票，其中不乏和歐巴馬一樣的少數族裔，生平首次選總統。第3段則聲明歐巴馬要作全民的總統，感謝全國不分黨派，不分膚色，不分老少，都傾全力支持。

歐巴馬此役主打的是改變與希望兩張牌，而這兩個主題首次出現在第4與第5段。第4段形容國人「把手放在歷史拱弧」（put their hands on the arc of history）──典故是黑人民權領袖馬丁‧路德‧金恩博士（Dr. Martin Luther King Jr.）一九六七年的演說「此後往哪走？」（Where do we go from here?）：

Let us realize the arc of the moral universe is long, but it bends toward justice.

（我們要明白道德宇宙的弧線很長，但它卻彎向正義。）

第5段呼應首段強調在此關鍵性時刻，「改變已降臨美國」（change has come to America）──這句話被多家媒體用作全篇演說的標題。

6-11段

歐巴馬利用6至11段致謝詞：第6段感謝競選對手麥肯（John McCain），強調他在軍中服役的背景，將他稱為國家英雄（national hero）。第7段感謝的是副手拜登（Joe Biden），特別提到他的平民作風──替賓州鄉親發聲，和民眾一同搭火車上班。

第8段則感謝妻女，以及選舉揭曉前過世的外祖母；第9段提及自己同母異父的妹妹和同父異母的姊姊──特別點名這幾位親屬和歐巴馬獨特的身世有關。歐巴馬的母親是美國白人，父親是肯亞黑人，兩人結婚時，其父在肯亞早已有家室，當時育有一男一女，女兒即歐巴馬口中的姊姊奧瑪（Auma Obama）──姊弟倆成年後才相認。歐巴馬父母婚後三年離婚──母親隨後改嫁印尼人，生下了歐巴馬的妹妹瑪亞（Maya Obama），全家移居印尼居住四年。四年後十歲的歐巴馬搬回夏威夷與外祖父母同住，就讀夏威夷著名的普納侯（Punahou）貴族中學。在夏威夷，歐巴馬一直是由外祖父母帶大的──外公在一九九二年過世，而外婆瑪德琳（Madelyn Lee Payne Dunham）在二〇〇八年選舉揭曉前一週往生，不巧未能看到外孫成為美國首位黑人總統。

12-14段

12到14段展現的是歐巴馬的平民作風。第12段說明他並不是有什麼高官貴人在華府作後盾，而是靠著像愛荷華州的第蒙市（Des moines, Iowa）、新罕布夏州的康科特市（Concord, New Hampshire），和南卡羅萊納州的查爾斯敦（Charleston, South Carolina）這些名不見經傳的小地方的平民百姓力挺，才有機會選上。第15段補充說明競選經費是靠勞工階級掏腰包五塊錢、十塊錢慢慢的累積而來的，感謝那些幫他挨家挨戶去籌錢的熱心義工，表示如此

實現了林肯「民有、民治、民享」的建國精神。以下是第15段末句，與其出處——林肯（Abraham Lincoln）的「蓋茲堡演說」（Gettysburg Address）——相比較：

　　林肯這篇在南北戰爭（一八六一～一八六五）時所發表的精鍊演說，在短短三百字之中道出自由與平等的精髓，並鼓吹解放黑奴，使人類不分膚色一律平等。而一百五十年後黑人當選美國最高領袖，重新再引用林肯的話語，也可算是理想的實現、種族平等概念的昇華。

歐巴馬「當選感言」 （2008年11月4日）	林肯「蓋茨堡演說」 （1863年11月9日）
...and proved that more than two centuries later a government of the people, by the people, and for the people has not perished from the Earth.	...this nation under God shall have a new birth of freedom, and that government of the people, by the people, for the people shall not perish from the earth.
⋯⋯證明這個民有、民治、民享的政府，在兩百多年之後，沒有從地球上消失。	⋯⋯要使這個國家在上帝庇佑之下，得到新生的自由——要使那民有、民治、民享的政府不致從地球上消失。

　　15-22段

　　有人說歐巴馬在位的四年，將是美國有史以來最艱辛的一段總統任期：國內有超級金融風暴，海外還有伊拉克、阿富汗兩場未了戰爭，加上國家嚴重負債，總統想要做得好，簡直是不可能。在第15和16段，歐巴馬表示

他明白這其中的困難。他說，路途將是陡峭的（our climb will be steep），會有很多挫折（setbacks），會多次揮棒落空（false starts），而且一個任期（one term）內無法完成。然而他並不因而氣餒：他呼籲大家要勇於犧牲（sacrifice），要有愛國情操 （patriotism），要更加努力（work harder），一磚一瓦（block by block, brick by brick）地去將國家重建。

在18、19兩段特別強調同甘共苦。18段針對當前的金融風暴，譴責那些拿老百姓血汗錢揮霍的銀行家與投資客，說不容華爾街（Wall Street）獨善其身，而家鄉老街（Main Street）卻窮苦潦倒。19段譴責那些小鼻子、小眼睛，只搞政黨惡鬥而看不到國家大局的政客。

21段末再度引用林肯總統的名言。一八六一年，美國內戰伊始，國家分裂為二，南北各自選出總統。聯邦的林肯總統在就職演說苦苦哀求，說儘管不是所有人都樂見他當選，然而畢竟都是同胞，致詞結束時語重心長地向敵對陣營喊話：「我們不是敵人，而是朋友。我們的友誼或曾出現僵局，卻不影響彼此之間感情的維繫。」（We are not enemies but friends. Though passion may have strained, it must not break our bonds of affection.）。歐巴馬藉此提醒民主、共和兩黨選戰已結束，此後要攜手合作。

22-34段

歐巴馬是美國第一位黑人總統，此次當選對於三千六百萬美國黑人意義非凡。歐巴馬演說最後幾段，藉著一位一百零六歲美國黑人人瑞的一生，回憶美國黑人爭取民權的歷史，也回顧美國近百年的民主發展，見證人民辛苦得來的進步，中間不時穿插著「我們做得到！」（Yes we can）的高亢口號，帶領群眾進入高潮。

24段提醒大家，百年前奴隸制度才剛剛廢除不久，女人和黑人都還無權投票。27段提醒民眾，一九三〇年代的經濟大蕭條及平原沙塵暴，破壞力不

亞於當前的金融問題，然而羅斯福總統（Franklin D. Roosevelt）也是靠著新政策的制訂一步步地帶領國家走出困境──這是做得到的！

　　29段是美國黑人民權運動的總回顧：歐巴馬將民權運動中幾幕最鮮明的畫面擺在世人眼前，提醒大家進步得來不易：五〇年代聲援羅莎・帕克斯（Rosa Parks），抗議黑白隔離的「蒙哥馬利公車罷乘運動」；一九六三年遭警察以高壓水柱阻撓的伯明罕民權示威；一九六五年遊行至賽爾瑪市橋上爆發的警民流血衝突；一九六三年華府草坪上的萬人大遊行；民權運動之父──金恩博士「我有一個夢」的著名演說──個個都是爭取民權路途中的里程碑。

　　演說最後，在30至31段提醒大家要拋開懷疑，擁有自信，相信夢想是能夠實現的──第30段以鮮明的事證相佐：人類登上月球、柏林圍牆倒塌──有什麼是不可能做到的？31段把焦點再拉回老人瑞身上：走過一百年，看到美國的進步，更要相信明天能夠更好。歐巴馬反問，百年而後，我們的子孫是否也能享受我們打拚的成果？答案是：Yes we can。

Berlin, Germany | July 24, 2008

Remarks of Senator Barack Obama:

A World that Stands as One

德國柏林市，2008年7月24日

歐巴馬參議員演說：

四海一家

◎ 深度導讀：陸以正（無任所大使）

◎ 單字、文句解析：李文肇（美國舊金山州立大學外文系副教授、國立台灣師範大學翻譯研究所特約兼任副教授）

◎ 翻譯：田思怡（聯合報國際新聞中心編譯組）

◎ 審訂：彭鏡禧（國立臺灣大學外文系及戲劇系特聘教授）

第一部分　深度導讀

我們需要一個團結的世界

二○○八年七月二十四日在柏林演講

◎陸以正（無任所大使）

　　意氣風發的歐巴馬，九天前剛在華府暢談他贏得大選後的外交政策，隨即應邀到柏林，向戰後早已唾棄希特勒種族優越思想的第三代德國人，闡述他的世界觀。

　　雖然他在國外，這仍是一篇給美國人聽的競選演說。歐巴馬的用意，是效法甘迺迪總統一九六三年六月二十四日，在西柏林對十六萬德國人用德語說「我也是個柏林人」（Ich bin ein Berliner）的著名故事。

　　二次大戰德國敗後，領土分由美、英、法、蘇四國佔領，蘇軍佔領區最大。柏林因係首都，雖在蘇軍區之內，卻由四國共管，成為孤城，對外交通及補給全賴空運。史達林故意設置種種障礙，要逼使柏林人屈膝，甘迺迪那次演說的用意，是向所有西德人民顯示，西方盟國絕不向蘇聯讓步。

　　甘迺迪是戰後民主黨最有魅力的總統，他從柏林回美五個月後，便遇刺身亡。歐巴馬不遠千里飛到柏林去發表演說，目標仍是美國國內選民。本篇標題 "A World that Stands as One" 極難翻譯，如作「一個團結的世界」，似乎不夠有力。副題「探索作為世界公民的職責」又嫌囉唆，且意義不大。

　　本篇風格也與其他各篇有很大差異。第13段起，引用六十前柏林市長的話，以修辭學中的頓呼法（apostrophe）大聲疾呼：「全世界的人啊！你看看柏林。」如此重複四次，達到非常戲劇化的效果。接著才點明正題，空運接濟柏林六十年，柏林圍牆倒塌十年後，歐巴馬說：世界正面臨新的危機。

　　什麼危機呢？第一是美國與歐洲盟國間有道無形的圍牆。他不必解釋，聽眾自然明白他在暗指布希總統的「單邊主義（unilateralism）」，導致美國與歐洲盟友格格不入的現狀。大西洋兩岸都忘記了彼此命運不可分割的道理，他們之間有一道新的牆，正如同富國和窮國間、不同種族間、不同宗教間，都有一道圍牆阻隔一樣，這些高牆必須和柏林圍牆一樣被拆除。

　　不注意時事的讀者可能不清楚，北約部隊已經大部取代了美軍在阿富汗追捕恐怖分子的角色。德國有三千三百名官兵，即將增加到四千五百人，參加歐盟派遣的「國際協助安全部隊」（International Security Assistance Force，簡稱ISAF）。歐巴馬感謝德軍的貢獻，坦承美國無法獨力應付恐怖集團的活動。

　　他說：沒有人喜歡戰爭，但美國和德國需要合作對恐怖集團反擊，不能半途而廢。他一連用了五次「時刻已經來臨了（Now is the time ...）」，重申他對外交關係的理想：

　　第一，逐步達成一個沒有核子武器的世界；

　　第二，歐洲所有國家需有選擇自身前途的機會，丟棄陳舊的冷戰觀念，可能時並與俄國合作，共存共榮；

　　第三，開放市場，鼓勵自由公平貿易，共享財富；

　　第四，在中東，迫使伊朗放棄核武野心，支持黎巴嫩走向民主，謀求以色列與巴勒斯坦和平共處，協助伊拉克自行解決內戰問題；

　　第五，減少排放二氧化碳，拯救地球，把未來還給子孫。

　　到結尾時，歐巴馬又使用喊叫方式行文。他向不僅住在柏林的德國人，而是全世界的人，呼籲說：我們面對無比的挑戰，前面的路途也很遙遠，但我們必須繼承這場為自由的鬥爭，堅持到底，重建一個團結為一的世界，藉此回到全篇的標題。

第二部分 主文/中譯

主文中譯◎田思怡（聯合報國際新聞中心編譯組）
單字解說◎李文肇（美國舊金山州立大學外文系副教授、國立台灣師範大學翻譯研究所特約兼任副教授）

 Thank you to the citizens of Berlin and to the people of Germany. Let me thank **Chancellor Merkel** and **Foreign Minister Steinmeier** for welcoming me earlier today. Thank you **Mayor Wowereit**, the **Berlin Senate**, the police, and most of all thanks to all of you for this welcome.

 I come to Berlin as so many of my countrymen have come before. Tonight, I speak to you not as a candidate for President, but as a citizen–a proud citizen of the United States, and a fellow citizen of the world.

 I know that I don't look like the Americans who've previously spoken in this great city. The journey that led me here is **improbable**–My mother was born in the **heartland** of America, but my father grew up **herding** goats in **Kenya**. His father–my grandfather–was a cook, a **domestic servant** to the British.

◎ Chancellor Merkel（n.）德國總理梅克爾（Angela Merkel）—— 德國史上首位女總理，也是二次大戰以來最年輕的德國總理。「總理」頭銜，在德國稱為chancellor。
◎ Foreign Minister Steinmeier（n.）德國外長史坦邁爾（Frank-Walter Steinmeier）。foreign minister（n.）外交部長。
◎ Mayor Wowereit（n.）柏林市長渥瑞特（Klaus Wowereit）。mayor（n.）市長。
◎ Berlin Senate（n.）柏林參議院（指柏林市政府行政部門）。

1 柏林市民和德國人民，謝謝你們。感謝梅克爾總理和史坦麥爾外長今天稍早的接待。感謝渥瑞特市長、柏林參議院、警方，尤其感謝在場各位這麼熱情的歡迎。

2 我來柏林，很多我的同胞過去也來過。今晚，我不是以總統候選人的身分對你們演說，而是以公民身分──驕傲的美國公民和世界公民身分。

3 我知道，我的外表不像過去在這個偉大城市演說過的美國人。引領我來到這裡的旅程不可思議。我的母親在美國中部出生，但我的父親在肯亞牧羊長大。他的父親──我的祖父──是廚師，是英國的僕人。

◎ improbable（adj.）可能性不大的；不太可能發生的。與第10段unlikely同義。
◎ heartland（n.）指美國中西部心臟地帶；最純正、最具代表性的美國。
◎ herd（v.）放牧。herd goats（v.）放牧山羊。
◎ Kenya（n.）（非洲）肯亞。
◎ domestic servant（n.）僕人；傭人。

At the height of the **Cold War**, my father decided, like so many others in the forgotten corners of the world, that his **yearning**–his dream–required the freedom and opportunity promised by the West. And so he wrote letter after letter to universities all across America until somebody, somewhere answered his prayer for a better life.

 That is why I'm here. And you are here because you too know that yearning. This city, of all cities, knows the dream of freedom. And you know that the only reason we stand here tonight is because men and women from both of our nations came together to work, and struggle, and sacrifice for that better life.

 Ours is a **partnership** that truly began sixty years ago this summer, on the day when the first American plane touched down at **Templehof**.

 On that day, much of this continent still lay **in ruin**. The **rubble** of this city had yet to be built into a wall. The **Soviet** shadow had swept across Eastern Europe, while in the West, America, Britain, and France **took stock** of their losses, and **pondered** how the world might be **remade**.

 This is where the two sides met. And on the twenty-fourth of June, 1948, the **Communists** chose to **blockade** the western part of the city. They cut off food and supplies to more than two million Germans in an effort to **extinguish** the last flame of freedom in Berlin.

◎ Cold War（n.）冷戰——指一九四〇年代中期至一九九〇年代初，美國與蘇聯兩大超級強國的軍事對峙與心理戰爭。
◎ yearning（n.）渴望。動詞用法見第38段 yearn（v.）渴望。
◎ partnership（n.）合作夥伴關係。

◎ Templehof（n.）柏林譚貝霍夫國際機場——二戰期間曾為歐洲三大機場之一，航廈大樓躋身世界二十大建築，然而由於逐漸沒落，機場已於二〇〇八年關閉。
◎ in ruin（片語）破壞殆盡；處於廢墟狀態。
◎ rubble（n.）瓦礫堆。

在冷戰高峰期，我的父親和許多世界被遺忘角落的人們一樣，認定他的憧憬、他的夢想，需要西方世界所承諾的自由和機會才能實現。因此，他寫信給美國各地的大學，一封接著一封，直到某處的某人回應他追求更好生活的願望。

因此我才站在這裡。你們站在這裡，是因為你們也明瞭我父親的憧憬。在所有城市中，這個城市最明瞭自由的夢想。你們明瞭，今晚我們能夠站在這裡的唯一原因，是因為我們兩國的男男女女曾經一起為了更好的生活而努力、奮鬥和犧牲。

我們兩國真正展開夥伴關係是在六十年前的夏天，從美國飛機降落在譚貝霍夫機場的那一天開始。

那天，歐洲大部分地區仍是廢墟。這個城市的瓦礫尚待築成圍牆。蘇聯的陰影籠罩全東歐，而在西方，美國、英國和法國清點他們的損失，並苦思如何再造世界。

這裡是東西方的交會點。一九四八年六月二十四日，共產黨選擇封鎖這個城市的西半部，他們切斷兩百多萬德國人的食物與物資，為的是熄滅柏林市僅存的自由火苗。

◎ Soviet（adj.）蘇聯的。可參考第21段蘇維埃聯邦（蘇聯）Soviet Union。
◎ take stock（片語）盤貨；評估狀況。
◎ ponder（v.）仔細思索；沈思。
◎ remake（v.）再造；重建。
◎ Communists（n.）共產黨；共產黨員；共產

主義國家（又見第9段 Communism共產主義）。
◎ blockade（v./n.）封鎖。
◎ extinguish（v.）滅火；使（火焰）熄滅。

The size of our forces was no match for the much larger Soviet Army. And yet **retreat** would have allowed **Communism** to march across Europe. Where the last war had ended, another **World War** could have easily begun. All that stood in the way was Berlin.

 And that's when the **airlift** began–when the largest and most **unlikely** rescue in history brought food and hope to the people of this city.

 The **odds were stacked against** success. In the winter, a heavy fog filled the sky above, and many planes were forced to turn back without dropping off the needed supplies. The streets where we stand were filled with hungry families who had no comfort from the cold.

 But in the darkest hours, the people of Berlin kept the flame of hope burning. The people of Berlin refused to give up. And on one fall day, hundreds of thousands of Berliners came here, to the **Tiergarten**, and heard the city's mayor **implore** the world not to give up on freedom. "There is only one possibility," he said. "For us to stand together united until this battle is won...The people of Berlin have spoken. We have done our duty, and we will keep on doing our duty. People of the world: now do your duty...People of the world, look at Berlin!"

◎ retreat（v./n.）撤退。
◎ Communism（n.）共產主義（又見第8段Communist共產黨員）。
◎ World War（n.）世界大戰。
◎ airlift（n.）空投物資；此指Berlin airlift。二次大戰後，德國分為東西兩半，分別由蘇俄及英、美勢力掌管；而首善之都柏林亦分東西兩區，東柏林屬俄國，西柏林交由英、美治理。然而問題在於柏林地理上屬東德，由英、美掌控的西柏林事實上是東德領土中的孤島。一九四八年六月到一九四九年五月，蘇聯切斷西柏林對外的一切陸路交通，然而英、美不死心，硬是靠美軍空投物資讓西柏林

9 我軍的規模遠不及蘇聯大軍。但撤退將讓共產主義席捲全歐洲。上個戰爭結束的地方，可能輕易開啓另一次世界大戰。擋住共產黨去路的唯有柏林。

10 這時開始空投——有史以來最大規模和最想像不到的救援行動，為這個城市的居民帶來食物和希望。

11 成功的勝算不大。冬天，濃霧籠罩天空，許多飛機還沒空投民生必需物資就被迫折返。今天我們所站的街道擠滿飢餓的家庭，在寒冷中等不到慰藉。

12 但在最黑暗的時刻，柏林人讓希望的火苗繼續燃燒。柏林市民不放棄。一個秋天，幾十萬柏林人來到這裡，來到狩獵公園，聆聽市長懇求世人不要放棄自由。他說：「只有一個選擇，那就是讓我們團結一致，直到贏得戰爭……柏林人開口說話了。我們盡我們的義務，我們會繼續盡我們的義務。全世界的人們：現在盡你們的義務……全世界的人們，看看柏林！」

得以撐下去，而不被蘇聯吞噬，日後傳為佳話。
◎ unlikely（adj.）希望不大的；不太可能的。與第3段improbable同義。
◎ odds are stacked against...（片語）原為賭博用語——指某項結果的投注賠率偏低；此處用以比喻成功的機率不大；希望極為渺茫。
◎ Tiergarten（n.）柏林狩獵公園——柏林市區的大公園（相當於台北的大安森林公園）。此為歐巴馬本次演講的場地。
◎ implore（v.）懇求；乞求；哀求。

13 People of the world─look at Berlin! Look at Berlin, where Germans and Americans learned to work together and trust each other less than three years after facing each other on the field of battle.

14 Look at Berlin, where the **determination** of a people met the **generosity** of the **Marshall Plan** and created a German miracle; where a victory over **tyranny** gave rise to **NATO**, the greatest **alliance** ever formed to defend our common security.

15 Look at Berlin, where the bullet holes in the buildings and the **somber** stones and **pillars** near the **Brandenburg Gate** insist that we never forget our **common humanity**.

16 People of the world─look at Berlin, where a wall came down, a continent came together, and history proved that there is no challenge too great for a world that **stands as one**.

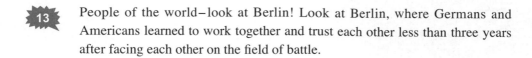

◎ determination（n.）決心。
◎ generosity（n.）慷慨；大方。
◎ Marshall Plan（n.）馬歇爾計畫──又名「歐洲復興計畫」（European Recovery Program），為二次大戰後由美國在一九四七年向歐洲十七國提供的一百三十億美元經援計畫（合今日千億美元）。該計畫因主事者國務卿喬治‧馬歇爾（George Marshall）而得名，推動期間（一九四八～一九五二），西歐經濟增長神速，使得歐洲得以從戰後的經濟破碎走向復甦。
◎ tyranny（n.）暴政；專制統治。
◎ NATO（n.）North Atlantic Treaty Organization 的縮寫，亦即北大西洋公約組織（北約）──一九四九年由美、加及西歐各國所成立的共同軍事防衛組織，目的在於協力阻止以俄國為首的東歐

13　全世界的人們——看看柏林！看看柏林，在這裡，德國人和美國人在戰場上兵戎相見不到三年後，學習合作與互信。

14　看看柏林，在這裡，一個民族的決心結合馬歇爾計畫的慷慨援助，創造了德國奇蹟；在這裡，抗暴勝利促成了北大西洋公約組織，這是為防禦我們共同安全所組成的最偉大聯盟。

15　看看柏林，建築物上的彈孔和布蘭登堡門附近嚴肅的紀念碑和紀念柱堅持要我們不可忘記共有的人道精神。

16　全世界的人們——看看柏林，在這裡，圍牆倒塌了，歐洲大陸融為一體，歷史證明，世界團結一致，沒有克服不了的挑戰。

　共產國家擴張與入侵。
◎ alliance（n.）聯盟；同盟。可參考第26段ally（n.）盟國；友邦。
◎ somber（adj.）肅穆的；深沈的；幽暗的。
◎ pillar（n.）柱子；石柱。
◎ Brandenburg Gate（n.）布蘭登堡大門——柏林市指標性建築，位於直通皇宮的菩提大道（Unter den Linden）入口，十八世紀末由普魯士王腓特烈‧威廉二世（Frederick William II）所興建。
◎ common humanity（n.）（人類所共有的）人性。
◎ stand as one（片語）同心協力；不被分化。

Sixty years after the airlift, we are called upon again. History has led us to a new **crossroad**, with new promise and new **peril**. When you, the German people, tore down that wall–a wall that divided East and West; freedom and tyranny; fear and hope–walls came tumbling down around the world. From **Kiev** to **Cape Town**, **prison camps** were closed, and the doors of democracy were opened. Markets opened too, and the spread of information and technology reduced **barriers** to opportunity and prosperity. While the 20th century taught us that we share a common destiny, the 21st has revealed a world more **intertwined** than at any time in human history.

 The fall of the **Berlin Wall** brought new hope. But that very **closeness** has given rise to new dangers–dangers that cannot be **contained** within the borders of a country or by the distance of an ocean.

 The terrorists of September 11th plotted in **Hamburg** and trained in **Kandahar** and **Karachi** before killing thousands from all over the globe on American soil.

 As we speak, cars in **Boston** and factories in Beijing are melting the **ice caps** in the Arctic, shrinking **coastlines** in **the Atlantic**, and bringing **drought** to farms from **Kansas** to Kenya.

單字解說

◎ crossroad（n.）十字路口（比喻作抉擇的時刻）。
◎ peril（n.）危險；危機。
◎ Kiev（n.）（烏克蘭）基輔。
◎ Cape Town（n.）（南非共和國首都）開普敦。
◎ prison camp（n.）戰俘營；集中營。
◎ barrier（n.）障礙；阻礙；路障。reduce barriers 排除障礙。
◎ intertwined（adj.）糾纏在一起的；緊密相連、不可分割的。
◎ Berlin Wall（n.）柏林圍牆──一九六一年興建，區隔東德與西德領土的圍牆。柏林圍牆在一九八九年被拆除，東德政府此時垮台，東、西德也因而統一。

17 在空投的六十年後，我們又被召喚。歷史帶領我們走上新的十字路口，帶著新的希望和危險。當你們，德國人民，拆掉分隔東方與西方、分隔自由與專制、分隔恐懼與希望的圍牆時，全世界的圍牆都倒塌了。從基輔到開普敦，戰俘營關了，民主的大門開啟。市場也開放了，資訊和科技的流通，降低了通往機會與繁榮的障礙。二十世紀教導我們休戚與共，二十一世紀揭開一個人類史上最緊密交織的世界。

18 柏林圍牆倒塌帶來新希望。但繼之而來的是新危險，一國的國界或海洋的距離都擋不住這些危險。

19 發動九一一攻擊事件的恐怖分子，在美國土地上殺死幾千名來自全世界的人們之前，是在漢堡策畫，在坎達哈和喀拉蚩接受訓練。

20 在我們發表談話的同時，波士頓的汽車和北京的工廠正在融化北極冰帽，大西洋的海岸線正在縮小，為堪薩斯到肯亞的農場帶來乾旱。

◎ closeness（n.）親近；熟悉。
◎ contain（v.）隔離；防止擴散。
◎ Hamburg（n.）（德國）漢堡市。
◎ Kandahar（n.）坎達哈市，阿富汗第三大城。
◎ Karachi（n.）喀拉蚩，巴基斯坦第一大城。
◎ Boston（n.）（美國麻州）波士頓。

◎ ice cap（n.）（北極常年不化的）冰帽。
◎ coastline（n.）海岸線。
◎ the Arctic（n.）北極；北極海。
◎ drought（n.）乾旱；旱災。
◎ Kansas（n.）（美國）堪薩斯州；美國穀倉之一，被譽為美國之心臟地帶（heartland——見第3段）。

Poorly **secured** nuclear material in the former **Soviet Union**, or secrets from a scientist in **Pakistan** could help build a bomb that **detonates** in Paris. The **poppies** in **Afghanistan** become the **heroin** in Berlin. The poverty and violence in **Somalia breeds** the terror of tomorrow. The **genocide** in **Darfur shames** the **conscience** of us all.

 In this new world, such dangerous **currents** have swept along faster than our efforts to contain them. That is why we cannot afford to be **divided**. No one nation, no matter how large or powerful, can defeat such challenges alone. None of us can deny these **threats**, or escape responsibility in meeting them. Yet, in the absence of Soviet tanks and a terrible wall, it has become easy to forget this truth. And if we're honest with each other, we know that sometimes, on both sides of the Atlantic, we have **drifted apart**, and forgotten our **shared destiny**.

◎ secure（v.）保護；保衛。
◎ Soviet Union（n.）蘇維埃社會主義聯邦共和國（蘇聯）。
◎ Pakistan（n.）巴基斯坦。巴基斯坦人為 Pakistani（s）。
◎ detonate（v.）引爆（炸彈）。
◎ poppy（n.）罌粟花。
◎ Afghanistan（n.）阿富汗。阿富汗人為Afghan（s）。
◎ heroin（n.）海洛因（毒品）。
◎ Somalia（n.）（非洲東部的）索馬利亞——二〇〇六年起便陷入內戰，大量難民流入鄰國衣索比亞，而衣索比亞隨即出兵犯境，兩國處於戰爭狀態。
◎ breed（v.）引起；遭惹。
◎ genocide（n.）種族滅絕；種族屠殺。

21 前蘇聯境內的核子原料疏於保安，或巴基斯坦科學家的研究機密外洩，很可能讓有心人士製造炸彈，在巴黎引爆。阿富汗的罌粟成為柏林的海洛因。索馬利亞的貧窮和暴力滋養明天的恐怖活動。達富爾的種族屠殺讓我們所有人的良心蒙羞。

22 在這個新世界，這些危險洪流的侵襲速度之快，讓我們來不及阻擋。這是為什麼我們承擔不起分裂。沒有一個國家，不管再大再強，能單獨戰勝這些挑戰。我們任何人都不能否認這些威脅的存在，或逃避迎戰它們的責任。然而，少了蘇聯坦克和可怕的圍牆，很容易忘記這個事實。如果我們彼此坦誠以對，我們很清楚，有時候，在大西洋兩岸，我們漸行漸遠，忘了我們共同的命運。

◎ Darfur（n.）非洲蘇丹的達富爾區——二〇〇三年起一場大規模種族滅絕戰爭的所在地，至今已有四十萬人葬身其中，戰爭中兒童被濫殺、婦人遭強姦、民眾被集體屠殺，慘狀堪比二戰期間德國納粹黨追殺猶太人的情景（Holocaust），同時也有為數龐大的難民潮流亡至蘇丹鄰國。二戰後歐美政府曾發誓絕不再讓種族滅絕事件再現（never again），然而達富爾卻令其汗顏。
◎ shame（v.）使人感到羞愧。
◎ conscience（n.）良心；良知。
◎ current（n.）潮流；思潮。
◎ divided（adj.）處於分裂的；意見不合的；不合作的。afford to be divided 有本錢處於分裂。
◎ threat（n.）威脅。
◎ drift apart（片語）漸行漸遠；慢慢由熟悉變得疏離。
◎ shared destiny（n.）共同的命運。

In Europe, the view that America is part of what has gone wrong in our world, rather than a force to help make it right, has become all too common. In America, there are voices that **deride** and deny the importance of Europe's role in our security and our future. Both views **miss the truth**–that Europeans today are bearing new **burdens** and taking more responsibility in **critical** parts of the world; and that just as American **bases** built in the last century still help to defend the security of this continent, so does our country still sacrifice greatly for freedom around the globe.

 Yes, there have been **differences** between America and Europe. No doubt, there will be differences in the future. But the burdens of **global citizenship** continue to **bind** us together. A **change of leadership** in Washington will not **lift this burden**. In this new century, Americans and Europeans alike will be required to do more–not less. Partnership and cooperation among nations is not a choice; it is the one way, the only way, to protect our common security and advance our common humanity.

 That is why the greatest danger of all is to allow new walls to divide us from one another.

 The walls between old **allies** on either side of the Atlantic cannot stand. The walls between the countries with the most and those with the least cannot stand. The walls between races and tribes; natives and immigrants; Christian and Muslim and Jew cannot stand. These now are the walls we must tear down.

◎ deride（v.）嘲笑；諷刺。
◎ miss the truth（片語）沒說中事實；與事實偏離。
◎ burden（n.）重擔；負擔。

◎ critical（adj.）關鍵性的。
◎ base（n.）（軍事）基地。
◎ differences（n.）意見不合；意見有分歧。
◎ global citizenship（n.）世界公民身分。

23 在歐洲，認為美國是這個世界裡出差錯的一部分，而不是協助世界導正的力量，已是很普遍的觀點。在美國，也有聲音嘲笑和否認歐洲對我們的安全和前途所扮演角色的重要性。兩種觀點都偏離了事實，今天的歐洲人在全世界重要地區承擔新的負擔和更多責任；就如同上一世紀建造的美國基地迄今仍協助防衛歐洲安全，我國仍對全球的自由做了很大的犧牲。

24 是的，美國和歐洲之間存有歧異。毫無疑問，未來仍會有。但全球公民的重擔把我們綁在一起。華盛頓領袖的更迭不會解除重擔。在這個新世紀，美國人和歐洲人都需要貢獻更多，不是更少。各國之間的夥伴關係和合作不是一種選擇；是保護我們共同安全和促進我們共同人道主義的單一途徑，是唯一途徑。

25 因此最大的危險是容許築起分裂我們的新牆。

26 大西洋兩岸的舊盟邦之間不容有牆。最富國和最貧國之間不容有牆。種族和部落之間；原住民和移民之間；基督徒、穆斯林和猶太教徒之間，不容有牆。這是我們現在必須拆除的牆。

◎ bind（v.）結合；綑綁；相繫。過去式bound 見第29段。
◎ change of leadership（片語）政黨輪替；改朝換代；「變天」。
◎ lift a burden（片語）減輕負擔。
◎ ally（n.）盟國；盟友；又可參考第14段 alliance聯盟。

We know they have fallen before. After centuries of **strife**, the people of Europe have formed a **Union** of promise and prosperity. Here, at the base of a **column** built to mark victory in war, we meet in the center of a Europe at peace. Not only have walls come down in Berlin, but they have come down in **Belfast**, where **Protestant** and **Catholic** found a way to live together; in **the Balkans**, where our **Atlantic alliance** ended wars and **brought savage war criminals to justice**; and in **South Africa**, where the struggle of a courageous people defeated **apartheid**.

 History reminds us that walls can be torn down. But the task is never easy. True partnership and true progress requires **constant** work and **sustained** sacrifice. They require sharing the burdens of **development** and **diplomacy**; of progress and peace. They require allies who will listen to each other, learn from each other and, most of all, trust each other.

◎ strife（n.）衝突；鬥爭；爭吵。
◎ Union（n.）此處指European Union——歐洲聯盟（歐盟）。
◎ column（n.）柱子——此處指柏林狩獵公園（Tiergarten）的勝利女神紀念碑（Siegessäule）——歐巴馬站在此紀念柱前演講。
◎ Belfast（n.）北愛爾蘭首都貝爾法斯特。愛爾蘭本為天主教多數國，然而北愛爾蘭由信奉（基督教）新教的英國政府統治，使得北愛爾蘭的「獨派」民族主義者（Nationalists）與支持英國統治的「統派」（Unionists）水火不容，恐怖暴力事件層出不窮，直到一九九八年雙方簽署貝爾法斯特協議（Belfast Agreement），戰火才停歇。
◎ Protestant（adj./n.）（基督教的）新教徒。
◎ Catholic（adj./n.）天主教徒。
◎ the Balkans（n.）巴爾幹半島（the Balkan Peninsula）的簡稱，此處特別指巴爾幹半島上的前南斯拉夫 former Yugoslavia（今分裂為波士尼亞Bosnia and Herzegovina、塞爾維亞 Servia、克羅埃西亞 Croatia、斯洛文尼亞 Slovenia、馬其頓 Macedonia）。九〇年代南國分裂的過程中，各族裔彼此屠殺，數十萬民眾喪命。當時由英、美主導的北大西洋公約組織（北約 NATO）派軍機轟炸，試圖阻止殘酷的戰爭罪行。

我們知道這些牆過去曾倒下。在歷經幾個世紀的衝突後，歐洲人建了一個有遠景和繁榮的聯盟。在這裡，在紀念戰時勝利的紀念柱基底，我們在承平時期的歐洲中心交會。不只柏林圍牆倒了，貝爾法斯特的牆也倒了，新教徒和天主教徒找到了共存之道；在巴爾幹半島，我們的大西洋盟國結束戰爭，將殘暴的戰犯繩之以法；在南非，英勇人民的奮鬥，戰勝了種族隔離政策。

28 歷史提醒我們，圍牆可以拆除，但任務艱鉅。真正的夥伴關係和真正的進步，需要持續不斷的努力和持久的犧牲。需要分擔發展與外交責任；分擔進步與和平責任。需要能彼此傾聽、相互學習，最重要的，需要能夠互信的盟邦。

◎ Atlantic alliance（n.）此處指 Northern Atlantic Treaty Organization（NATO）—— 北大西洋公約組織（北約）。
◎ bring...to justice（片語）使受到法律制裁；將之繩之以法。
◎ savage（adj.）野蠻的；如同禽獸的；未開化的。
◎ war criminal（n.）戰爭罪犯（指戰爭中犯下濫殺無辜、屠殺種族等違反人道之重大罪行者）。
◎ South Africa（n.）南非。
◎ apartheid（n.）（南非在一九四八至一九九四年實施的）種族隔離制——有色人種無法享受與白人相同的基本權利。此制度引發國際社會對南非的經濟制裁，也激起了國內的抗議聲浪。南非的種族隔離制於九〇年代初廢止，促成此事的白人總統戴克拉克（Frederik Willem de Klerk）與黑人民權領袖曼德拉（Nelson Mandela）共同獲得諾貝爾和平獎。
◎ constant（adj.）不時的；不斷的。constant work不斷的努力。
◎ sustained（adj.）持續的；持久的。sustained sacrifice持續不斷的犧牲。
◎ development（n.）發展（此處指救助貧窮國家，使其得到進步發展）。
◎ diplomacy（n.）外交手段（相對於使用武力）。

That is why America cannot turn inward. That is why Europe cannot **turn inward**. America has no better partner than Europe. Now is the time to build new bridges across the globe as strong as the one that bound us across the Atlantic. Now is the time to join together, through constant cooperation, strong **institutions**, shared sacrifice, and a global **commitment** to progress, to meet the challenges of the 21st century. It was this spirit that led airlift planes to appear in the sky above our heads, and people to assemble where we stand today. And this is the moment when our nations—and all nations—must **summon** that spirit anew.

 This is the moment when we must defeat **terror** and dry up the well of **extremism** that supports it. This threat is real and we cannot **shrink from** our responsibility to **combat** it. If we could create NATO to **face down** the Soviet Union, we can join in a new and global partnership to **dismantle** the networks that have struck in **Madrid** and **Amman**; in **London** and **Bali**; in **Washington** and **New York**. If we could win a battle of ideas against the communists, we can stand with the vast majority of **Muslims** who **reject** the extremism that leads to hate instead of hope.

單 字 解 說

◎ turn inward（v.）焦點向內：只注意國內事務，不重視國際情勢發展。
◎ institution（n.）組織；機構。
◎ commitment（n.）承諾。global commitment to progress追求進步的全球性承諾。
◎ summon（v.）喚起。
◎ terror（n.）恐怖行為；恐怖分子的活動。可參考第31段terrorist（n.）恐怖分子。
◎ extremism（n.）極端主義；過激主義。
◎ shrink from（v.）躲避；推卸；推諉。
◎ combat（v.）對抗；與……戰鬥。
◎ face down（片語）在對峙中以聲勢壓倒對方，令對方退卻。
◎ dismantle（v.）拆卸；拆除。
◎ Madrid（n.）馬德里——指二〇〇四年三月十一日（又稱三一一事件），西班牙大選前夕，恐怖分子利用上班尖峰時間炸毀首都馬德里的多個火車班次，造成一百九十一死、一千八百人受傷。
◎ Amman（n.）安曼——指二〇〇五年十一月九日，恐怖分子在約旦首都安曼的三家外國使節往來的飯店中放置炸彈，造成六十死一百一十五傷的慘劇。

此所以美國不能向內發展，歐洲不能向內發展。歐洲是美國最佳夥伴。現在是在全球各地搭建新橋的時候了，就像橫跨大西洋，把我們連接在一起的橋一樣堅固。現在是聯手的時候了，透過不斷的合作、堅強的機構、共同的犧牲，以及全球對進步的承諾，來迎接二十一世紀的挑戰。就是這種精神引領空投飛機飛到我們頭頂上的天空，民眾聚集在我們今天所站的位置。此刻，我們這些國家，所有國家，必須重新喚起這種精神。

此刻我們必須戰勝恐怖活動，把支持恐怖活動的激進主義井水抽乾。威脅確實存在，我們不能逃避對抗它的責任。既然我們能創造北大西洋公約組織，使蘇聯懾服，我們也能建立一個全新的全球夥伴關係，拆除在馬德里和安曼、在倫敦和峇里島、在紐約和華盛頓發動攻擊的網絡。既然我們能贏得對抗共產主義分子的思想戰，我們也能和絕大多數拒絕激進主義的穆斯林站在一起；激進主義通往仇恨，而不是希望。

◎ London（n.）倫敦──指二○○五年七月七日，英國伊斯蘭激進分子為了抗議英國政府協助美軍攻打伊拉克，於早晨尖峰時刻在倫敦的巴士與地鐵中引爆炸彈，炸死五十二名民眾，造成七百人受傷，並使得倫敦市交通系統全線癱瘓。
◎ Bali（n.）峇里島──指印尼史上傷亡最慘重的恐怖攻擊行動：二○○二年十月十二日，印尼的伊斯蘭激進組織派出自殺炸彈客在觀光鬧區引爆炸彈，造成二百零二人喪生、二百零九人受傷，其中死傷者多為外國觀光客。
◎ Washington（n.）指二○○一年九月十一日的九一一恐怖攻擊，其中位於美國首都華盛頓特區的國防部五角大廈遭挾持客機撞擊，大廈部分倒塌並起火燃燒，造成一百二十五人死亡。
◎ New York（n.）指二○○一年九月十一日的九一一恐怖攻擊，其中位於紐約的世界貿易中心（World Trade Center）南、北兩塔遭到兩架被挾持的民航機直接撞擊，起火後雙雙倒塌，造成機上及塔中兩千九百多人喪生。
◎ Muslim（n.）穆斯林信徒：伊斯蘭教徒。
◎ reject（v.）拒絕：反對。

This is the moment when we must renew our **resolve** to **rout** the **terrorists** who **threaten** our security in **Afghanistan**, and the **traffickers** who sell drugs on your streets. No one welcomes war. I recognize the enormous difficulties in Afghanistan. But my country and yours have a **stake** in seeing that NATO's first **mission** beyond Europe's borders is a success. For the people of Afghanistan, and for our shared security, the work must be done. America cannot do this alone. The Afghan people need our troops and your **troops**; our support and your support to defeat the **Taliban** and **al Qaeda**, to develop their economy, and to help them rebuild their nation. We have too much at stake to turn back now.

 This is the moment when we must renew the goal of a world without nuclear weapons. The two **superpowers** that faced each other across the wall of this city came too close too often to destroying all we have built and all that we love. With that wall gone, we need not stand **idly** by and watch the further spread of the deadly **atom**. It is time to secure all loose nuclear materials; to stop the spread of **nuclear** weapons; and to reduce the **arsenals** from another **era**. This is the moment to begin the work of seeking the peace of a world without nuclear weapons.

◎ resolve（n.）決心。亦可作動詞「下定決心」（見第36段）。
◎ rout（v.）使（敵軍）潰散；使崩潰；打得對方潰不成軍。
◎ terrorist（n.）恐怖分子。
◎ threaten（v.）威脅。
◎ Afghanistan（n.）阿富汗。九一一事件後，美國在二〇〇一年十月七日出兵阿富汗，試圖推翻包庇恐怖分子的塔利班神學士政權（見下Taliban），並揪出九一一主謀奧薩瑪・賓拉登（Osama bin Laden），及其所屬的蓋達組織（見下al Qaeda）。
◎ trafficker（n.）走私（毒品）者；毒梟。
◎ stake（n.）自身利益；利害關係。at stake（片語）攸關自身利益。
◎ mission（n.）任務。

此刻我們必須重新下決心擊潰那些在阿富汗威脅我們安全的恐怖分子，以及在你們的街頭販賣毒品的走私客。沒人歡迎戰爭。我知道阿富汗的情勢極艱難。但這場戰爭和你我的國家都有切身的利害關係——北約跨出歐洲邊界的首次任務務必成功。為了阿富汗人民，為了我們共同的安全，必須執行任務。美國不能單獨行動。阿富汗人需要我們的軍隊和你們的軍隊，需要我們和你們的支持去打敗神學士和蓋達組織，去發展他們的經濟，去協助他們重建國家。我們現在要走回頭路的風險太大。

此刻我們必須重新將沒有核武的世界訂為目標。過去在這個城市的圍牆兩邊，兩大超級強權劍拔弩張，隨時會摧毀我們建造的一切和我們所愛的一切。現在圍牆不在了，我們不需要閒閒地任由致命的核武繼續擴散。現在是確保所有管理鬆散的核子原料安全無虞的時候了；是阻止核武擴散的時候了；是裁減上個時代遺留下來的武器的時候了。此刻是開始追求沒有核武的和平世界的時候了。

◎ troops（n.）部隊；軍隊。
◎ Taliban（n.）塔利班——阿富汗篤信伊斯蘭基本教義派的神學士政權。
◎ al Qaeda（n.）蓋達組織；又譯為基地組織。以奧薩瑪‧賓拉登（Osama bin Laden）為首，反對美軍在阿拉伯國家活動的恐怖組織。
◎ superpower（n.）超級強國（指美、俄兩國）。
◎ idly（adv.）閒閒地；無所事事地。idle（adj.）閒置的；沒有在做事的。
◎ atom（n.）原子；此指原子彈。
◎ nuclear（adj.）核子的。nuclear weapons核子武器。nuclear materials核子物料；核材料。
◎ arsenal（n.）武器庫存；軍械庫存。
◎ era（n.）時代；時期；紀元。

This is the moment when every nation in Europe must have the chance to choose its own tomorrow free from the shadows of yesterday. In this century, we need a strong **European Union** that deepens the security and **prosperity** of this **continent**, while **extending a hand** abroad. In this century－in this **city of all cities**－we must reject the Cold War **mindset** of the past, and resolve to work with Russia when we can, to stand up for our values when we must, and to seek a partnership that extends across this entire continent.

 This is the moment when we must **build on** the wealth that **open markets** have created, and share its benefits more **equitably**. Trade has been a **cornerstone** of our growth and global development. But we will not be able to sustain this growth if it favors the few, and not the many. Together, we must **forge** trade that truly rewards the work that creates **wealth**, with meaningful protections for our people and our **planet**. This is the moment for trade that is free and fair for all.

◎ European Union（n.）歐洲聯盟。
◎ prosperity（n.）繁榮；富庶。
◎ continent（n.）洲；大陸。
◎ extend a hand（片語）伸出援手。
◎ city of all cities（n.）城市中的城市；最偉大的城市。
◎ mindset（n.）心態；思考方式。Cold War mindset指冷戰時期美、蘇對峙的思考方式。
◎ build on（v.）建立在……的基礎上；以……為基礎繼續前進。

此刻，歐洲每個國家必須有機會擺脫歷史陰影，選擇自己的明天。在本世紀，我們需要強大的歐洲聯盟，加強歐洲大陸的安全和繁榮，同時擴大海外責任。在本世紀，特別是這個城市，我們必須摒棄過去的冷戰心態，下決心盡可能與俄羅斯合作，在必要時挺身而出維護我們的價值，尋求與整個歐洲大陸建立夥伴關係。

 此刻我們必須在開放市場所創造的財富上建設，並力求雨露均霑。貿易一向是我們經濟成長和全球發展的基石。如果貿易只讓少數人獲利，而不是多數人，我們無法維持這樣的成長。我們必須攜手打造真正回饋創造財富工作的貿易，並對我們的人民和我們的地球採取有意義的保護措施。現在是對全人類推動自由和公平貿易的時候了。

◎ open market（n.）開放市場。
◎ equitably（adv.）均等的；公平分配的。
◎ cornerstone（n.）基石；根基。
◎ forge（v.）鑄造；建造；建立。
◎ wealth（n.）財富；create wealth 創造財富。
◎ planet（n.）星球──此處指地球。

098 ▶▶▶ 敢於大膽希望——歐巴馬七篇關鍵演說

This is the moment when we must help answer the **call for** a new dawn in the **Middle East**. My country must stand with yours and with Europe in sending a direct message to **Iran** that it must **abandon** its nuclear **ambitions**. We must support the **Lebanese** who have marched and bled for democracy, and the **Israelis** and **Palestinians** who seek a **secure** and **lasting** peace. And despite past differences, this is the moment when the world should support the millions of **Iraqis** who seek to rebuild their lives, even as we pass responsibility to the Iraqi government and finally bring this war to a close.

This is the moment when we must come together to save this planet. Let us resolve that we will not leave our children a world where the oceans rise and **famine** spreads and terrible storms **devastate** our lands. Let us **resolve** that all nations—including my own—will act with the same **seriousness of purpose** as has your nation, and reduce the **carbon** we send into our **atmosphere**. This is the moment to give our children back their future. This is the moment to stand as one.

單字解說

◎ call for（v.）鼓吹；提倡。
◎ Middle East（n.）中東地區。
◎ Iran（n.）伊朗。
◎ abandon（v.）放棄。
◎ ambition（n.）野心；企圖心。nuclear ambitions核野心；建造核子彈的野心。
◎ Lebanese（n.）黎巴嫩人。Lebanon黎巴嫩。此指黎巴嫩的「雪松革命」（Cedar Revolution）：二○○五年三月十四日，五百萬名黎巴嫩人走上首都貝魯特街頭，抗議總理哈里里（Rafik Hariri）被刺殺，並要求敘利亞自黎巴嫩南部撤軍。
◎ Israeli（n.）以色列人。Israel以色列。
◎ Palestinian（n.）巴勒斯坦人。（註：巴勒斯坦人與以色列人有領土糾紛——巴勒斯坦人故居目前屬以色列領土，巴勒斯坦至今無法立國，巴、以雙方為此征戰不休。）

此刻是我們必須協助響應中東新黎明號召的時候了。我的國家必須與你們的國家和歐洲站在一起，對伊朗直接發出訊息，要求伊朗必須放棄核武野心。我們必須支持走上街頭、為民主流血的黎巴嫩人，協助尋求穩定和永久和平的以色列人和巴勒斯坦人。儘管過去有歧見，現在是全世界應支持數以百萬計想重建生活的伊拉克人的時候了，即便我們已將責任交給伊拉克政府，終於結束戰爭。

此刻是我們必須攜手拯救地球的時候了。讓我們下定決心，我們不要留給我們的孩子一個海平面上升、饑荒擴大、可怕的風暴毀壞我們土地的世界。讓我們下定決心，包括我的國家在內的所有國家，拿出與你們國家同樣認真的決心，減少我們送入大氣層的碳。此刻是我們把我們孩子的未來還給他們的時候了。此刻是團結一致的時候了。

◎ secure（adj.）安全的；安穩的。
◎ lasting（adj.）持久的；永續的。
◎ Iraqi（n.）伊拉克人。Iraq伊拉克。此指二〇〇三年三月美國出兵伊拉克，推翻海珊（Sadam Hussein）政權，之後伊拉克境內內戰不斷，美國仍有待建立秩序，再將統治權歸還伊拉克民選政府。
◎ famine（n.）饑荒。
◎ devastate（v.）蹂躪；毀壞。
◎ resolve（v.）下定決心。亦可作名詞（見第31段）。
◎ seriousness of purpose（n.）認真的面對態度；正視的心態。
◎ carbon（n.）碳；此指二氧化碳（排放到空氣中的二氧化碳——是全球暖化的元兇）。
◎ atmosphere（n.）大氣層。

And this is the moment when we must give hope to those **left behind** in a **globalized** world. We must remember that the Cold War born in this city was not a battle for land or treasure. Sixty years ago, the planes that flew over Berlin did not drop bombs; instead they delivered food, and **coal**, and candy to grateful children. And in that show of **solidarity**, those pilots won more than a military victory. They won hearts and minds; love and loyalty and trust—not just from the people in this city, but from all those who heard the story of what they did here.

 Now the world will watch and remember what we do here—what we do with this moment. Will we extend our hand to the people in the forgotten corners of this world who **yearn** for lives marked by **dignity** and opportunity; by **security** and **justice**? Will we lift the child in **Bangladesh** from **poverty**, **shelter** the **refugee** in Chad, and **banish** the **scourge** of **AIDS in our time**?

 Will we stand for the human rights of the **dissident** in Burma, the **blogger** in Iran, or the voter in **Zimbabwe**? Will we give meaning to the words "never again" in Darfur?

單字解說

◎ left behind（adj.）被拋棄的；遠遠落後的；
　leave behind（v.）丟下不管。
◎ globalized（adj.）全球化的；globalize
　（v.）全球化。
◎ coal（n.）煤炭。
◎ solidarity（n.）團結；上下一心。
◎ yearn（v.）渴望；非常希望。
◎ dignity（n.）尊嚴。
◎ security（n.）人身安全。
◎ justice（n.）公平正義。

◎ Bangladesh（n.）孟加拉。
◎ poverty（n.）貧窮。lift from poverty 使脫離貧窮。
◎ shelter（v.）為……提供庇護；為……提供居留之處。
◎ refugee（n.）難民；流亡者。
◎ Chad（n.）查德共和國——為蘇丹鄰國，同時也是達富爾大屠殺（見第21段）難民潮群聚之地，因而引發暴力與戰亂。
◎ banish（v.）驅逐；消弭。

此刻我們必須給那些在全球化世界裡落後的人們希望。我們必須記住，誕生於這個城市的冷戰，不是為了爭奪土地和財富的戰役。六十年前，飛越在柏林上空的飛機沒有扔炸彈；他們空投食物和煤，為滿心感激的孩子送來糖果。在展現團結的行動中，飛行員不只贏得軍事勝利，他們贏得了人心，贏得愛、忠誠和信任，不只出於這個城市的人民，也出於所有聽說他們事蹟的人。

現在全世界將注視、記住我們在這裡的作為，看著我們此刻做了什麼。我們會向世界被遺忘角落、渴望過著有尊嚴和機會、有安全和正義的生活的人們伸出援手嗎？我們會解除孟加拉孩子的貧窮、提供查德難民住處、在我們有生之年消除愛滋病的苦難根源嗎？

我們會出面保障緬甸異議分子，伊朗部落格作家，和辛巴威選民的人權嗎？「永不容許」的誓言，我們在達富爾做得到嗎？

◎ scourge（n.）天災；大災難；大瘟疫。
◎ AIDS（n.）愛滋病——Acquired Immune Deficiency Syndrome（後天免疫缺乏症候群）的縮寫。
◎ in our time（片語）在我們有生之年。
◎ dissident（n.）異議分子；持反對意見者。
◎ Burma（n.）緬甸。（註：緬甸軍政府以逮捕異議分子著稱，其中以一九九一年獲得諾貝爾和平獎的異議分子翁山蘇姬〔Aung San Suu Kyi〕最為出名。）
◎ blogger（n.）寫部落格的人。blog（n.）部落格。此指伊朗以反革命、間諜等罪名逮捕在部落格上批評政府的網民，並判以重刑，引起世界各地保衛言論自由與新聞自由的組織大加撻伐。
◎ Zimbabwe（n.）辛巴威。二○○八年辛巴威總統選舉，執政長達二十八年的穆加比（Robert Mugabe）動用軍隊以暴力恐嚇人民，威脅其投支持票，使得選舉公平性盡失，引起國際撻伐。

40 Will we **acknowledge** that there is no more powerful example than the one each of our nations **projects** to the world? Will we reject **torture** and stand for the **rule of law**? Will we welcome **immigrants** from different lands, and **shun discrimination** against those who don't look like us or **worship** like we do, and keep the promise of **equality** and opportunity for all of our people?

41 People of Berlin–people of the world–this is our moment. This is our time.

42 I know my country has not **perfected** itself. At times, we've struggled to keep the promise of **liberty** and equality for all of our people. We've made our share of mistakes, and there are times when our actions around the world have not lived up to our best **intentions**.

43 But I also know how much I love America. I know that for more than two centuries, we have **strived–at great cost** and great sacrifice–to form a more perfect **union**; to seek, with other nations, a more hopeful world. Our **allegiance** has never been to any particular tribe or kingdom–indeed, every language is spoken in our country; every culture has left its **imprint** on ours; every point of view is expressed in our public squares. What has always united us–what has always **driven** our people; what drew my father to America's shores–is a set of ideals that **speak to aspirations** shared by all people: that we can live free from fear and free from **want**; that we can speak our minds and **assemble** with whomever we choose and **worship** as we please.

◎ acknowledge（v.）承認；認知；認識到。
◎ project（v.）投射。
◎ torture（n.）嚴刑拷打；使用酷刑。
◎ rule of law（片語）法治。
◎ immigrant（n.）移民。
◎ shun（v.）避開；遠離。

◎ discrimination（n.）歧視。
◎ worship（v.）信仰；拜神。
◎ equality（n.）平等。
◎ perfect（v.）使趨於完美；使完美無缺。
◎ liberty（n.）自由。
◎ intention（n.）心意；best intentions好意。

我們能夠體認我們每個國家對全世界的示範作用強大無比嗎？我們會摒棄刑求而維護法治？我們會歡迎來自不同國家的移民，不去歧視長相和我們不同或祈禱儀式不同的人，並謹遵全人類平等和機會均等的承諾？

柏林人，全世界的人，這是我們的時刻。這是我們的時代。

我知道我的國家本身不完美。有時，我們履行維護國人自由和平等的承諾有些力不從心。我們也有錯誤，有些時候，我們在全球的行動不符合我們最良善的意圖。

但我知道我多麼愛美國。我知道，兩個世紀多以來，我們努力奮鬥建立更完美的聯邦，付出了極高的代價和犧牲；與其他國家共同追求更有希望的世界。我們從未向某個部族或王國效忠——確實，我們國家裡操什麼語言的人都有；每一種文化都在我們的文化裡留下印記。我們的公共廣場可供表達各種觀點。從來，凝聚我們、激勵我們的人民、吸引我父親來到美國海岸的，是一套理想，迎合所有人共同的抱負：我們能過著免於恐懼和匱乏的生活；我們能把心裡的話說出來；我們能和任何人集會，能信奉任何信仰。

◎ strive（v.）奮鬥；努力。
◎ at great cost（片語）付出了很大的代價。
◎ union（n.）聯邦；United States的別稱。
◎ allegiance（n.）效忠；忠誠。
◎ imprint（n.）印記；印象。
◎ drive（v.）驅動；驅使；促使前進。

◎ speak to（v.）能得到認同；能得到青睞。
◎ aspiration（n.）志向；抱負；理想。
◎ want（n.）缺乏；不足。
◎ assemble（v.）聚集；集會（指憲法保障的人民集會權）。
◎ worship（v.）信仰；信奉神明（指憲法保障的人民信仰自由）。

These are the aspirations that joined the fates of all nations in this city. These aspirations are bigger than anything that drives us apart. It is because of these aspirations that the airlift began. It is because of these aspirations that all free people–everywhere–became citizens of Berlin. It is in pursuit of these aspirations that a new generation–our generation–must make our mark on the world.

People of Berlin–and people of the world–the scale of our challenge is great. The road ahead will be long. But I come before you to say that we are **heirs** to a struggle for freedom. We are a people of improbable hope. With an eye toward the future, with resolve in our hearts, let us remember this history, and answer our destiny, and remake the world once again.

單 字 解 說

◎heir（n.）繼承人。

這些抱負在這個城市裡連結過所有國家的命運。這些抱負大於任何將我們分開的力量。因為這些抱負過，空投展開了。因為這些抱負，來自各地的所有自由的人們，成為柏林市民。透過追求這些抱負，新世代，我們這一代，必在世上留下功名。

柏林人，還有全世界的人，我們的挑戰範圍很大。前路漫長。但我來到你們面前說，我們繼承先人爭取自由的奮鬥精神。我們懷有看似不可能的希望。把眼光放遠，我們心裡下定決心，讓我們記住這段歷史，回應我們的命運，再造世界。

第三部分 🏆 文句解析

◎李文肇（美國舊金山州立大學外文系副教授、國立台灣師範大學翻譯研究所特約兼任副教授）

　　八家國際媒體調查顯示，二〇〇八年美國總統選舉若開放給全世界投票，歐巴馬將成為囊括八成普選票的大贏家。歐巴馬在海外的支持度遠超過美國本土，而從他二〇〇八年七月在柏林狩獵公園（Tiergarten）勝利女神紀念碑（Siegessäule）前的這場演說不難看出端倪——英國「衛報」（Guardian）形容場面猶如搖滾巨星的大陣仗，德國「每日鏡報」（Der Tagesspiegel）將之比作救世主降臨，百萬年輕人擠爆了布蘭登堡大門（Brandenburg）通往狩獵公園的大道，前來聆聽這位未來領袖談保護地球，談歐美合作，談世界和平——當時歐巴馬還未獲民主黨提名，更別說當選美國總統，然而魅力已銳不可擋。歐巴馬在演說中一反布希總統（George W. Bush）的唯我獨尊，發言顯得謙和審慎，為美國過去的失策表歉意，贏得如雷的掌聲。本篇充分表現出領袖人物的親和力，也算是彰顯歐巴馬國際觀的代表作。

　　1-12段

　　演說開場，歐巴馬刻意放低身段，說自己不是候選人（candidate）而是世界公民（citizen of the world），是傭人（domestic servant）和牧羊人（goat herder）的子嗣。然而也正因為出身卑微，了解幸福得來不易，所以才特別珍惜美國人所享有的自由，一如飽經戰亂、死裡逃生的柏林人也特別能夠體會自由的珍貴。

　　歐巴馬以美、德兩國共同奮鬥的歷史拉近兩國人民的距離。6至11段細述二次大戰後共產勢力西進，一九四八至一九四九蘇聯切斷柏林聯外交通，

人民靠的是美國空軍空投物資（airlift），才讓柏林免於淪陷鐵幕。

　　第12段特別引述圍城期間西柏林市長路透（Ernst Reuter）同樣在狩獵公園對受困民眾的精神喊話，強調絕不屈服、絕不向共產勢力投降。當時美、德密切合作，路透曾向美軍將領克雷（Lucius Clay）表示，你負責物資，我負責人民士氣。兩國的合作，讓柏林市民度過了飢餓的寒冬，也讓共軍圍城終究功虧一簣。

　　13-21段

　　第14段則提到戰後德國窮苦潦倒之際，美國大方地提出了馬歇爾計畫（Marshall Plan）的百億援助，讓整個歐洲經濟得以發展成今日的規模；而當蘇聯共產勢力伸入歐洲之時，美國組織北大西洋公約組織（NATO）嚇阻其西進，讓西歐得以保有今日的自由與民主。

　　16與18段兩度提到一九八九年柏林圍牆倒塌（第16段：a wall came down；第18段：the fall of the Berlin Wall）、東西德因此統一，藉以象徵共產主義式微、民主自由勝利。歐巴馬在第16段藉此強調，如果連共產與自由之間的藩籬都能擊垮，那麼世界上有什麼不可能的事？六十年前短兵相接的同盟國與軸心國，如今泯滅國界（a continent came together）組織歐洲聯盟（European Union）。但歐巴馬在第18段同時也呼籲，戰爭的型態改變了——過去是軍隊與軍隊的戰爭，敵人處於國界之外，或可用大海隔開（contained within the borders or a country, or by the distance of an ocean），今則分界幾近不存在，各國命運緊密相連（intertwined），19至21段以實例舉證：阿富汗的罌粟花搖身一變成為德國街頭的毒品；北京和波士頓的工廠廢氣融化了北極的冰山，致使美國中西部乾旱；在德國密謀、阿富汗受訓的恐怖分子，最終攻擊美國紐約。

　　22-29段

22、23兩段反映近八年不少歐洲人深感美國窮兵黷武、獨斷獨行的行徑在擾亂世界，而反之美國也有人視歐洲為不敢有所作為的紙老虎。歐巴馬呼籲兩邊放棄成見，建立合作與夥伴關係（第24段：partnership and cooperation）。

第26段，歐巴馬再度回到拆牆的比喻，藉此闡述他在各篇演說中力倡的多元文化觀：不但要拆除歐美兩邊之間的圍牆，也要拆除種族之間的圍牆，要拆除宗教之間的圍牆，要拆除貧富之間的圍牆，要拆除新舊移民之間的圍牆。第27段回顧九〇年代至今，各種無形「圍牆」的拆除：南非種族隔離的終結、北愛爾蘭宗教紛爭的結束、南斯拉夫族群屠殺的遏止、歐洲聯盟與共同市場的建立。

30-32段

30到31段提到了當前世界所面臨的恐怖主義威脅，以及歐巴馬的因應之道。

第30段完整列舉了千禧年以來佔據報紙頭條的五大國際恐怖攻擊事件。二〇〇一年的九一一恐怖攻擊，伊斯蘭激進分子在美國本土劫持民航客機撞擊紐約世貿大樓南、北兩塔以及華府五角大廈周遭建築，造成數千人死亡，雙塔焚燒倒塌的駭人畫面震驚全球。二〇〇二年，伊斯蘭基本教義派在印尼觀光勝地峇里島鬧區引爆炸彈，炸死數百國際遊客。二〇〇四年西班牙大選前夕，恐怖分子在交通尖峰時間炸毀首都馬德里的通勤火車，造成百死千傷。二〇〇五年七月，英國倫敦的巴士與地鐵遭人放置炸彈，炸死五十二名民眾，七百人受傷，倫敦交通全線癱瘓。同年十一月，約旦首都安曼三家外國使節往來的飯店被炸，造成六十死一百一十五傷。

五年內發生五大恐怖攻擊，歐巴馬在第31段的因應之道，是歐美聯合揪出藏匿在阿富汗的元兇，擊敗蓋達組織（al Qaeda）與塔利班政權

（Taliban）。恐怖主義之外，伊朗、北韓等國發展核子武器，對自由世界也是一大威脅——對此，歐巴馬在第32段力促歐美共同防止核擴散，消滅核子武器。

33-36段

33到36段歐巴馬談到未來的願景，要讓歷史對我們作何評價，要留給子孫怎樣的家園。第33段著眼歐洲政治，認為必須拋棄過去西歐與蘇聯對峙的冷戰思維，要主動拉攏俄國，讓整個歐洲處於互助、共榮的氣氛中。第34段說到貧富差距，認為自由市場所創造的財富要讓全民共同分享才有意義，而不是集中在少數人手中。他說貿易必須兼顧公平以及對於環境的保護。

第35段主攻中東議題，提倡主動幫助伊拉克、黎巴嫩等地區爭取民主與安定，調停以色列與巴勒斯坦間的領土糾紛，同時由歐、美雙方出面，堅定地說服伊朗放棄製造核子武器。

第36段宣示了美國保護地球環境的決心：在全球暖化，海平面上升，颶風肆虐之際，歐巴馬誓言配合國際減少美國的二氧化碳排放量，降低對大氣層的破壞，留給子孫一個能夠永續發展的地球。

37-41段

37至40段體現的是歐巴馬關心世界、悲天憫人的胸懷，列舉的是近十年世界各角落的人道悲劇。其中第39段所提到的達富爾（Darfur）種族大屠殺（又見第21段），讓人聯想起二次大戰期間德國納粹黨撲殺猶太人，事後西方國家承諾再也不容許此類行徑重現（never again），然而眼看達富爾慘劇有過之而無不及，四十萬生靈遭姦殺擄掠，甚至波及鄰國查德，讓旁觀者不勝欷歔。同段還提到了遭伊朗當局監禁的部落格作家、被緬甸軍政府軟禁的異議分子、被總統御軍恐嚇拷打的辛巴威選民——個個都需要西方伸出援手，保障人權，保障尊嚴。

　　第40段強調，富裕的西方國家必須以身作則，本身就要尊重法治、保障人權，對各族裔一律平等，才能被世界看得起──而此時此刻正是這種種理想付諸實行的時候。

42-45段

　　在第42段中，歐巴馬一改過去布希總統單邊主義的強硬作風，在此為美國所犯下的錯誤向世人道歉──為此贏得了群眾的掌聲。他承認美國心有餘而力不足，在國際上的所作所為還未臻完美，也犯下了不該犯的錯誤。然而從43段起，他便開始闡述崇尚自由、執著理想的美國精神。45段最後作出的結論是，美國是一個無比樂觀的民族（a people of improbable hope），願意帶領世界迎接新世紀的挑戰，創造更美好的命運。

　　四十五年前，也曾有一位年輕帥氣的美國總統來到德國柏林，以「我是柏林人」（Ich bin ein Berliner）為號召發表演說，讓身陷冷戰恐懼中的柏林居民士氣再起。當年的甘迺迪（John F. Kennedy）總統意氣風發，讓世界為之瘋狂，也成為流行文化中的代表人物。四十五年後的歐巴馬面對這群反戰、反恐、關心人權、關心地球的柏林人，似乎也贏得了人心，重振美國的金字招牌，可供後世傳為佳話。

D.C, July 15, 2008

A New Strategy for a New World

Rebuilding Our Alliances

2008年7月15日於華府

新世界的新戰略

重建我們的盟友關係

◎ 深度導讀：陸以正（無任所大使）
◎ 單字、文句解析：楊人凱
◎ 翻譯：蔡繼光（聯合報國際新聞中心編譯組）
◎ 審訂：彭鏡禧（國立臺灣大學外文系及戲劇系特聘教授）

第一部分 深度導讀

新的世界 需要新戰略

二〇〇八年七月十五日在華盛頓演講

◎陸以正（無任所大使）

　　歐巴馬在競選期間發表的這篇演說，目的原在勾劃出一個輪廓，如果他當選總統，美國會如何與其他國家相處。要記得他講話時間是七月中旬，與雷曼兄弟公司（Lehman Brothers）破產之日巧合，離十一月五日的選舉則幾乎早了四個月。

　　等到美國大選日，全世界已被金融海嘯的浪潮捲入怒海波濤中，載浮載沈。歐巴馬預計將援外預算加倍的理想，在他第一任四年內恐怕難以兌現。但各國仍可從豪氣干雲的本篇裡，了解美國新總統的世界觀，以及他對許多國際問題的看法。

　　演講之日，雖然民主黨總統全代會尚未開始，歐巴馬已經累積了足夠出席代表（convention delegates）的票，確定會擊敗希拉蕊，獲得提名。他主要目的是解釋他外交政策的藍圖。

　　本篇多少也有針對全代會的含意，所以他一開頭就提到六十餘年前民主黨全盛期的外交團隊，包括杜魯門總統（Harry S. Truman）、艾契遜國務卿（Dean Acheson）、創議對蘇聯「圍堵政策（containment policy）」的外交家肯南（George F. Kennan），和從五星上將轉任國務卿的馬歇爾將軍（George C. Marshall）。

　　歐巴馬的用意很明顯，他要追隨這些先進的腳步，但會善用包括民主理念、經濟實力、情報蒐集與外交手段等工具，達到不戰而勝目的。講到對九一一事件的反應，他批評布希總統坐失良機，一連用了六次「我們原可（we could have...）」如

何如何，指責共和黨政府所採外交與軍事對策的錯誤。

　　反對伊拉克戰爭是歐巴馬競選的招牌。他列舉五項外交與國防政策的重點：終止伊戰，剿滅恐怖集團，阻止流氓國家獲得核武，確保能源安全，重整美與盟邦關係，迎接二十一世紀的挑戰。這些也都是布希的目標，只是說來比做到容易而已。

　　仔細咀嚼歐巴馬的宣示，其實他是個「鷹派（hawks）」而非「鴿派（doves）」。他誓言要在阿富汗和巴基斯坦追殺賓拉登（Osama bin Laden）和蓋達（al Qaeda）分子，至少加派兩個旅的兵力，不受北大西洋公約盟國的牽制。

　　舉馬歇爾計畫成功的前例，歐巴馬承諾將每年增加十億美元對阿富汗的經濟援助，不只給首都喀布爾（Kabul）一地，而是供邊遠省份作基礎建設之用。唯有改善阿國貧苦農民的生活，才能根絕他們種植鴉片，輸出貽害世界的習慣。

　　冷戰時期只有美、蘇兩強擁有核子武器，但今日全世界有四十幾個國家、民間總共持有超過五十噸的濃縮鈾。歐巴馬要跟俄國談判彼此減低核武數量，阻止核武擴散，尤其不能讓北韓或伊朗製造或持有原子彈。他說，必要時他願意會晤伊朗政府的領袖，但時間與地點要由他來決定。

　　美國一天要花費七億元從國外進口石油，歐巴馬說他當選後，將投資一千五百億美元，研究與發展替代品，以確保能源安全，不再受石油輸出國家組織（OPEC）的箝制。他也要在二〇五〇年之前，做到全球總共減少排放80％的溫室氣體。

　　歐巴馬細數他的整體外交政策：與歐洲盟友共同面對二十一世紀的挑戰；與日、韓、澳洲、印度合作安定亞洲；與中國就共同利益合作，但也鼓勵大陸更加開放，更朝市場經濟移動；與北約盟邦更緊密合作，更尊重它們的立場；改造聯合國，使美國有更大影響力；解決以色列與巴勒斯坦爭執，使以國有安全感，而巴勒斯坦終能建國。

　　天下政治領袖都喜歡開一大堆天花亂墜的支票，歐巴馬也不能免俗。他要將對外援助到二〇一二年增至五百億美元，支持所謂「失敗國家」改革，幫助非洲經濟成長，將全球貧窮率減半，並使疾病不再肆虐人間；信不信就由你了。

第二部分  主文/中譯

主文中譯◎蔡繼光（聯合報國際新聞中心編譯組）
單字解說◎楊人凱

 Sixty-one years ago, George Marshall announced the plan that would come to bear his name. Much of Europe **lay in ruins**. The United States faced a powerful and **ideological enemy intent on world domination**. This menace was magnified by the recently discovered capability to destroy life on an unimaginable scale. The Soviet Union didn't yet have an atomic bomb, but **before long** it would.

 The challenge facing the greatest generation of Americans—the generation that had **vanquished fascism on the battlefield**—was how to **contain this threat** while extending freedom's frontiers. Leaders like Truman and Acheson, Kennan and Marshall, knew that there was no single decisive blow that could be struck for freedom. We needed a new **overarching** strategy to meet the challenges of a new and dangerous world.

單 字 解 說

◎ to lie in ruins：躺在一片廢墟之中。這裡，lay是lie的過去式，過去分詞是lain，這是大學入學考試常考的一個字。

◎ an ideological enemy intent on world domination：一個專注於支配全世界的意識形態上的敵人。這裡指的是蘇聯（the Soviet Union），intent作名詞解釋時是意圖的意思，to be intent on（doing something）是片語，這裡intent是當形容詞，意思是「專注於」。

六十一年前，馬歇爾宣布了日後以他為名的計畫。歐洲斷垣殘壁四處可見，美國面臨一個國力強大，意識形態鮮明，處心積慮想獨霸世界的敵國。最新又發現它擁有殺人如麻的利器，使得這項威脅更加可怕。雖然蘇聯尚未造出原子彈，但那只是早晚的事。

在戰場上擊潰法西斯主義的這個世代，是美國最偉大的一代，但他們卻面臨該如何遏阻這個威脅，並拓展自由疆域的挑戰。國家領袖，如杜魯門和艾契遜、肯南和馬歇爾都知道，自由乃非一蹴可幾者。面對一個嶄新、危險的世界挑戰，我們也必須有全面的新戰略。

◎ before long（片語）：不久，這是成語式的片語。long在這裡是名詞，before long可以與soon交換使用。如：I will see you again before long.（我不久就會再見到你。）
◎ vanquished fascism on the battlefield：在戰場上消滅了法西斯主義，指打敗了納粹德國。
◎ to contain a threat：contain是指把一個東西包起來，不讓它外流。
◎ overarching（adj.）：是一種弓形的拱狀物，這裡是分詞當形容詞用。

Such a strategy would join overwhelming military strength with sound judgment. It would shape events not just through military force, but through the force of our ideas; through economic power, intelligence and diplomacy. It would support strong allies that freely shared our ideals of liberty and democracy; open markets and the rule of law. It would foster new international institutions like the United Nations, NATO, and the World Bank, and focus on every corner of the globe. It was a strategy that saw clearly the world's dangers, while seizing its promise.

As a general, Marshall had spent years helping FDR wage war. But the Marshall Plan—which was just one part of this strategy—helped rebuild not just allies, but also the nation that Marshall had plotted to defeat. In the speech announcing his plan, he concluded not with tough talk or **definitive** declarations—but rather with questions and a call for perspective. "The whole world of the future," Marshall said, "**hangs on** a proper judgment." To make that judgment, he asked the American people to examine distant events that directly affected their security and prosperity. He closed by asking: "What is needed? What can best be done? What must be done?"

What is needed? What can best be done? What must be done?

◎ definitive：（adj.）決定性的；最後的。

這個新戰略，要以無敵的軍力和睿智的判斷為後盾：不可光憑武力，要以創意取勝；以經濟實力、情報和外交成事。凡是無條件與我們共享自由民主理念，開放市場，崇尚法治的堅強友邦，都該支持。新國際機構，如聯合國、北大西洋公約組織和世界銀行，要照顧；全球每個角落都要關懷。這個新戰略，不僅洞悉世界危機，也抓緊發展的契機。

 馬歇爾將軍為羅斯福總統運籌帷幄，作戰多年；馬歇爾計畫雖僅是這個戰略的一部分，卻不僅幫助盟邦，也幫費心用計擊敗的敵國重建。馬歇爾在宣布計畫的演說中，沒有強硬的語彙或不容妥協的宣言，而是以疑問和前瞻的呼籲作結。「全世界的未來，」馬歇爾說，「端賴睿智的判斷。」為了這個判斷，他要求全美民眾審視直接影響他們安全與繁榮的長遠因素。他在總結時問道：「需要的是什麼？做什麼最有用？該做些什麼？」

 需要的是什麼？什麼最能奏效？該做些什麼？

◎ hang on：（片語）有握住不放的意思，在此也可以解釋為仰賴。

Today's dangers are different, though no less **grave**. The power to destroy life **on a catastrophic scale** now risks falling into the hands of terrorists. The future of our security—and our planet—is held hostage to our dependence on foreign oil and gas. From the cave-spotted mountains of northwest Pakistan, to the **centrifuges spinning beneath Iranian soil**, we know that the American people cannot be protected by oceans or the **sheer might** of our military alone.

 The attacks of September 11 brought this new reality into a terrible and ominous focus. On that bright and beautiful day, the world of peace and prosperity that was the legacy of our Cold War victory seemed to suddenly vanish under rubble, and twisted steel, and clouds of smoke.

 But the depth of this **tragedy** also **drew out** the decency and determination of our nation. At blood banks and vigils; in schools and in the United States Congress, Americans were united—more united, even, than we were at the dawn of the **Cold War**. The world, too, was united against the perpetrators of this evil act, as old allies, new friends, and even long—time adversaries stood by our side. It was time—once again—for America's might and **moral suasion** to be harnessed; it was time to once again shape a new security strategy for an ever-changing world.

◎ grave：嚴重的。如：grave responsibilities嚴重的責任。
◎ on a catastrophic scale：浩劫式的規模。浩劫式的災難英文叫catastrophe。
◎ centrifuge spinning beneath Iranian soil：在伊朗土地下運轉的離心機。centrifuge離心機是製造濃縮鈾必須使用的機器。歐巴馬在此指稱伊朗在製造核子武器。
◎ sheer might：sheer是純粹的、全然的意思，如a sheer impossibility絕對不可能之事。might在這裡不是助動詞may的過去式，而是個名詞，代表力量，如：This is beyond my might.（這事超出我的

今天的危險，本質不同，嚴重性卻毫不稍遜。傷人無數，能使人間變成煉獄的武器，如今有落入恐怖分子手中的風險。由於我們對外國石油和天然氣的依賴，使我們的身家，乃至於整個地球未來的安全，淪為人質。從巴基斯坦西北山洞錯落的山脈，到伊朗地底旋轉不停的離心機，我們了解，徒有兩大洋的屏障，或光憑我們的武力，不足以保護美國人民。

 九一一恐怖攻擊，讓這個新事實成為可怕不祥的焦點。就在那個清朗美麗的日子，我們冷戰勝利所得來的世界和平與繁榮遺緒，好像就在瓦礫、扭曲的鋼筋和陣陣煙幕底下，突然消失無蹤。

 但這場悲劇的深刻，也激發了我國的道德與決心。在血庫與守靈地點；在學校及美國國會，美國民眾團結起來——甚至比冷戰伊始，更加團結。全世界也團結起來，新朋舊友，甚至連宿敵都站到我們這一邊，聲討幹下這起邪惡勾當的劊子手。那是美國力量和道德勸說再度被動員起來的時刻；那同時也是針對這個變動不斷之世界，新安全戰略再度成形的時刻。

能力之外。）
◎ tragedy（n.）：悲劇性事件、災難。
◎ draw out（片語）：有拔出、取出的意思，在此可解釋為激發。
◎ cold War（片語）：冷戰。
◎ moral（adj.）：道德（上）的。
◎ suasion（n.）：說服、勸告。

Imagine, for a moment, what we could have done in those days, and months, and years after 9/11.

 We could have **deployed** the full force of American power to **hunt down** and **destroy** Osama bin Laden, al Qaeda, the Taliban, and all of the **terrorists** responsible for 9/11, while supporting real **security** in Afghanistan.

 We could have secured **loose nuclear** materials around the world, and updated a 20th century non-proliferation **framework** to meet the challenges of the 21st.

 We could have invested hundreds of billions of dollars in **alternative** sources of energy to grow our economy, save our planet, and end the **tyranny** of oil.

 We could have strengthened old **alliances**, formed new partnerships, and renewed international institutions to advance peace and **prosperity**.

 We could have called on a new generation to step into the strong currents of history, and to serve their country as troops and teachers, Peace Corps volunteers and police officers.

◎ deploy（v.）：展開、部署。
◎ hunt down（片語）：追捕到。
◎ destroy（v.）：毀壞、破壞。

◎ terrorist（n.）：恐怖主義者、恐怖分子。
◎ security（n.）：安全。
◎ loose（adj.）：未控制的、四處散放的。

9 想像一下，九一一後的這些日、月、年中，我們原可完成的許多事情。

10 我們原可全力部署美國的兵力，追捕並殲滅賓拉登、蓋達、神學士和所有涉及九一一的恐怖分子，同時支持阿富汗的真正安全。

11 我們原可嚴格管制散處全球各地的核子材料；針對二十一世紀新挑戰，更新二十世紀禁核擴散條約架構。

12 我們原可投資上兆美元研發替代能源，促進我們的經濟成長，拯救我們的地球，並終結石油的專橫亂象。

13 我們原可鞏固舊盟友，締結新夥伴關係，重整國際組織，促進和平與繁榮。

14 我們原可呼籲新生代投入這股歷史洪流，或從軍、或擔任教師、或加入和平團志工及警察。

◎ nuclear（adj.）：原子能的、原子彈的。
◎ framework（n.）：架構、組織。
◎ alternative（adj.）：替代的、供選擇的。
◎ tyranny（n.）：壟斷、專橫。
◎ alliances（n.）：聯盟、同盟。
◎ prosperity（n.）：繁榮、昌盛。

We could have secured our **homeland** – investing in sophisticated new protection for our ports, our trains and our power plants.

 We could have rebuilt our roads and bridges, laid down new rail and broadband and electricity systems, and made college **affordable** for every American to strengthen our ability to compete.

 We could have done that.

 Instead, we have lost thousands of American lives, spent nearly a **trillion** dollars, **alienated** allies and **neglected emerging** threats – all in the cause of fighting a war for well over five years in a country that had absolutely nothing to do with the 9/11 attacks.

 Our men and women in uniform have accomplished every mission we have given them. What's missing in our debate about Iraq – what has been missing since before the war began – is a discussion of the strategic consequences of Iraq and its dominance of our foreign policy. This war distracts us from every threat that we face and so many opportunities we could seize. This war diminishes our security, our standing in the world, our military, our economy, and the resources that we need to confront the challenges of the 21st century. **By any measure**, our single-minded and open-ended focus on Iraq is not a sound strategy for keeping America safe.

◎ homeland（n.）：祖國、故國。
◎ affordable（adj.）：負擔得起的。
◎ instead（副詞）：反而、卻。

◎ trillion（adj.）：萬億的、兆的。
◎ alienate（vt.）：使疏遠。
◎ neglecte（v.）：疏忽、疏漏。

15 我們原可加強國土安全——投資新科技，為我們的港埠、火車及電廠提供新安全保障。

16 我們原可重修道路橋梁，鋪新軌道及建設寬頻與電力系統，讓每個美國國民都讀得起大學，提升我們的競爭力。

17 這些都是我們原可以做到的。

18 但是，我們卻在一個和九一一恐怖攻擊毫無瓜葛的國家發動戰爭，打了五年多的仗，付出數以千計美軍捐軀、近兆美元戰費、盟友逐一疏遠及坐視新威脅浮現而不顧的代價。

19 我們的軍隊已達成每一個交付的任務。我們辯論伊拉克議題時所欠缺的，也是這場戰爭發動之前就一直欠缺的，就是伊拉克的戰略後果，以及它可能宰制我國外交政策的討論。這場戰爭讓我們分心，無法注意我們所面臨的每一個威脅，也喪失許多我們可以掌握的契機。這場戰爭削弱我們的安全、我們的世界地位、我們的軍隊、我們的經濟，以及我們面對二十一世紀挑戰所需的各種資源。無論怎麼看，我們這種一心一意、無止無休地聚焦於伊拉克，並非維護美國安全的健全策略。

◎ emerging（adj.）：新興的。
◎ by any measure：以任何方式來評估。如: By any measure, you were wrong from the start.（不管怎麼看，你一開始就錯了。）

I am running for President of the United States to lead this country in a new direction—to **seize** this moment's promise. Instead of being **distracted** from the most pressing threats that we face, I want to overcome them. Instead of pushing the entire **burden** of our foreign policy on to the brave men and women of our military, I want to use all elements of American power to keep us safe, and prosperous, and free. Instead of alienating ourselves from the world, I want America—once again—to lead.

 As President, I will **pursue** a tough, smart and principled national security strategy—one that recognizes that we have interests not just in Baghdad, but in Kandahar and Karachi, in Tokyo and London, in Beijing and Berlin. I will focus this strategy on five goals essential to making America safer: ending the war in Iraq responsibly; finishing the fight against al Qaeda and the Taliban; securing all nuclear weapons and materials from terrorists and **rogue states**; achieving true energy security; and **rebuilding our alliances** to meet the challenges of the 21st century.

 My **opponent** in this campaign has served this country with honor, and we all respect his **sacrifice**. We both want to do what we think is best to defend the American people. But we've made different judgments, and would lead in very different directions. That starts with Iraq.

◎ seize（v.）：抓住、捉取。
◎ distracted（vt.）：使分心、轉移。
◎ burden（n.）：沈重的責任、重擔。
◎ pursue（vt.）：追求。
◎ rogue states：流氓國家。這是美國政府對北韓、伊朗等擁有核子武器卻又不願接受約束的一些國家的稱呼。

我競選美國總統，就是要帶領這個國家邁入新方向：抓住此刻的契機。我不會因為我們所面臨的緊迫威脅而分心；相反的，我要克服它們。我不會把外交政策重責，全部推給我們勇敢的軍人；相反的，我要運用美國全部國力，確保我們的安全、繁榮與自由。我不會讓我們和這個世界疏離；相反的，我要讓美國再度成為世界領袖。

 如果當選總統，我將追求強硬、聰明、有原則的國家安全戰略——一個能夠體認我們不僅在巴格達，而是在坎達哈和喀拉蚩、東京和倫敦、北京和柏林，也存在著利益的戰略。我這個戰略，要把重點放在讓美國更安全的五個不可或缺的目標上：負責任地結束伊拉克戰爭；打完對抗蓋達和神學士的戰事；嚴格控管所有核子武器與材料，不讓恐怖分子及流氓國家得手；達成真正能源安全的目標；重建我們的盟友關係，迎接二十一世紀挑戰。

 我的競選對手對國家貢獻不凡，我們對他的犧牲也很尊敬。我們倆都想用我們認為最佳的方式，保國衛民。但我們各有判斷，未來領導的方向也截然不同。這個分歧就從伊拉克開始。

◎ rebuilding our alliance：ally是盟邦。與盟邦的聯盟關係是alliance。在英文中，alliance, league, confederation, union都有聯盟的意思，但alliance是指對雙方有利的聯盟，league是指為特殊目的組成的聯盟（如美國職棒聯盟），confederation是指兩個或三個以上政府所組成的聯盟，有邦聯的涵意，union 則是指密切而且永久性的聯盟，如美國汽車工人聯合工會United Autoworkers Union.
◎ opponent（n.）：對手、敵手。
◎ sacrifice（n.）：犧牲、犧牲的行為。

I opposed going to war in Iraq; Senator McCain was one of Washington's biggest supporters for war. I warned that the invasion of a country posing no imminent threat would **fan the flames** of extremism, and **distract** us from the fight against al Qaeda and the Taliban; Senator McCain claimed that we would be greeted as liberators, and that democracy would spread across the Middle East. Those were the judgments we made on the most important strategic question since the end of the Cold War.

Now, all of us recognize that we must do more than look back─we must make a judgment about how to move forward. What is needed? What can best be done? What must be done? Senator McCain wants to talk of our **tactics** in Iraq; I want to focus on a new strategy for Iraq and the wider world.

It has been 18 months since President Bush announced the surge. As I have said many times, our troops have performed **brilliantly** in lowering the level of violence. General Petraeus has used new tactics to protect the Iraqi population. We have talked directly to Sunni tribes that used to be **hostile** to America, and supported their fight against al Qaeda. Shiite militias have generally respected a cease-fire. Those are the facts, and all Americans welcome them.

For weeks, now, Senator McCain has argued that the gains of the surge mean that I should change my **commitment** to end the war. But this argument **misconstrues** what is necessary to succeed in Iraq, and **stubbornly ignores** the facts of the broader strategic picture that we face.

◎ to fan the flames：fan是扇子,這裡當動詞用,是煽風的意思。flame是火焰。
◎ to distract（someone）from（something）：讓某人自某事分心。如：Playing video games distracts me from my studies.（玩電動遊戲讓我無法專心於學習。）
◎ tactics（n.）：戰術、策略。
◎ brilliantly（ad.）：燦爛的、出色的。

我反對派兵到伊拉克作戰；麥肯參議員是華府支持伊戰最力者之一。我當時警告，入侵一個未構成立即威脅的國家，會煽起極端主義的火焰，讓我們無法專心對付蓋達與神學士；麥肯參議員聲稱，我們會受到歡迎，被奉為解放者，民主將普傳中東。那是我們對這個冷戰結束以來最重要的戰略問題所作的判斷。

 我們都了解，我們不能一味回顧──我們必須對如何向前邁進，作出判斷。需要的是什麼？什麼最能奏效？該做什麼？麥肯參議員要談的，是我們在伊拉克的戰術；我則要把焦點集中在一個適用於伊拉克及更廣大世界的新戰略。

 布希總統宣布伊拉克增兵計畫，迄今已十八個月。我說過很多遍，我們的軍隊在降低暴亂方面，表現亮眼。裴卓斯將軍已啟用保護伊拉克人民的新戰術。我們已直接和一向敵視美國的正統教派會談，支持他們對抗蓋達的戰事。什葉派民兵對停火協議，大抵是尊重的。這些都是事實，美國民眾對這些事實表示歡迎。

 這幾星期以來，麥肯參議員聲稱，增兵計畫所獲致的成果，意謂著我該改變結束戰爭的主張。這種說法誤解在伊拉克成功的必要因素，刻意漠視我們所面對，戰略情勢較為寬廣的事實。

◎ hostile（adj.）：敵人的、敵方的。
◎ commitment（n.）：承諾、保證。
◎ misconstrue（vt.）：作出錯誤的解釋。
　explain是說明，construe有解讀的意思。

◎ stubbornly（vt.）：倔強地、刻意地。
◎ ignore（vt.）：不理會、忽視。

In the 18 months since the surge began, the strain on our military has increased, our troops and their families have borne an enormous burden, and American **taxpayers** have spent another $200 billion in Iraq. That's over $10 billion each month. That is a **consequence** of our current strategy.

 In the 18 months since the surge began, the situation in Afghanistan has **deteriorated**. June was our highest **casualty** month of the war. The Taliban has been on the offensive, even launching a **brazen** attack on one of our bases. Al Qaeda has a growing **sanctuary** in Pakistan. That is a consequence of our current strategy.

 In the 18 months since the surge began, as I warned **at the outset**－Iraq's leaders have not made the political progress that was the purpose of the surge. They have not invested tens of billions of dollars in oil **revenues** to rebuild their country. They have not resolved their differences or shaped **a new political compact**.

 That's why I strongly stand by my plan to end this war. Now, Prime Minister Maliki's call for a **timetable** for the **removal** of U.S. forces presents a real opportunity. It comes at a time when the American general in charge of training Iraq's Security Forces has **testified** that Iraq's Army and Police will be ready to assume responsibility for Iraq's security in 2009. Now is the time for a responsible redeployment of our **combat** troops that pushes Iraq's leaders toward a political solution, rebuilds our military, and refocuses on Afghanistan and our broader security interests.

◎ taxpayers（n.）：納稅人。
◎ consequence（n.）：結果、後果。
◎ deteriorated（vi）：惡化、質量或價值下降。
◎ casualty（n.）：（軍隊的）傷亡人員。

◎ brazen：厚顏無恥的。常作brazen-faced面無愧色的。
◎ sanctuary：庇護所，也有神殿、聖堂的意思。
◎ at the outset：在開始的時候、起初。From

27　在增兵計畫開始實施以來的十八個月中，我們軍方的壓力大增，我們部隊和他們的眷屬承受巨大的負擔，美國納稅人在伊拉克也額外花了兩千億美元，平均每個月超過一百億美元。這就是我們目前戰略的後果。

28　在增兵計畫開始實施以來的十八個月中，阿富汗情勢惡化。今年六月成為開戰以來傷亡最高的月份。神學士不斷發動攻勢，甚至明目張膽地攻擊我們的一個基地。蓋達在巴基斯坦的巢穴日益壯大。這就是我們目前戰略的後果。

29　在增兵計畫開始實施以來的十八個月中，一如我一開始的警告，伊拉克領導階層並未達成增兵計畫要求的政治進展。他們未將數百億美元的石油收益用來重建他們的國家。他們並未解決他們對新政治協定的歧見，或擬定新協約。

30　這是我力挺伊戰結束計畫的原因。現在，伊拉克總理馬立基提出訂定美軍撤離時間表的呼籲，是個好機會。這項呼籲提出之時，美國負責訓練伊拉克安全部隊的將領也正好作證指出，伊拉克軍隊和警察可望在二〇〇九年負起伊拉克安全責任。現在，正是負責任地重新部署我們的戰鬥部隊，迫使伊拉克領導階層達成政治解決方案，重建我們的軍隊，把重點重新放在阿富汗和我們更廣大的安全利益上的時機。

---

the outset則是從一開始就如何如何。
◎ revenues（n.）：收入、收益。
◎ a new political compact：一個新的政治協定。
◎ timetable（n.）：時間表、時刻表。
◎ removal（n.）：撤離。
◎ testifiy（vi.）：作證、證明。
◎ combat（n.）：戰鬥、搏鬥。

George Bush and John McCain don't have a strategy for success in Iraq—they have a strategy for staying in Iraq. They said we couldn't leave when violence was up, they say we can't leave when violence is down. They refuse to press the Iraqis to make **tough** choices, and they **label** any timetable to redeploy our troops "**surrender**," even though we would be turning Iraq over to a sovereign Iraqi government—not to a terrorist enemy. Theirs is an endless focus on tactics inside Iraq, with no consideration of our strategy to face threats beyond Iraq's borders.

 At some point, a judgment must be made. Iraq is not going to be a perfect place, and we don't have **unlimited** resources to try to make it one. We are not going to kill every al Qaeda sympathizer, eliminate every trace of Iranian influence, or stand up a flawless democracy before we leave—General Petraeus and Ambassador Crocker acknowledged this to me when they testified last April. That is why the accusation of surrender is **false rhetoric** used to justify a failed policy. In fact, true success in Iraq—victory in Iraq—will not take place in a surrender ceremony where an enemy lays down their arms. True success will take place when we leave Iraq to a government that is taking responsibility for its future—a government that prevents **sectarian conflict**, and ensures that the al Qaeda threat which has been beaten back by our troops does not **reemerge**. That is an achievable goal if we pursue a **comprehensive** plan to press the Iraqis to stand up.

◎ tough（adj.）：棘手的、困難的。
◎ label（vt.）：把⋯⋯稱為。
◎ surrender（vi.）：投降、自首。

◎ unlimited（a.）：無限制的、無約束的。
◎ false rhetoric：虛偽的說詞。rhetoric也作修辭學。

布希總統和麥肯根本沒有要在伊拉克成功的策略——他們只有在伊拉克駐留的策略。他們說過當地暴亂方殷時，我們不能離開；現在當地暴亂稍歇，他們又說，我們不能離開。他們拒絕向伊拉克人施壓，要他們作出困難的抉擇；他們把所有重新部署我們部隊的時間表，形容為「投降」，雖然我們要移交的對象，是伊拉克合法政府，而非遂行恐怖主義的敵人。他們在伊拉克境內的戰術上，有談不完的議題，對我們該如何面對來自伊拉克境外的威脅，卻隻字未提。

在某個時點上，必須作出判斷。伊拉克不會是個完美的地方，我們也沒有使它變成完美的無限資源。我們不會在離開之前，殺死每一個蓋達的同路人，抹除伊朗所有的影響，或成立一個完美無瑕的民主政府——裴卓斯將軍和柯洛克大使四月作證時，即就此對我坦承以告。之所以譴責投降是個假議題，用以支持一個失敗的政策。事實上，伊拉克真正的成功——亦即在伊拉克的勝利，是不可能發生在敵對一方放下武器的投降儀式上的。唯有我們把伊拉克交給一個願為自己國家未來負責的政府時，真正的成功才會出現。這個政府必須有能力預防派系衝突，確保被我們部隊擊潰的蓋達威脅不會重現。如果我們推動的，正是迫使伊拉克人自己站起來的包羅萬象的計畫，這種目標才可能實現。

◎ sectarian conflict：派系之間的矛盾與衝突。sect是一個宗教或政治團體內部的派系。sectarian是它的形容詞。

◎ reemerge（vi）：再度出現。
◎ comprehensive（a.）：無所不包的、包羅萬象的。

To **achieve** that success, I will give our military a new mission on my first day in office: ending this war. Let me be clear: we must be as careful getting out of Iraq as we were careless getting in. We can safely redeploy our combat brigades at a pace that would remove them in 16 months. That would be the summer of 2010–one year after Iraqi Security Forces will be prepared to stand up; two years from now, and more than seven years after the war began. After this **redeployment**, we'll **keep a residual force** to perform specific missions in Iraq: targeting any remnants of al Qaeda; protecting our service members and diplomats; and training and supporting Iraq's Security Forces, so long as the Iraqis make political progress.

We will make **tactical** adjustments as we **implement** this strategy–that is what any responsible Commander-in-Chief must do. As I have consistently said, I will consult with commanders on the ground and the Iraqi government. We will redeploy from secure areas first and **volatile** areas later. We will **commit** $2 billion to a meaningful international effort to support the more than 4 million displaced Iraqis. We will forge a new **coalition** to support Iraq's future–one that includes all of Iraq's neighbors, and also the United Nations, the World Bank, and the European Union–because we all have a stake in stability. And we will make it clear that the United States seeks no permanent bases in Iraq.

◎ achieve（vt.）：完成、達到。
◎ redeployment（n.）：整編、重做部署。
◎ keep a residual force：保存一支殘留的武

力。residual是 residue（剩餘物）的形容詞，是剩餘的意思。
◎ tactical（adj.）：作戰的、戰術的。

要達成這個成功的目標，我上任首日，將賦予我們的軍隊新使命：結束這場戰爭。我要清楚說明：如何當初我們如何倉促投入伊拉克，我們撤離時也必須如何謹慎。我們可以十六個月內撤離的速度，安全地重新部署我們的戰鬥部隊。那個時間應該是在二〇一〇年夏季——即伊拉克安全部隊準備自立的一年之後；距離現在還有兩年，而距伊戰開始，已七年有餘。經過這番整編，我們將維持一支留守的部隊，在伊拉克境內負責特定的任務：鎖定任何蓋達餘孽；保護我們的服務和外交人員；訓練及支持伊拉克安全部隊，只要伊拉克人在政治上有所進展即可。

我們執行這項戰略時，戰術上會加以調整，這是任何負責任的三軍統帥都該盡的責任。我常說，我會諮詢戰地指揮官和伊拉克政府。我們的整編，會先從安全的地區開始，不寧靖的地區略後。我們會撥款二十億美元投入有意義的國際努力，以支持四百多萬流離失所的伊拉克百姓。我們會締結新聯盟，支持伊拉克的未來——這項聯盟要納入伊拉克所有鄰邦，外加聯合國、世界銀行和歐洲聯盟——因為舉凡國際的安定，我們全都休戚與共。我們會清楚表白，美國沒有在伊拉克建立永久基地的打算。

◎ implement（vt.）：實施、執行。
◎ volatile：有揮發性的，短暫的，不穩定的。
◎ commit（vt.）：撥出。

◎ coalition（n.）：政黨、國家等臨時結成的聯盟。

This is the future that Iraqis want. This is the future that the American people want. And this is what our common interests demand. Both America and Iraq will be more **secure** when the terrorist in Anbar is taken out by the Iraqi Army, and the criminal in Baghdad fears Iraqi Police, not just coalition forces. Both America and Iraq will succeed when every Arab government has an embassy open in Baghdad, and the child in Basra benefits from services provided by Iraqi dinars, not American tax dollars.

 And this is the future we need for our military. We cannot tolerate this strain on our forces to fight a war that hasn't made us safer. I will restore our strength by ending this war, completing the increase of our ground forces by 65,000 soldiers and 27,000 marines, and investing in the capabilities we need to defeat **conventional foes** and meet the unconventional challenges of our time.

 So let's be clear. Senator McCain would have our troops continue to fight tour after tour of duty, and our taxpayers keep spending $10 billion a month indefinitely; I want Iraqis to take responsibility for their own future, and to reach the political **accommodation** necessary for long-term stability. That's victory. That's success. That's what's best for Iraq, that's what's best for America, and that's why I will end this war as President.

 In fact—as should have been apparent to President Bush and Senator McCain—the central front in the war on terror is not Iraq, and it never was. That's why the second goal of my new strategy will be taking the fight to al Qaeda in Afghanistan and Pakistan.

◎ secure（a.）：安全的、無危險的。　　◎ conventional（a.）：傳統式的。

35 這是伊拉克想要的未來；這是美國民眾想要的未來；這更是我們共同利益的要求。當安巴爾的恐怖分子被伊拉克軍隊消滅，巴格達的歹徒不僅害怕盟軍，也對伊拉克警方心存忌憚之時，美國和伊拉克都會更安全。當每一個阿拉伯政府都在巴格達開設大使館，巴斯拉的兒童能從服務中獲得利益，而且付費的是伊拉克國幣第納爾，而不是美國納稅人的美鈔時，美國和伊拉克才能算成功。

36 這是我們希望我們軍方所擁有的未來。要我們的部隊承受壓力，去打一場並沒有讓我們更安全的仗，這是我們不能容忍的。我要結束這場戰爭，完成增加六萬五千名地面部隊及兩萬七千名陸戰隊的計畫，為我們擊敗傳統敵人的能力投資，迎接當代非傳統挑戰，藉以恢復我們的國力。

37 所以，讓我們搞清楚。麥肯參議員將讓我們的部隊不斷輪調作戰，我們的納稅人每月將繼續花費一百億美元，永無止期；我則要求伊拉克人對他們自己的未來負責，達成維持長治久安所需的政治妥協。這才是勝利，才是成功；對伊拉克才最好，對美國也最好。這是我當總統要結束這場戰爭的原因。

38 其實，伊拉克從來不是，現在也不是反恐作戰的核心戰線。對此，布希總統和麥肯參議員應該心知肚明。所以，我新戰略的第二個目標，就是要把反恐戰爭的對象，轉為阿富汗和巴基斯坦境內的蓋達組織。

◎ foe（n.）：敵人。　　　　　◎ accommodation（n.）：和解、妥協。

It is unacceptable that almost seven years after nearly 3,000 Americans were killed on our soil, the terrorists who attacked us on 9/11 are still **at large**– Osama bin Laden and Ayman al-Zawahari are recording messages to their followers and plotting more terror. The Taliban controls parts of Afghanistan. Al Qaeda has an **expanding base** in Pakistan that is probably no farther from their old Afghan sanctuary than a train ride from Washington to Philadelphia. If another attack on our homeland comes, it will likely come from the same region where 9/11 was planned. And yet today, we have five times more troops in Iraq than Afghanistan.

 Senator McCain said–just months ago–that "Afghanistan is not in trouble because of our **diversion** to Iraq." I could not disagree more. Our troops and our NATO allies are performing **heroically** in Afghanistan, but I have argued for years that we lack the resources to finish the job because of our commitment to Iraq. That's what the Chairman of the Joint Chiefs of Staff said earlier this month. And that's why, as President, I will make the fight against al Qaeda and the Taliban the top priority that it should be. This is a war that we have to win.

 I will send at least two additional combat **brigades** to Afghanistan, and use this commitment to seek greater **contributions**–with fewer restrictions–from NATO allies. I will focus on training Afghan security forces and supporting an Afghan **judiciary**, with more resources and **incentives** for American officers who perform these missions. Just as we succeeded in the Cold War by supporting allies who could **sustain** their own security, we must realize that the 21st century's frontlines are not only on the field of battle–they are found in the training exercise near Kabul, in the police station in Kandahar, and in the rule of law in Herat.

◎ at large：逍遙於法網之外。它有好幾個意思，在法律上是特指一個罪犯仍然逍遙法外。

◎ expand（vt.）：發展、擴大。
◎ base（n.）：基地。
◎ diversion（n.）：分散注意力、牽制。

39 將近三千名美國人在自己的國土上被殺害，迄今將屆滿七年，但對我們發動九一一攻擊的元兇仍逍遙法外，實在令人難以接受。賓拉登和札瓦希里仍在錄製發給追隨者的訊息，籌畫更多恐怖活動。神學士仍控制著阿富汗部分地區。蓋達在巴基斯坦有一個仍繼續壯大的基地，這個基地距他們過去在阿富汗的巢穴，可能連從華府車站到費城的距離都不到。如果我們的本土遭受另一波攻擊，極可能就來自這個與九一一策畫地相同的地區。但是今日，我們在伊拉克駐紮比阿富汗多五倍的兵力。

40 僅在數月前，麥肯參議員說：「阿富汗有問題，與我們轉移目標到伊拉克無關。」這話我完全無法苟同。我們的部隊和北大西洋公約組織盟軍在阿富汗的表現極為英勇，但我多年來不斷強調，我們缺乏完成此一任務的資源，因為我們受困於伊拉克。參謀首長聯席會議主席本月初也這麼說。這是我當選總統後，要恢復打擊蓋達和神學士的優先地位的原因。這場戰爭，我們非勝不可。

41 我至少要額外增派兩個戰鬥旅到阿富汗，藉此承諾爭取北約盟邦更多，但限制更少的奉獻。我要把焦點放在阿富汗安全部隊的訓練上，支持阿富汗司法體制，不但提供更多資源，還要提供獎勵誘因給從事這項任務的美國軍官。我們打贏冷戰，是靠支持能維護自身安全的盟邦，同理，我們必須體認，二十一世紀的前線，不再只是戰場——喀布爾附近的訓練演習、坎達哈的警察局、赫拉特的法治等，都是前線。

◎ heroically（ad.）：英勇地。　　　◎ judiciary（n.）：司法制度。
◎ brigade（n.）：（軍）旅。　　　　◎ incentive（n.）：鼓勵、獎勵。
◎ contribution（n.）：奉獻。　　　◎ sustain（vt.）：支持、鼓舞。

Moreover, lasting security will only come if we heed Marshall's lesson, and help Afghans grow their economy from the bottom up. That's why I've proposed an additional $1 billion in non-military assistance each year, with meaningful safeguards to prevent **corruption** and to make sure investments are made–not just in Kabul but out in Afghanistan's provinces. As a part of this program, we'll invest in alternative livelihoods to poppy-growing for Afghan farmers, just as we crack down on heroin trafficking. We cannot lose Afghanistan to a future of **narco–terrorism**. The Afghan people must know that our commitment to their future is enduring, because the security of Afghanistan and the United States is shared.

 The greatest threat to that security lies in the tribal regions of Pakistan, where terrorists train and insurgents strike into Afghanistan. We cannot tolerate a terrorist sanctuary, and as President, I won't. We need a stronger and sustained partnership between Afghanistan, Pakistan and NATO to secure the border, to take out terrorist camps, and to crack down on **cross–border insurgents**. We need more troops, more helicopters, more satellites, more **Predator drones** in the Afghan border region. And we must make it clear that if Pakistan cannot or will not act, we will take out high-level terrorist targets like bin Laden if we have them in our sights.

◎ corruption (n.)：貪污。
◎ narco–terrorism：與毒品相關的恐怖主義narco是narcotics（毒品）的簡寫。
◎ cross–border insurgents：穿越邊境的叛軍。基地組織的游擊部隊經常穿梭於阿富汗和巴基斯坦的邊

此外，我們唯有謹遵馬歇爾的教誨，協助阿富汗從頭建設經濟，才有可能長治久安。所以，我要每年額外提撥十億美元的非軍事援助，加上必要的防範貪污措施，以確保投資能確實到位——不光是在喀布爾，還要遍及阿富汗各省分。由於我們要掃蕩海洛因走私，所以這項計畫還要協助阿富汗的罌粟農民，替他們找別的生計。我們不能讓阿富汗成為未來毒品恐怖主義的溫床。阿富汗人民必須了解，我們的承諾永久有效，因為阿富汗的安全和美國休戚與共。

但是這項安全最大的威脅，來自巴基斯坦部落地區，恐怖分子就在那裡訓練，叛軍也從那裡進擊阿富汗。我們不能容忍這種恐怖分子巢穴，而我身為總統，不會容忍。我們需要阿富汗、巴基斯坦和北約締結更堅固永續的夥伴關係，以鞏固邊界的安全，殲滅恐怖分子巢穴，掃蕩越界活動的叛軍。我們需要增派部隊、直升機、衛星及「掠奪者」無人飛機，到阿富汗邊界地區。而且我們必須清楚表示，假如巴基斯坦不能，或不願採取行動，只要像賓拉登這類高階恐怖組織頭目落入我們的視界，將逕予消滅。

境，讓美軍和聯軍很難掌握他們的行動。insurgent的字根意思是內部竄起來的反抗，亦作反抗軍。
◎ Predator drone：predator是掠食者動物，drone是一種無人駕駛的遙控飛機；Predator drone這種美軍用的無人遙控飛機可裝上兩具導彈，對阿富汗境內的恐怖分子武力有很大的殺傷力。

Make no mistake: we can't succeed in Afghanistan or secure our homeland unless we change our Pakistan policy. We must expect more of the Pakistani government, but we must offer more than **a blank check** to a General who has lost the confidence of his people. It's time to strengthen stability by standing up for the aspirations of the Pakistani people. That's why I'm cosponsoring a bill with Joe Biden and Richard Lugar to triple non-military aid to the Pakistani people and to sustain it for a decade, while ensuring that the military assistance we do provide is used to take the fight to the Taliban and al Qaeda. We must move beyond a purely military alliance built on convenience, or face mounting popular opposition in a nuclear-armed nation **at the nexus of terror and radical Islam**.

 Only a strong Pakistani democracy can help us move toward my third goal–securing all nuclear weapons and materials from terrorists and rogue states. One of the terrible ironies of the Iraq War is that President Bush used the threat of nuclear terrorism to **invade** a country that had no active nuclear program. But the fact that the President misled us into a **misguided** war doesn't **diminish** the threat of a terrorist with a weapon of mass destruction– in fact, it has only increased it.

◎ a blank check：空白支票。沒有填上金額，可以讓收支票人任意填寫的支票，意指無條件的支持。
◎ at the nexus of terror and radical Islam：在恐怖（主義）與激進伊斯蘭主義相互聯結的情形之下。
◎ invade（vt.）：入侵。

別搞錯：除非我們的巴基斯坦政策改絃更張，否則非但我們在阿富汗的目標無法達成，本土安全也將不保。我們必須要求巴基斯坦負起更多責任，但是不能只是無條件支持一個已喪失自己子民信心的將軍。目前正是聲援巴國人民之渴望，強化安定的時機。所以，我要和拜登、魯加兩位聯邦參議員共同起草法案，將撥給巴國人民的非軍事援助增為三倍，期間長達十年，同時確保我們提供的軍事援助，全都用在打擊神學士和蓋達恐怖組織上面。我們必須跳脫純軍事結盟的傳統舊思維，否則就得面對這個處於恐怖與激進伊斯蘭核心的核武國家日益強大的民意反彈。

只有堅強的巴基斯坦民主體制，才能幫我們朝我的第三個目標邁進：確保所有核子武器和材料安全，不可落入恐怖分子和流氓國家手中。伊拉克戰爭最大的反諷之一，就是布希總統以核武恐怖主義威脅為由，入侵一個連實際核武計畫都沒有的國家。不過，恐怖分子以大規模毀滅武器出擊的威脅，並不因為總統誤導我們發起一場誤入歧途的戰爭就降低；事實上，這種威脅反而增強。

◎ misguided（adj.）：被錯誤指導的。
◎ diminish（vt.）：減少。

In those years after World War II, we worried about the deadly atom falling into the hands of the Kremlin. Now, we worry about 50 tons of highly enriched uranium–some of it poorly secured–at civilian nuclear facilities in over forty countries. Now, we worry about the breakdown of a **non-proliferation framework** that was designed for the bipolar world of the Cold War. Now, we worry–most of all–about a rogue state or nuclear scientist transferring the world's deadliest weapons to the world's most dangerous people: terrorists who won't **think twice** about killing themselves and hundreds of thousands in Tel Aviv or Moscow, in London or New York.

We cannot wait any longer to protect the American people. I've made this a priority in the Senate, where I worked with Republican Senator Dick Lugar to pass a law accelerating our pursuit of loose nuclear materials. I'll lead a global effort to secure all loose nuclear materials around the world during my first term as President. And I'll develop new defenses to protect against the 21st century threat of biological weapons and **cyber–terrorism**–threats that I'll discuss in more detail tomorrow.

◎ non–proliferation framework：一個防止（核武）擴散的架構。proliferate是擴散，滋長。non-proliferation是專指防止核子武器擴散的條約和公約。
◎ to think twice：想上第二遍，也就是猶疑，躊躇的意思。

二戰結束後這些年，我們擔心致命原子武器落入克里姆林宮手中。現在，我們憂心散處四十國民間核子設施的五十噸左右高濃縮鈾，因為有些的安全管理廢弛。現在，我們擔心冷戰兩極世界時代所設計的禁止核子擴散架構瓦解。現在，我們最憂慮某個流氓國家或核子科學家將這種最致命的武器，移轉給全世界最危險的人手中：毫不思索就會在特拉維夫或莫斯科，在倫敦或紐約，自殺或殺死數十萬人的恐怖分子。

47 為了保護美國人民，我們不能等。我在參院把此事列為優先急務，和共和黨參議員魯加合作，通過一項加緊追蹤廢弛管制之核子材料的法案。我在第一個總統任期內，要領導全球確保管制廢弛之核子材料的安全。我要發展新防衛方案，保護並對抗二十一世紀生物武器和網路恐怖主義的威脅。我明天會針對這些威脅，再詳加討論。

◎ cyber–terrorism（n.）：利用網路的恐怖主義。cyber是形容任何與網路相關的事物，如cybercafe網咖，cyberspace網路空間等。

Beyond taking these immediate, urgent steps, it's time to send a clear message: America seeks a world with no nuclear weapons. As long as nuclear weapons exist, we must retain a strong **deterrent**. But instead of threatening to kick them out of the G−8, we need to work with Russia to take U.S. and Russian ballistic missiles off **hair−trigger alert**; to dramatically reduce the **stockpiles** of our nuclear weapons and material; to seek a global ban on the production of **fissile material** for weapons; and to expand the U.S.−Russian ban on intermediate−range **missiles** so that the agreement is global. By keeping our commitment under the Nuclear Non−Proliferation Treaty, we'll be in a better position to press nations like North Korea and Iran to keep theirs. In particular, it will give us more **credibility** and **leverage** in dealing with Iran.

We cannot tolerate nuclear weapons in the hands of nations that support terror. Preventing Iran from developing nuclear weapons is a vital national security interest of the United States. No tool of statecraft should be taken off the table, but Senator McCain would continue a failed policy that has seen Iran strengthen its position, advance its nuclear program, and stockpile 150 kilos of low **enriched uranium**. I will use all elements of American power to pressure the Iranian **regime**, starting with aggressive, principled and direct diplomacy− diplomacy backed with strong **sanctions** and without **preconditions**.

◎deterrent（n.）：威嚇力量、制止物。
◎hair−trigger alert：一觸即發的警戒狀態。這是核子武器時代的用語。因為當敵國的核彈發射之後，被攻擊的國家往往只有幾分鐘的時間可以回應，所以它必須將本身的核子武器處於一觸即發的備戰警戒狀態。hair是頭髮，是極細微的事物，但是即使是最微小的事件也可能引發毀滅性的戰爭，正如中文中所形容的千鈞一髮。trigger是扳機，扣扳機或是觸發也可用trigger。
◎ stockpile（n.）：應急用的儲備物資，如原料、武器等。

除了採取上開立即而且緊急的手段外，目前也是傳播明確訊息的時機：追求無核武世界，是美國的目標。只要核武還在，我們就必須維持強有力的嚇阻工具。不過，除了威脅將它們趕出G8外，我們必須和俄羅斯合作，解除美俄兩國彈道飛彈的高度戰備狀態；大幅削減我們彼此的核武及材料庫存；設法通過全球禁令，禁止生產製造核武所需的核分裂材料；擴大美俄禁止中程飛彈協定，使其全球化。只有遵守我們對禁止核子擴散條約的承諾，我們才有立場向北韓和伊朗施壓，要求他們遵守他們的承諾。特別是伊朗，這種作法可以讓我們在打交道時，更具可信度與影響力。

---

49 我們絕不容忍核武落入支持恐怖活動國家的手中。預防伊朗發展核武，攸關美國重大國家安全利益。任何防制工具都不應遺漏，但麥肯參議員卻會延續坐視伊朗鞏固其立場，推進其核武計畫，儲存一百五十公斤低濃縮鈾的錯誤政策。我會運用美國一切力量向伊朗政權施壓，從採取積極、堅守原則的直接外交途徑——以強力制裁和沒有先決條件為後盾的外交手段——做起。

◎ fissile materials：可產生核子分裂的物質。fissile是指會分裂的。
◎ missiles（n.）：飛彈、導彈。
◎ credibility（n.）：可信度。
◎ leverage：槓桿作用，也可引申作對己方有利的影響力。

◎ enriched uranium（片語）：濃縮鈾。
◎ regime（n.）：政權。
◎ sanctions：這裡是指制裁的意思。
◎ preconditions（n.）：先決條件。

There will be careful preparation. I commend the work of our European allies on this important matter, and we should be full partners in that effort. Ultimately the measure of any effort is whether it leads to a change in Iranian behavior. That's why we must pursue these tough negotiations in full coordination with our allies, bringing to bear our full influence—including, if it will advance our interests, my meeting with the appropriate Iranian leader at a time and place of my choosing.

 We will pursue this diplomacy with no illusions about the Iranian regime. Instead, we will present a clear choice. If you abandon your nuclear program, support for terror, and threats to Israel, there will be meaningful **incentives**. If you refuse, then we will ratchet up the pressure, with stronger unilateral sanctions; stronger multilateral sanctions in the Security Council, and sustained action outside the UN to isolate the Iranian regime. That's the diplomacy we need. And the Iranians should negotiate now; by waiting, they will only face mounting pressure.

 The surest way to increase our leverage against Iran **in the long-run** is to stop bankrolling its ambitions. That will depend on achieving my fourth goal: ending the tyranny of oil in our time.

 One of the most dangerous weapons in the world today is the price of oil. We ship nearly $700 million a day to unstable or hostile nations for their oil. It pays for terrorist bombs going off from Baghdad to Beirut. It funds **petro-diplomacy** in Caracas and radical **madrasas** from Karachi to Khartoum. It takes leverage away from America and shifts it to dictators.

◎ incentive（n.）：誘因。許多公司為鼓勵員工，會提出一些誘因，如加薪、放假等，就叫incentive programs誘因計畫。
◎ in the long-run（片語）：終久。相反的用語是in the short run在短期之內。

這件事要有妥善的準備。我推崇我們歐洲盟邦對此一重要事件的努力，我們應加入，成為完全的夥伴。努力的成效最終還是要看是否能改變伊朗的行為。所以，我們必須和我們的盟邦充分協調，推動這些艱辛的談判，充分發揮我們的影響力──包括：若能促進我們的利益，我願意在由我挑選的時間和地點，與合適的伊朗領袖晤談。

 我們從事這項外交努力時，不會對伊朗心存幻想。相反的，我們會提出明確的選項。如果你放棄你們的核武計畫，不支持恐怖活動，不威脅以色列，就會有夠多的誘因。如果你拒絕，我們就要加緊施壓，祭出更嚴厲的片面制裁，在安全理事會通過更嚴厲的多方制裁，不斷的在聯合國以外的地方，採取孤立伊朗政權的行動。這是我們所需要的外交途徑。伊朗最好現在就同意談判，拖延等待，只會面臨更大的壓力。

 長期而言，增加我們對抗伊朗的籌碼的最保險作法，就是抽掉支持其野心的銀根。那就要看我的第四個目標是否能達成：終結我們這個時代的石油暴政。

 今天這個世界最危險的武器，就是油價。我們每天送出近七億美元，向政治不安定或懷有敵意的國家買石油。這些錢被用來支付從巴格達到貝魯特引爆的恐怖攻擊炸彈；在委內瑞拉首都加拉加斯成立石油外交基金，以及創辦從喀拉蚩到喀土木的伊斯蘭學校。它奪走美國對抗的籌碼，轉而厚植獨裁者的實力。

◎ petro-diplomacy（n.）：石油外交。petro是petroleum石油的縮寫式。
◎ madrasas（n.）：回教學校或回教大學。

This immediate danger is **eclipsed** only by the long−term threat from climate change, which will lead to devastating weather **patterns**, terrible storms, drought, and famine. That means people competing for food and water in the next fifty years in the very places that have known **horrific** violence in the last fifty: Africa, the Middle East, and South Asia. Most **disastrously**, that could mean **destructive** storms on our shores, and the disappearance of our coastline.

 This is not just an economic issue or an environmental concern - this is a national security crisis. For the sake of our security−and for every American family that is paying the price at the pump−we must end this dependence on foreign oil. And as President, that's exactly what I'll do. Small steps and political **gimmickry** just won't do. I'll invest $150 billion over the next ten years to put America on the path to true energy security. This fund will fast track investments in a new green energy business sector that will end our addiction to oil and create up to 5 million jobs over the next two decades, and help secure the future of our country and our planet. We'll invest in research and development of every form of alternative energy−solar, wind, and biofuels, as well as technologies that can make coal clean and nuclear power safe. And from the moment I take office, I will let it be known that the United States of America is ready to lead again.

◎ eclipse：日月之蝕。月蝕叫lunar eclipse，當動詞用時，它的意思是把某件事物遮蓋住了或是減損了它原有的光彩。
◎ pattern（n.）：形態、樣式。
◎ horrific（adj）：可怕的。

前途迫在眉睫的危險，僅次於氣候變遷帶來的長期威脅：破壞性大的氣象形態、可怕的暴風雨、苦旱和饑荒。也就是說，一些過去五十年來爆發駭人聽聞之動亂的地方，如非洲、中東，南亞等地，在未來五十年內，人們必將競逐糧食與飲水。而最慘重者，可能意味我們的沿海地區遭毀滅性的暴風雨侵襲，整個海岸線消失無蹤。

這不僅是一個經濟議題或環境問題；這是國家安全危機。為了我們國家的安全，也為了每一個在加油機旁付錢的美國家庭，我們必須終結對外國石油的依賴。身為總統，這正是我要做的。小規模的行動和政治小動作根本無濟於事。我要在未來十年內投資一千五百億美元，讓美國踏上真正的能源安全道路。這個基金能加速綠色新能源行業的投資，終結我們的石油癮，在未來二十年內創造五百萬個工作，讓我們的國家和地球的未來更安全。我們要投資每一種替代能源形式的研發──太陽能、風力、生質燃料，以及可讓煤炭乾淨，核能安全的科技。從我上任那一刻起，我要讓全世界知道，這個領袖角色，美國已準備好了。

◎ disastrously（ad.）：悲慘地。
◎ destructive（adj）：毀滅性的。
◎ gimmickry：噱頭的總稱。gimmick是指魔術表演中巧妙裝置或是行銷手法中的一些噱頭。

Never again will we sit on the sidelines, or stand in the way of global action to **tackle** this **global** challenge. I will reach out to the leaders of the biggest **carbon** emitting nations and ask them to join a new Global Energy Forum that will lay the foundation for the next generation of climate **protocols**. We will also build an alliance of oil-importing nations and work together to reduce our demand, and to break the grip of OPEC on the global economy. We'll set a goal of an 80% reduction in global **emissions** by 2050. And as we develop new forms of clean energy here at home, we will share our technology and our **innovations** with all the nations of the world.

That is the tradition of American leadership on behalf of the global good. And that will be my fifth goal—rebuilding our alliances to meet the common challenges of the 21st century.

For all of our power, America is strongest when we act alongside strong partners. We **faced down** fascism with the greatest war−time alliance the world has ever known. We stood shoulder to shoulder with our NATO allies against the Soviet threat, and paid a far smaller price for the first Gulf War because we acted together with a broad coalition. We helped create the United Nations−not to constrain America's influence, but to **amplify** it by advancing our values.

◎ tackle（vt.）：著手處理。
◎ global（adj.）：全世界的。

◎ carbon（n.）：碳。
◎ protocol（n.）：議定書。

我們絕不再從旁坐視，或妨礙應付此一全球危機的全球行動。我會向排碳最多的國家領袖展臂，要求他們參加嶄新的全球能源論壇，為未來世代的氣候公約奠下基礎。我們也要建立一個石油進口國聯盟，共同努力減少我們的需求，打破石油輸出國家組織對全球經濟的箝制。我們將把二○五○年全球減碳排放目標，設定減少80%。我們在國內研發新形式乾淨能源之時，也要和全球所有國家分享我們的科技和創意。

 這是美國帶頭，謀求全球利益的傳統。那也是我第五個目標：重建我們的聯盟關係，迎接二十一世紀的共同挑戰。

58 無論我們國力多強，只有在和堅強的夥伴一起採取行動時，美國才最強大。我們和全球歷來僅見，最偉大的戰時聯盟，迫使法西斯主義崩盤。我們和我們的北約盟邦併肩對抗蘇聯威脅；也因為我們和一個包羅廣泛的聯盟一起行動，第一次波斯灣戰爭才能付出遠較預期為小的代價。我們幫忙創立聯合國——不是要限制美國影響力，而是藉此推廣我們的價值觀，放大我們的影響力。

◎ emission（n.）：排放。
◎ innovation（n.）：創新、創意。
◎ face down：對抗。
◎ amplify（vt.）：宣揚、擴展。

We will have to provide meaningful resources to meet critical priorities. I know development assistance is not the most popular program, but as President, I will make the case to the American people that it can be our best investment in increasing the common security of the entire world. That was true with the Marshall Plan, and that must be true today. That's why I'll double our foreign assistance to $50 billion by 2012, and use it to support a stable future in failing states, and sustainable growth in Africa; to halve global poverty and to roll back disease. To send once more a message to those yearning faces beyond our shores that says, "You matter to us. Your future is our future. And our moment is now."

This must be the moment when we answer the call of history. For eight years, we have paid the price for a foreign policy that lectures without listening; that divides us from one another–and from the world–instead of calling us to a common purpose; that focuses on our tactics in fighting a war without end in Iraq instead of forging a new strategy to face down the true threats that we face. We cannot afford four more years of a strategy that is out of balance and out of step with this defining moment.

None of this will be easy, but we have faced great odds before. When General Marshall first spoke about the plan that would bear his name, the rubble of Berlin had not yet been built into a wall. But Marshall knew that even the fiercest of adversaries could forge bonds of friendship founded in freedom. He had the confidence to know that the purpose and pragmatism of the American people could outlast any foe. Today, the dangers and divisions that came with the dawn of the Cold War have receded. Now, the defeat of the threats of the past has been replaced by the transnational threats of today. We know what is needed. We know what can best be done. We know what must be done. Now it falls to us to act with the same sense of purpose and pragmatism as an earlier generation, to join with friends and partners to lead the world anew.

我們必須提供夠多的資源，以因應這些優先急務之所需。我知道，開發援助並非最受歡迎的計畫，但身為總統，我會向全美民眾解釋，這些援助計畫可以成為我們加強全世界共同安全的最佳投資。所以，我要在二○一二年以前，把對外援款加倍，成為五百億美元，用這些錢來讓失敗的國家有安定的未來，讓非洲永續成長，讓全球貧窮減半，疾病大幅消失。我要再度向我們境外那些渴望的面孔傳送一個訊息，「我們關心你們。你們的未來就是我們的未來。我們要把握現在。」

 現在必定是我們回應歷史呼喚的時刻。八年來，我們為只會說教而不曾虛心聆聽的外交政策而付上代價；令我們區分彼此，也與世界分離，而非號召大家為共同目標努力；只關心我們在伊拉克那場永無止境戰爭的戰術細節，而不是擬定新戰略，對抗我們所面臨之真正威脅。我們不能為失衡、與此關鍵時刻脫節的戰略，再浪費四年。

 以上所說的，沒有一樣是容易的，但我們曾經面臨過大危機。當馬歇爾將軍第一次發表這個以他為名的計畫，柏林的瓦礫尚未被築成一道牆。但是，馬歇爾知道，即使是最強悍的敵人，也可以透過自由機制建立堅強的友誼。他有自信，知道美國人民的目標和務實作風，可以戰勝任何敵人。今天，伴隨冷戰肇端而來的危險與分裂，業已消退。如今，敗北的昔日威脅，已被今日的跨國威脅取代。我們知道，需要的是什麼。我們知道，什麼最能奏效。我們知道，該做什麼。現在，輪到我們用和上一代同樣的目標感和務實作風採取行動，和朋友與夥伴共同攜手，再次領導世界。

第三部分 🏆 文句解析

◎楊人凱

二〇〇八年七月，歐巴馬的選情進入白熱化。他知道他應可擊敗同黨的候選人希拉蕊贏得民主黨的總統提名，但是他不能確定能否贏過他的共和黨對手，來自亞利桑那州的參議員約翰・麥肯。麥肯曾是個越戰英雄，而且曾被越共俘虜，深得美國保守派人士的愛戴。歐巴馬知道他的兩大弱點：一是他的膚色，一是他的國際觀與處理國際事務的經驗。於是，他發表了這篇名之為「新世界的新戰略」的主題演說，將他的國際政策作了一次較完整的闡述。

「新世界的新戰略」這個觀念和名詞源自於二次大戰戰後擔任美國國務卿的喬治・馬歇爾將軍。

那時，世界陷入美國和蘇聯兩個超級強權的對立，所有的其他國家被迫選邊，形成一個兩極（bi-polar）的狀態，冷戰正要開始。蘇聯正要擁有核子武器，對美國造成莫大的威脅，而美國的盟邦，包括英法等國，因大戰受到巨大的傷害，亟待重建。面對這樣的一個新世界情勢，馬歇爾提出一個「歐洲恢復計畫」（Europe Recovery Program），主張美國應大力協助歐洲國家重建。這個計畫後來就被稱之為「馬歇爾計畫」（The Marshall Plan）。

歐巴馬認為，在馬歇爾計畫實施六十一年之後，美國面臨一個新的世界形態。蘇聯已經解體，亞洲的力量正在崛起。更令人憂心的是，回教恐怖主義盛行，世界能源短缺，對於石油過度依賴。而且，有一些所謂的「流氓國家」（rogue states），如伊朗、北韓等，正在不負責任地發展核子武器。面對這種新世界形勢，他引用馬歇爾當年問美國人民的三個問題：「需要的是什麼？什麼最能奏效？該做什麼？」（What is needed? What can best be done? What must be done?）

　　馬歇爾當年並沒有為他所提出的問題提供答案。但是，作為總統候選人，歐巴馬提出了他的五大政策，作為他的新戰略（new strategy）的重大宣示。在這篇等同於是他的政策白皮書的演講稿之中，歐巴馬不遺餘力地抨擊布希總統的伊拉克政策，包括進兵攻打一個與九一一恐怖事件毫無關連的國家，導致許多軍人犧牲寶貴的生命，每月花費美國納稅人一百億美元，卻不能保證讓美國更安全，反而讓一些盟邦與美國的關係更為疏離等等（最明顯的是法國）。所以，他說，他當選美國總統要做的第一件事，就是要終止伊拉克戰爭，並且在二○一○年前自伊拉克撤兵。事後證明，歐巴馬的這個宣示贏得了美國多數的民心。

　　其次，他認為恐怖主義的大本營不在於伊拉克而是在於阿富汗境內和巴基斯坦邊境的基地組織，而由於錯誤的進兵伊拉克的政策，使得美國無法全力對付在阿富汗的賓拉登。所以，他將重新部署（redeploy）美國的軍事力量，重點放在對付基地組織和賓拉登身上。因此，他反對給予巴基斯坦統治者無條件的支持（offer him a blank check）。但是，如同馬歇爾，他贊成撥款協助伊拉克和阿富汗重建，讓人民過較好的生活並學習民主。

　　對於伊朗等「流氓國家」，歐巴馬主張要用各種制裁的手段，來防止製造核子武器的原料流入這些國家的手中。這些制裁手段包括美國的單邊制裁及透過聯合國安理會（the Security Council of the United Nations）的多邊制裁。他甚至表示願意與伊朗領導人會面，並且答應給予伊朗許多的誘因（incentive），如果伊朗願意合作的話。

　　美國每天要花費七千萬美元購買石油，而這些錢多半流入實施恐怖主義的阿拉伯國家的手中。歐巴馬認為這是不能忍受的情況，所以，他的第四項重要政策，就是要投資一千五百億發展替代能源，以脫離石油的暴政統治（the tyranny of oil）。

　　最後，歐巴馬主張強化與盟邦的關係，包括歐盟，北大西洋公約組織國家等。

　　他期待經由多國合作解決以色列和巴勒斯坦的問題，並且打擊世界性的恐怖主義。他也承諾經援非洲的落後國家。

　　毫無疑問的是，歐巴馬的這些政見受到了馬歇爾的啟發，也為他贏得了美國大選。但是，他真正的問題才要開始。尤其是，他要做這麼多事，美國又面臨空前的經濟不景氣，錢從哪裡來？

Philadelphia, PA | March 18, 2008

Remarks of Senator Barack Obama:

A More Perfect Union

2008年3月18日於賓州費城

歐巴馬參議員演說：

一個更完美的聯邦

◎ 深度導讀：陸以正（無任所大使）
◎ 單字、文句解析：楊人凱
◎ 翻譯：王麗娟（聯合報國際中心編譯組）
◎ 審訂：彭鏡禧（國立臺灣大學外文系及戲劇系特聘教授）

第一部分 🎗 深度導讀

更完美的美利堅聯邦
二〇〇八年三月十八日在賓州費城的演說

◎陸以正（無任所大使）

　　美國民主的特色是兩黨政治，若非共和黨，就是民主黨，沒有第三種選擇。好處是非楊即墨，不像法國或許多新興國家每逢選舉，一大堆小黨派搶得烏煙瘴氣。它的壞處是黨內為競逐總統候選人提名，常常爭得面紅耳赤，破壞團結。

　　從二〇〇七年二月宣佈他要競選總統起，到第二年八月底在丹佛城民主黨全國代表大會獲得提名，歐巴馬和希拉蕊・柯林頓（Hillary Rodney Clinton）整整纏鬥了一年半時間，才確定勝出。此後他與共和黨提名的麥肯（John McCann）參議員競爭總統職位，總共不滿三個月，後半遠不如前段既冗長又辛苦。

　　有黑人出來競選白宮主人的位置，自然轟動一時，美國凡是非洲裔人，不管先來後到，也不論是否黑奴後裔，全都興奮莫名，紛紛為他加油打氣。本篇就是因友好熱心過度，弄巧成拙，反而幫了倒忙，累得他臨危搶救最顯著的事例。

　　歐巴馬夫妻都是基督教徒。他早在進哈佛法學院之前，就認識在芝加哥貧民區居住的西區三一聯合教堂（Trinity United Church）的萊特牧師（Jeremiah Wright）；歐巴馬的婚禮和他們兩個女兒的受洗禮，都由萊特主持。媒體爆料說，歐氏凡有重大決定，事前總找萊特商榷，真相如何，沒有人敢確定。

　　二〇〇八年三月十八日，萊特在教堂講道，忽然大罵希拉蕊，使用黑人慣用語

法說：「希拉蕊從來沒被叫過『黑鬼』（Hillary ain't never been called a nigger!）」還有許多更不堪入耳的抨擊，充滿種族仇視，全美為之震驚。

打鐵趁熱，歐巴馬當機立斷，同天夜晚就在賓州費城（Philadelphia, PA）發表本篇演說。正因為事出倉促，沒有時間咬文嚼字，可能也未備講稿，更顯得難能可貴。

本篇演說的標題〈A More Perfect Union〉一詞，出自一七八七年五月到九月在費城獨立廳召開的制憲議會（Constitutional Assembly）通過的「聯邦條款（Articles of Confederation）」。當時華盛頓是議長，麥迪遜（James Madison）擔任記錄。這份文件最後並未完成，由於交通困難，參加的十三州代表也只能在會議期間陸續趕到。更多的獨立革命的領袖因反對而未參加。

反對什麼呢？意見紛歧的原因之一，是買賣黑奴問題無法解決；最後決定延至二十年後再議。歐巴馬說，可見在羊皮紙上簽署的莊嚴契約，不足以解除奴隸頸上的枷鎖。必須後繼世世代代的美國人經過一次內戰，走上街頭，到法院訴訟，和風起雲湧的非暴力反抗（公民不合作主義）等等階段，才達成最後平等。

他縷述自己的身世，強調美國人必須團結一致，解決殘存的種族分離現象。中下階級的白人同樣有被歧視的感覺，他們也是被遺忘的一群。歐巴馬把這些歸罪於華府的政客與華爾街的大老闆們。

Union一字在此指聯邦制的美國。歐巴馬獲得民主黨提名，與麥肯競逐總統職位時，最令人驚訝的是黨內初選的對手希拉蕊能捐棄前嫌，全力為他助選。歐巴馬勝利後，立即請她出任國務卿，可謂惺惺惜惺惺，英雄識英雄，也成為歷史的佳話。

作為本篇註腳，萊特牧師成為新聞人物後，接受電視訪問之外，甚至還到華府全國記者俱樂部去演講。歐巴馬不得不使用「悲哀」（saddened）和「生氣」（outraged）等字眼形容他的反應。過了兩個月，他終於辭去在「三一聯合教堂」的教友資格，和萊特切斷了關係。

第二部分  主文/中譯

主文中譯◎王麗娟（聯合報國際新聞中心編譯組）
單字解説◎楊人凱

 "We, the people, in order to form a more perfect union."

 Two hundred and twenty one years ago, in a hall that still stands across the street, a group of men gathered and, with these simple words, **launched** America's **improbable** experiment in democracy. Farmers and scholars, statesmen and patriots who had traveled across an ocean to escape tyranny and persecution finally made real their **declaration of independence** at a Philadelphia convention that lasted through the spring of 1787.

 The document they produced was **eventually signed but ultimately unfinished**. It was stained by this nation's original sin of slavery, a question that divided the colonies and brought the convention to a stalemate until the founders chose to allow the slave trade to continue for at least twenty more years, and **to leave any final resolution to future generations**.

單 字 解 説

◎ launched（v.）：多半是當動詞用，意指開辦，創辦，使船入水，發射飛彈等，少數情形下亦作形容詞，指「首創的」，如The launch issue of the new magazine had a story on Obama.（新雜誌的創刊號有一篇歐巴馬的故事）。
◎ Improbable和impossible這兩個形容詞經常被混用。前者指的是可能的，但發生機率不高，如中大樂透。後者指的是不可能發生的，如死人復生。
◎ declaration of independence（n.）獨立宣言。若首字大寫，則通常指美國的獨立宣言。台灣獨立運

「我們人民，為創建更完美的聯邦。」

兩百二十一年前，在迄今仍屹立在對街上的一個大廳中，一群人齊聚一室，並以像這般簡單的文字，啟動看似不可能的一項美國民主實驗。飄洋過海逃離暴政與迫害的農民、學者、政治家、愛國者，終於能在一七八七年一整個春天於費城召開的會議中，發表獨立宣言。

他們擬就的那份文件是完成簽署了，可惜文件最終仍有未竟之功。這個國家的原罪——奴隸制度，是文件的污點。此一問題造成殖民地的分裂，並讓大會陷入僵局，這個國家的創建者最後決定讓奴隸交易再延長至少二十年，將問題遺留給後世子孫解決。

動在英文裡就叫Taiwan Independence Movement。
◎ eventually signed but ultimately unfinished：eventual和ultimate意義相仿，eventual是單純指事件的終結，ultimate卻強調終極的限度。
◎ to leave any final resolution to future generations：來自這個片語to leave something to someone，指將某事留給某人。resolution是指會議中的決議案。動議案則叫motion。

Of course, the answer to the slavery question was already embedded within our Constitution–a Constitution that had at is very core the ideal of equal citizenship under the law; a Constitution that promised its people liberty, and justice, and a union that could be and should be perfected over time.

 And yet **words on a parchment** would not be enough to deliver slaves from bondage, or provide **men and women of every color and creed** their full rights and obligations as citizens of the United States. What would be needed were Americans in successive generations who were willing to do their part –through protests and struggle, on the streets and in the courts, through a civil war and civil disobedience and always at great risk–to narrow that gap between the promise of our ideals and the reality of their time.

 This was one of the tasks we set forth at the beginning of this campaign-to continue the long march of those who came before us, a march for a **more just**, **more equal**, **more free**, **more caring** and more prosperous America. I chose to run for the presidency at this moment in history because I believe deeply that we cannot solve the challenges of our time unless we solve them together - unless we perfect our union by understanding that we may have different stories, but we hold common hopes; that we may not look the same and we may not have come from the same place, but we all want to move in the same direction-towards a better future for our children and our grandchildren.

◎ words on a parchment（片語）：指寫在一張羊皮紙上的字（即美國獨立宣言）。parchment 是羊皮紙，但parch是指烘乾，烤乾，如parched soil枯乾的土地。
◎ men and women of every color and creed不同膚色和信仰的男女。creed是指宗教的教派。

4 當然，奴隸制度問題的解答，早已寫在憲法之中。法律之前人人平等的理想，是這部憲法的核心，它同時許諾人民自由、公義，以及一個應該、以及能夠與時並進，臻於完美的聯邦。

---

5 書寫於羊皮紙上的文字，並不足以讓黑奴脫離禁錮，或讓不同膚色與信仰的男女，享有美國公民的完整權利與義務。它仍需要其後世代代的美國人，善盡他們的一份職責，透過街頭與法院的抗爭，或是經由內戰與公民不合作主義，一再的甘冒大風險，才能縮短當年我們所承諾的理想與現實狀況兩者之間的距離。

---

6 這是選戰一開始，我們即已設定的任務──延續先人的長征道路，追求一個更公正、平等、自由、關懷、繁榮的美國。我選擇在歷史的這一刻參選，因為我深信，除非群策群力，我們難以戰勝這項挑戰，同時，除非我們能夠了解，雖然我們每個人有不同的故事，唯有懷抱共同的希望，聯邦才能更完美；儘管我們外表不同，且來自不同的地方，但我們都想朝同一方向前進，一個可讓後世子孫活得更好的將來。

◎ more just, more equal, more free, more caring：更公正，更平等，更自由，更關懷的。這裡，歐巴馬用了more free，而不用freer，是為了文章前後的統一性。就文法而言，free是單音節形容詞，理應用freer，如最自由的國家，英文一定用the freest nation in the world。不會說是the most free nation in the world。

This belief comes from my unyielding faith in the decency and generosity of the American people. But it also comes from my own American story.

I am the son of a black man from Kenya and a white woman from Kansas. I was raised with the help of a white grandfather who survived a Depression to serve in Patton's Army during World War II and a white grandmother who worked on a bomber assembly line at Fort Leavenworth while he was overseas. I've gone to some of the best schools in America and lived in one of the world's poorest nations. I am married to a black American who carries within her the blood of slaves and slaveowners—an inheritance we pass on to our two precious daughters. I have brothers, sisters, nieces, nephews, uncles and cousins, of every race and every hue, scattered across three continents, and for as long as I live, I will never forget that in no other country on Earth is my story even possible.

It's a story that hasn't made me the most **conventional** candidate. But it is a story that has seared into my genetic makeup the idea that this nation is more than the sum of its parts—that out of many, we are truly one.

Throughout the first year of this campaign, against all predictions **to the contrary**, we saw how hungry the American people were for this message of unity. Despite the temptation to view my candidacy through a purely racial lens, we won commanding victories in states with some of the whitest populations in the country. In South Carolina, where the Confederate Flag still flies, we built a powerful coalition of African Americans and white Americans.

◎conventional（a.）：指老套的，因襲的，陳舊的。

這種信念，來自我對美國人正直、仁厚的不變信心。這種信念，同時也來自我自己的美國故事。

 我的父母，一個是來自肯亞的黑人，一個是來自堪薩斯州的白人女性，我是白人外祖父母幫忙帶大的。熬過經濟大蕭條苦日子的外祖父，二戰時曾跟隨巴頓將軍，外祖母在外祖父於海外時，於李文渥斯堡當轟炸機的裝配線工人。我上過美國最好的學校，待過全球最貧窮的國家。我娶了一名黑人女性為妻，她的身體流著黑奴與黑奴主人的血液，而我的兩個寶貝女兒繼承了我們所有的血統。我有兄弟、姊妹、姪甥、姪甥女、叔伯、表親，所有膚色、種族都有，他們來自三個大陸，而我將沒齒難忘，我的故事，絕無可能發生於地球上的任何其他國家。

 這個故事並未讓我成為最傳統的總統參選人。但這個故事讓我打從骨子裡體認到，這個國家不僅是所有部分加起來的總和，它雖有許多部分，實則已合而為一。

 投入選戰的頭一整年，出乎意外，我們目睹美國人對團結這項訊息的想望。儘管有人想純粹地從種族的眼光，看待我的選舉，我們白人比例最高的一些州中獲致壓倒性勝利。在南部聯邦旗幟依舊飄揚的北卡州，我們在黑人與白人之間建立起強大的聯盟。

◎to the contrary是常用的介系詞片語，意指相反的。

This is not to say that race has not been an issue in the campaign. At various stages in the campaign, some commentators have deemed me either "too black" or "not black enough." We saw racial tensions bubble to the surface during the week before the South Carolina primary. **The press** has scoured every **exit poll** for the latest evidence of racial polarization, not just in terms of white and black, but black and brown as well.

 And yet, it has only been in the last couple of weeks that the discussion of race in this campaign has taken a particularly divisive turn.

 On one end of the spectrum, we've heard the implication that my candidacy is somehow an exercise in **affirmative** action; that it's based solely on the desire of wide-eyed liberals to purchase racial reconciliation on the cheap. On the other end, we've heard my former pastor, Reverend Jeremiah Wright, use incendiary language to express views that have the potential not only to widen the racial **divide**, but views that denigrate both the greatness and the goodness of our nation; that rightly offend white and black alike.

 I have already condemned, in unequivocal terms, the statements of Reverend Wright that have caused such controversy. For some, nagging questions remain. Did I know him to be an occasionally fierce critic of American domestic and foreign policy? Of course. Did I ever hear him make remarks that could be considered controversial while I sat in church? Yes. Did I strongly disagree with many of his political views? Absolutely—just as I'm sure many of you have heard remarks from your pastors, priests, or rabbis with which you strongly disagreed.

◎ the press（n.）是新聞媒體的總稱。它的原意是指the printing press印刷機。因為報紙、雜誌都需要用印刷機印刷，所以press就成了平面媒體的代號，後來又引申成為包括電子媒體在內，雖然電子媒體與印刷機扯不上關係。
◎ exit poll（n.）是指在投票亭附近對剛投票的民眾所作的民意調查，以作為選舉結果的預測用。

這不代表種族不是這場選戰的議題。在選戰的不同階段中,政論家有人說我「太黑」,有人說我「不夠黑」。南卡初選的前一週,我們目擊種族緊張關係浮上檯面。媒體問遍每個出口民調,尋找種族對立的最新證據,而且不光是找黑人與白人之間的對立,還有黑人與棕色人種之間的不和。

然而,這場選戰有關種族問題的討論,要到兩週前才變得格外兩極化。

在光譜的一端,有人說,我的參選,是美國平權法的一次練習;而我參選的想法很簡單,只是天真的自由派人士想撿種族大和解的便宜。在光譜的另一端,我們聽到我的前牧師耶利米·萊特,以煽動的語言表達觀點,他的論調不僅可能擴大種族隔閡,同時貶抑了我們國家的偉大與善良。

我已以明確的語言,對萊特牧師引起偌大爭議的言論加以譴責。但有人對我仍是不放心。他們問,我知不知道,萊特有時會痛批美國的內政、外交政策?當然。坐在教堂內,我是否聽他發表過具有爭議的言論?有的。在許多政治觀點上,我是否和他南轅北轍?絕對是。我相信我的情況和你們許多人雷同,都聽過你們的牧師、神父、猶太拉比說過你可能無法苟同的話。

◎ affirmative action(n.):字面的意義是正面肯定性的行動。在美國這個用語是特指美國政府為了保護民眾不因性別、種族、血緣受到歧視而提出的平等機會法案。
◎ divide,在此是名詞,意思是分隔。

But the remarks that have caused this recent firestorm weren't simply controversial. They weren't simply a religious leader's effort to speak out against perceived injustice. Instead, they expressed a profoundly distorted view of this country—a view that sees white racism as endemic, and that elevates what is wrong with America above all that we know is right with America; a view that sees the conflicts in the Middle East as rooted primarily in the actions of **stalwart allies** like Israel, instead of emanating from the perverse and hateful ideologies of radical Islam.

As such, Reverend Wright's comments were not only wrong but divisive, divisive at a time when we need unity; racially charged at a time when we need to come together to solve a set of monumental problems—two wars, a terrorist threat, a falling economy, a chronic health care crisis and potentially devastating climate change; problems that are neither black or white or Latino or Asian, but rather problems that confront us all.

Given my background, my politics, and my professed values and ideals, there will no doubt be those for whom my statements of condemnation are not enough. Why associate myself with Reverend Wright in the first place, they may ask? Why not join another church? And I confess that if all that I knew of Reverend Wright were the snippets of those sermons that have run in an endless loop on the television and You Tube, or if Trinity United Church of Christ conformed to the caricatures being peddled by some commentators, there is no doubt that I would react in much the same way.

單 字 解 說

◎ stalwart allies（n.）：stalwart是堅強的、強壯的意思。

但是最近引起風暴的言論，已不只是具爭議性。它不單是宗教領袖對自己感受到的不公不義嗆聲。相反的，它傳遞了對這個國家一項嚴重扭曲的觀點。它認為白人的種族歧視是通病，所以美國壞的地方多，好的地方少；同一觀點同時認為，中東衝突的禍根是以色列等美國堅定盟友的行為，而不是偏激伊斯蘭教徒的仇恨與反常的意識形態。

 萊特牧師的言論不僅錯誤，而且在我們亟需團結的時候，製造分裂，在我們亟需通力合作解決一連串棘手難題的時候，挑起種族情緒。我們手上有兩場戰爭、一項恐怖威脅、一個走下坡的經濟、一個長期存在的健保危機、可能持續惡化的氣候變遷。這些問題與我們是白人、黑人、拉丁裔、亞洲人無關，而是我們全民面對的難題。

就我的背景、政治立場，還有我公開談過的價值觀與理想，毫無疑問，有人定會認為，我光是譴責萊特是不夠的。最初為何要與萊特牧師打交道？為何不改上其他教會？我承認，若我對萊特牧師的認知，僅止於電視或是You Tube可一播再播的那些佈道短片，又或是三一聯合教會真如有些批評者諷刺的那般可笑，毫無疑問，我八成會這樣做。

◎ given（prep.）：有鑑於某些既成事實的習慣用法。如，Given the first lady's poor health, she is unlikely to go to jail.（既然第一夫人的健康情形不佳，她不太可能去坐牢。）

But the truth is, that isn't all that I know of the man. The man I met more than twenty years ago is a man who helped introduce me to my Christian faith, a man who spoke to me about our obligations to love one another; to care for the sick and lift up the poor. He is a man who served his country as a U.S. Marine; who has studied and lectured at some of the finest universities and seminaries in the country, and who for over thirty years led a church that serves the community by doing God's work here on Earth—by housing the homeless, ministering to the needy, providing day care services and scholarships and prison ministries, and reaching out to those suffering from HIV/AIDS.

 In my first book, *Dreams From My Father*, I described the experience of my first service at Trinity:

 "People began to shout, to rise from their seats and clap and cry out, a forceful wind carrying the reverend's voice up into the **rafters**.... And in that single note–hope!–I heard something else; at the foot of that cross, inside the thousands of churches across the city, I imagined the stories of ordinary black people merging with the stories of David and Goliath, Moses and Pharaoh, the Christians in the lion's den, Ezekiel's field of dry bones. Those stories– of survival, and freedom, and hope - became our story, my story; the blood that had spilled was our blood, the tears our tears; until this black church, on this bright day, seemed once more a vessel carrying the story of a people into future generations and into a larger world. Our trials and triumphs became at once unique and universal, black and more than black; in chronicling our journey, the stories and songs gave us a means to reclaim memories that we didn't need to feel shame about...memories that all people might study and cherish-and with which we could start to rebuild."

◎rafters（n.）：raft是竹筏的意思。rafter一般是指撐竹筏的人，但在這裡是指教堂裡的屋椽。

但事實上，我對這個人的認識不僅於此。我和他相識於二十多年前，他帶領我信仰基督，教導我說，愛人、關懷病患、扶助貧窮是我們的責任。他曾在美國陸戰隊報效國家，在美國最好的大學與神學院就讀與發表演講，而三十多年來，他帶領教會服務社區，做好上帝在世間的工作。他收容無家可歸者、照料窮人、提供日間托兒服務、獎學金，還到監獄佈道、向愛滋病毒／愛滋病患者伸援手。

在我的第一本書「歐巴馬的夢想之路——以父之名」中，我描述過第一次參加三一教會佈道的經驗：

「人們開始呼喊，從座位站起，拍手高喊，一股勁風，將牧師的聲音捲上了梁間……。而在眾人高喊『希望』這兩字時，我另有所悟。在那個十字架的下方，在這個城市數以千計的教會裡，我想像著平凡的黑人故事，正與大衛殺死巨人哥利亞、摩西與法老、基督徒與獅穴、以西結白骨回生的故事結合為一。那些生存、自由、希望的故事，變成我們的、我的故事。他們所流的血是我們的血，流的淚是我們的淚，而這所黑人教會，在這大白天中，再度化成一座方舟，承載著人們的故事，航向未來的世代以及一個更開闊的世界。我們經歷的試煉與勝利，既是獨一無二卻也萬有，它屬於黑人，又不只屬於黑人。在記錄我們的旅程時，所有的故事、歌謠，都將成為我們日後取回我們無須感到羞愧記憶的工具……這些記憶將為所有人所學習與珍惜，並以這些記憶從事改造。」

That has been my experience at Trinity. Like other **predominantly** black churches across the country, Trinity embodies the black community in its entirety–the doctor and the **welfare** mom, the model student and the former **gang–banger**. Like other black churches, Trinity's services are full of raucous laughter and sometimes bawdy humor. They are full of dancing, clapping, screaming and shouting that may seem jarring to the untrained ear. The church contains in full the kindness and cruelty, the fierce intelligence and the shocking ignorance, the struggles and successes, the love and yes, the bitterness and bias that make up the black experience in America.

 And this helps explain, perhaps, my relationship with Reverend Wright. As imperfect as he may be, he has been like family to me. He strengthened my faith, officiated my wedding, and **baptized** my children. Not once in my conversations with him have I heard him talk about any ethnic group in derogatory terms, or treat whites with whom he interacted with **anything but** courtesy and respect. He contains within him the contradictions–the good and the bad–of the community that he has served diligently for so many years.

 I can no more disown him than I can disown the black community. I can no more disown him than I can my white grandmother–a woman who helped raise me, a woman who sacrificed again and again for me, a woman who loves me as much as she loves anything in this world, but a woman who once confessed her fear of black men who passed by her on the street, and who on more than one occasion has uttered racial or ethnic stereotypes that made me cringe.

◎ predominantly（ad.）：佔主導地位地。
◎ welfare（adj.）：接受社會救濟的。
◎ gang-banger（n）：可以指一般的幫派分子，也可以指輪姦女性的人。在此文中歐巴馬是指一般的

這是我在三一教會的經驗。和全美其他黑人居多的教會一樣,三一教會是黑人社區的完整化身。它有醫生、有領社會救濟的母親,有模範學生和前少年幫派分子。和其他黑人教會一樣,三一教會的講道充滿喧鬧的笑聲,間或夾雜著低俗的幽默。它充滿舞蹈、擊掌、尖叫、呼喊,沒聽慣的人會覺得刺耳。這所教會無所不容,它有殘酷與善良、智慧過人與極度無知、奮鬥與成功、愛心,是的,還有仇恨與偏見,這些全是美國黑人經驗的組成。

 或許這有助於解釋我和萊特牧師的關係。他雖不完美,對我卻有如家人般。他堅定了我的信仰,為我證婚,領洗我的孩子。在和他的談話中,從未有任何一次,我聽到他貶抑任何族群,在與白人互動時,他的態度也總是守禮與尊重。他這個人充滿矛盾,有好有壞,這點和他長年勤於服務的社區的特色也不謀而合。

 我無法和他斷絕關係,一如我無法切斷與黑人族群的連繫。我無法和他斷絕關係,正如我無法和我的白人外祖母斷絕往來,這位女士一再為我犧牲,她愛我正如她愛這世上的萬事萬物,雖然她曾坦承,在街上與黑人擦身而過,心中難免恐懼,且不只一次,她提到一些種族的刻板印象時,曾讓我感到厭惡。

幫派分子。
◎ baptized(vt.):為……施洗禮。
◎ anything but:除了……之外的任何事物。在這裡,but是個介系詞,用法等同 except。

These people are a part of me. And they are a part of America, this country that I love.

Some will see this as an attempt to **justify** or excuse comments that are simply inexcusable. I can assure you it is not. I suppose the politically safe thing would be to move on from this episode and **just hope that it fades into the woodwork**. We can dismiss Reverend Wright as **a crank or a demagogue**, just as some have dismissed Geraldine Ferraro, in the aftermath of her recent statements, as harboring some deep-seated racial bias.

But race is an issue that I believe this nation cannot afford to ignore right now. We would be making the same mistake that Reverend Wright made in his **offending** sermons about America–to simplify and **stereotype** and amplify the negative to the point that it distorts reality.

The fact is that the comments that have been made and the issues that have surfaced over the last few weeks reflect the complexities of race in this country that we've never really worked through–a part of our union that we have yet to perfect. And if we walk away now, if we simply **retreat** into our **respective** corners, we will never be able to come together and solve challenges like health care, or education, or the need to find good jobs for every American.

◎ justify（vt.）：為……辯護。
◎ just hope that it fades into the woodwork是come out of the wooawork（突然令人不悅地出現）的反面用法。歐巴馬的意思是，他希望萊特牧師出言不遜的事件就此自然消失，不再被討論。
◎ a crank and a demagogue：crank一般指曲柄，也指有奇癖的怪人。demagogue 是指專門煽動群眾來達到自己私利的人。

這些人是我生命的部分。他們也是美國，這個我鍾愛國家的一部分。

 有人會說，我是在替無法原諒的言語辯白。我向你們保證絕對不是。我若想打政治安全牌，大可不必理會這件插曲，就這樣讓它消失於無形。我們可將萊特牧師斥為怪人或煽動者，情況和美國前副總統參選人潔若汀·費拉羅最近發表一些言論後，有人指責她種族偏見根深柢固類似。

 然而我相信種族問題此刻已是美國不容忽視的議題。若我們一味將這項負面問題簡化、定型，或者放大到扭曲事實的境地，將犯下和萊特牧師於講道中冒犯美國相同的錯。

 事實上，這幾週浮上檯面的議題，反映出美國從未能真正解決的種族問題的複雜性，也是這個聯邦至今仍美中不足的地方。不過，若是我們掉轉身，縮回各自的角落，將永遠無法群策群力，迎向醫療保健、教育，或是為所有美國人找到好工作等的挑戰。

◎ offending（adj.）：引起問題的。
◎ stereotype（vt.）：使成為陳規、定型。
◎ retreat（vi.）：撤退、退卻。
◎ respective（adj.）：各自的。

Understanding this reality requires a reminder of how we arrived at this point. As William Faulkner once wrote, "The past isn't dead and buried. In fact, it isn't even past." We do not need to recite here the history of racial injustice in this country. But we do need to remind ourselves that so many of the disparities that exist in the African-American community today can be directly traced to inequalities passed on from an earlier generation that suffered under the brutal **legacy** of slavery and **Jim Crow**.

 Segregated schools were, and are, inferior schools; we still haven't fixed them, fifty years after **Brown v. Board of Education**, and the inferior education they provided, then and now, helps explain the pervasive achievement gap between today's black and white students.

 Legalized discrimination—where blacks were prevented, often through violence, from owning property, or loans were not granted to African-American business owners, or black homeowners could not access FHA **mortgages**, or blacks were excluded from unions, or the police force, or fire departments—meant that black families could not amass any meaningful wealth **to bequeath to** future generations. That history helps explain the wealth and income gap between black and white, and the concentrated pockets of poverty that persists in so many of today's urban and rural communities.

◎ legacy（n.）：留給後人的東西。
◎ Jim Crow（n.）：吉姆克羅法。這是美國南北戰爭之後，美國南方所實施的一種法律，要求在公共設施如學校、軍隊、教會、餐廳裡將黑人與白人隔離。這個名字的來源是一首同名的歌。
◎ segregated（adj.）：種族隔離的。
◎ Brown v. Board of Education：是指美國最高法院於一九五四年通過的一項判決，裁定在公共設施裡實施種族隔離政策是違法的。自此，全美國就出現了黑白同校的教育制度。這項裁定被譽為是美國

28 要了解這項現實，我們必須清楚知道，最初是如何走上這步田地的。威廉·福克納曾寫道：「過去並未死亡，也未被埋葬，其實，過去甚至並未過去。」我們的確需要自我提醒，今天仍存在於黑人族群的許多不公平，可直接追溯到從上一代遺留的不平等待遇，那一代的人，因為奴隸制度與吉姆·克羅種族隔離法案的血腥餘毒而受盡苦難。

---

29 種族隔離的學校曾是，至今仍是，次等的學校；我們在「布朗對托皮卡教育局案」這樁判例過了五十年後，仍未能解決這些問題，而當時與現在所提供的次等教育，都可拿來解釋為何今天的白人與黑人學生，仍普遍存在個人成就的差距。

---

30 合法化的歧視，最常見的，是透過暴力，禁止黑人擁有財產，或是拒絕貸款給黑人生意人，不讓黑人購屋者申請聯邦住屋局的貸款，不讓黑人加入工會，進入警隊、消防隊等，使黑人家庭無法累積足夠的財富留給子孫。那段歷史足以說明為何黑白之間會存在收入與財富差距，以及時至今日，還有如此多的貧民區存在於都市與鄉村社區中。

司法史上的重要里程碑。
◎ legalized（vt.）：法律上認為……正當、使合法化。
◎ discrimination（n.）：不公平待遇、歧視。
◎ mortgages（n.）：抵押借款。
◎ to bequeath to（v.）：將某物件遺贈給或留傳給某人。如：After my death I shall bequeath my old house to my son.（我死後會把老房子留贈給我兒子。）

A lack of economic opportunity among black men, and the shame and frustration that came from not being able to provide for one's family, contributed to the erosion of black families—a problem that **welfare** policies for many years may have worsened. And the lack of basic services in so many urban black neighborhoods—parks for kids to play in, police walking the beat, regular garbage pick-up and building code enforcement—all helped create a cycle of violence, blight and neglect that continue to haunt us.

 This is the reality in which Reverend Wright and other African-Americans of his generation grew up. They came of age in the late fifties and early sixties, a time when segregation was still the law of the land and opportunity was systematically constricted. What's remarkable is not how many failed in the face of discrimination, but rather how many men and women overcame the odds; how many were able to make a way out of no way for those like me who would come after them.

 But for all those who scratched and clawed their way to get a piece of the American Dream, there were many who didn't make it—those who were ultimately defeated, in one way or another, by discrimination. That legacy of defeat was passed on to future generations—those young men and increasingly young women who we see standing on street corners or **languishing** in our prisons, without hope or prospects for the future. Even for those blacks who did make it, questions of race, and racism, continue to define their worldview in fundamental ways. For the men and women of Reverend Wright's generation, the memories of humiliation and doubt and fear have not gone away; nor has the anger and the bitterness of those years. That anger may not get expressed in public, in front of white co-workers or white friends. But it does find voice in the barbershop or around the kitchen table. At times, that anger is exploited by politicians, **to gin up** votes along racial lines, or to make up for a politician's own failings.

◎ welfare（adj.）：福利事業的。
◎ languishing（adj.）：漸漸衰弱的。

31 黑人男人欠缺賺錢機會，以及養不起家的羞愧與挫折感，造成黑人家庭問題層出不窮，而多年來的福利政策，導致問題更形惡化。許多市區的黑人社區基本服務付之闕如，例如沒有可供兒童遊戲的公園、無警察巡邏、無人定時收垃圾、建築法規執行不力，所有這些造就了一個暴力、破爛、輕視的循環，持續不斷地困擾著我們。

32 這項現實是萊特牧師以及他的世代的非裔美人的成長環境。他們在五○年代末期或是六○年代初期時成年，當時種族隔離制度仍是這塊土地上的法律，機會仍是有系統地受到限制。不過，更重要的，不是有多少人因種族歧視而失敗了，而是有多少男女克服了這項逆境，有多少人從絕境之中開闢出道路，嘉惠我和其他後人。

33 儘管有人歷經萬難成就了美國夢，但仍有許多人並不成功，他們被林林總總的歧視擊垮。而未來的世代繼承了這項挫敗的遺產，因此我們看到，一些少男以及越來越多的少女站在街角或在監獄中枯萎，了無希望與前景。而即使是出人頭地的黑人，種族問題或甚至種族歧視，依然持續根本地界定他們的世界觀。對萊特牧師一代的男女而言，屈辱、懷疑、恐懼仍是揮之不去，他們對那些年代的憤怒與仇恨也未消逝。在白人同事或白人友人面前，他們不會公然宣洩怒氣。但在理髮店或是廚房餐桌上，我們聽得到這些抱怨。有時，政治人物會利用這股怨氣，打種族牌拉選票，或用來彌補政治人物自身能力的不足。

◎ to gin up（片語）：gin一般是指英國產的琴酒（杜松子酒），所以gin up有藉喝酒來提神的涵意，後來成為一個俚語，也有創造，產生，使具有活力的意思。

And occasionally it finds voice in the church on Sunday morning, in the **pulpit** and in the **pews**. The fact that so many people are surprised to hear that anger in some of Reverend Wright's sermons simply reminds us of the old **truism** that the most segregated hour in American life occurs on Sunday morning. That anger is not always productive; indeed, all too often it distracts attention from solving real problems; it keeps us from squarely facing our own complicity in our condition, and prevents the African-American community from forging the alliances it needs to bring about real change. But the anger is real; it is powerful; and to simply wish it away, to condemn it without understanding its roots, only serves to widen the chasm of misunderstanding that exists between the races.

 In fact, a similar anger exists within segments of the white community. Most working—and middle-class white Americans don't feel that they have been particularly privileged by their race. Their experience is the **immigrant** experience—as far as they're concerned, no one's handed them anything, they've built it **from scratch**. They've worked hard all their lives, many times only to see their jobs shipped overseas or their pension dumped after a lifetime of labor. They are anxious about their futures, and feel their dreams slipping away; in an era of stagnant wages and global competition, opportunity comes to be seen as **a zero sum game**, in which your dreams come at my expense. So when they are told to bus their children to a school across town; when they hear that an African American is getting an advantage in landing a good job or a spot in a good college because of an injustice that they themselves never committed; when they're told that their fears about crime in urban neighborhoods are somehow prejudiced, resentment builds over time.

◎ pulpit（n.）：講道壇。
◎ pews（n.）：教堂座席。
◎ truism（n.）：是一些為多數所接受的老生常談。
◎ immigrant（adj.）：移民的。

偶爾，在週日上午的教堂中，從講道台或是從信眾席，我們也會聽到這種聲音。萊特牧師在講道時宣洩怒氣，讓這麼多人在聽到時感到訝異的這個事實，讓我聯想到一句老生常談：美國人生活中種族隔離最嚴重的時刻，就是週日上午。這種憤怒往往於事無補；確實是如此，許多時候，它分散我們解決真正問題的注意力；它讓我們無法真正面對一項事實，亦即我們是自己處境的共犯；它阻礙了黑人的族群團結，也未能帶動實質的改變。但這股怒氣真實存在且強大無比，只祈禱它會消失，或是不去了解根源地一味譴責，只會擴大族群之間的誤解。

 事實上，白人族群中的一些地區，也存在類似的憤怒。多數的勞工階級與中產階級的美國白人並不認為他的種族讓他享有什麼特權。他們的經驗是移民的經驗，對他們來說，沒人給過他們什麼，是他們讓自己從無到有。他們一輩子賣力工作，卻一再目睹老闆將工作移轉海外，或是辛苦一輩子的退休金最後化為烏有。他們對未來感到焦慮，也感到夢想正悄悄溜走；在一個薪資凍漲，全球競爭的年代，機會被視為是零和遊戲，你的美夢靠我犧牲成全。因此，當有人告訴他們必須讓孩子搭車到遠在這個城市另一頭的學校就讀；聽到黑人可以因為他們是黑人而在申請工作或名校享受保障名額時，同樣會怒不可遏，對黑人不公不義的又不是他們，卻要他們讓出機會；當他們對市區犯罪率攀升表達恐懼，而人們卻說這是他們的偏見時，這些白人的反感也在日積月累。

◎ from scratch：從頭開始。這是個常見的美國俚語，scratch是指在地上刻劃出來的一條起跑線，所以start from scratch就是從頭來過的意思。

◎ a zero sum game（n.）：零和遊戲。這是遊戲理論的一種，意思是當可分配的物件的總數是固定的時候，在兩個競爭者之間或多個競爭者之間某一方得到多些，另一方就會得到少些。而多的部分減去少的部分就永遠等於零。

Like the anger within the black community, these resentments aren't always expressed in polite company. But they have helped shape the political landscape for at least a generation. Anger over welfare and affirmative action helped forge the Reagan Coalition. Politicians routinely exploited fears of crime for their own electoral ends. Talk show hosts and conservative commentators built entire careers unmasking **bogus** claims of racism while dismissing legitimate discussions of racial injustice and inequality as mere **political correctness** or reverse racism.

Just as black anger often proved counterproductive, so have these white resentments distracted attention from the real culprits of the middle class squeeze—a corporate culture rife with inside dealing, questionable accounting practices, and short—term greed; a Washington dominated by lobbyists and special interests; economic policies that favor the few over the many. And yet, to wish away the resentments of white Americans, to label them as misguided or even racist, without recognizing they are grounded in legitimate concerns— this too widens the racial divide, and blocks the path to understanding.

This is where we are right now. It's a racial stalemate we've been stuck in for years. Contrary to the claims of some of my critics, black and white, I have never been so naïve as to believe that we can get beyond our racial divisions in a single election cycle, or with a single candidacy—particularly a candidacy as imperfect as my own.

But I have asserted a firm conviction—a conviction rooted in my faith in God and my faith in the American people—that working together we can move beyond some of our old racial wounds, and that in fact we have no choice if we are to continue on the path of a more perfect union.

◎bogus（a.）：假的，偽造的。如bogus watches是偽造的手錶，bogus government偽政府。

和黑人族群的憤怒一樣，這些反感並不總在禮貌的社交場合表達出來。不過，至少已有一個世代的時間，美國的政治景觀，是以這些反感形成。對福利與平權措施的不滿，也有助於雷根聯盟的形成。政治人物每每利用選民對犯罪的恐懼感，達到他們的選舉目的。談話節目主持人與保守派的評論員靠揭發不實的種族主義指控，建立起自己的整個事業，對種族主義不公不義的正當討論，卻斥為是政治正確或是逆向的種族歧視。

黑人的憤怒經常帶來不良後果，同樣地，這些白人的反感也產生了注意力轉移的結果，讓人們對中產階級受到擠壓的真正元兇視而不見。現代的企業文化充斥著內線交易、作假帳、短視近利；遊說人士與特殊利益者在華府予取予求；經濟政策獨厚少數而不是多數人。如果只是祈禱這些白人反感會自動消失，或者稱他們遭到誤導或甚至是種族主義者，不去認清他們其實是合理關切，這一切，只會擴大種族分裂，阻礙互諒的道路。

這是我們的現況。這是多年來我們深陷其中的種族歧視僵局。與那些批評我的人，無論是白人或黑人，所說的相反，我從未天真到相信，單靠一次選舉，或是一任總統，美國即能跨越種族歧見，尤是我還是這樣一個不完美的競選人。

但我有堅定的信念，一個來自我對上帝的信仰以及我對美國人的信心──只要我們同心協力，即能走出種族的舊創，事實上，我們若想持續走向一個更完美聯邦，就別無選擇。

◎ political correctness（n.）：政治正確。to be politically correct是指在政治上是符合當權派的喜好的，但是在道德上卻不一定正確。

For the African-American community, that path means embracing the burdens of our past without becoming victims of our past. It means continuing to insist on a full measure of justice in every aspect of American life. But it also means binding our particular grievances–for better health care, and better schools, and better jobs–to the larger aspirations of all Americans–the white woman struggling to break the glass ceiling, the white man who's been laid off, the immigrant trying to feed his family. And it means taking full responsibility for own lives–by demanding more from our fathers, and spending more time with our children, and reading to them, and teaching them that while they may face challenges and discrimination in their own lives, they must never **succumb to despair or cynicism**; they must always believe that they can write their own destiny.

 Ironically, this **quintessentially American**–and yes, conservative–notion of self-help found frequent expression in Reverend Wright's sermons. But what my former pastor too often failed to understand is that embarking on a program of self-help also requires a belief that society can change.

 The profound mistake of Reverend Wright's sermons is not that he spoke about racism in our society. It's that he spoke as if our society was static; as if no progress has been made; as if this country–a country that has made it possible for one of his own members to run for the highest office in the land and build a coalition of white and black, Latino and Asian, rich and poor, young and old–is still irrevocably bound to a tragic past. But what we know– what we have seen–is that America can change. That is true genius of this nation. What we have already achieved gives us hope-the audacity to hope– for what we can and must achieve tomorrow.

◎ to succumb to despair or cynicism：to succumb to是向某人或某件事屈服的意思。cynicism中文又叫犬儒主義。凡事懷疑別人誠意並且喜歡冷嘲熱諷的人就是一個cynic。

對非裔美人族群而言，這條道路代表我們必須欣然接受過去的包袱，停止成為過去的受害人。這意謂在美國生活的所有層面徹底落實公義的措施。它同時意謂黑人應該將他們希望能有更好的醫療保健、學校、工作的牢騷，與所有美國人，例如渴望粉碎職場無形障礙的白人女性、被裁員的白人男性、企求溫飽家人的移民的一些更大期望結合在一起。這意謂我們必須為自己的生活負起全責，例如對父親提出更多的要求，多花一點的時間陪伴孩子，讀書給他們聽，教導他們雖然他們可能在自己的生活遭遇挑戰和歧視，絕對不能因此變得絕望或憤世嫉俗；他們必須永遠相信，命運掌握在他們自己手中。

41 諷刺的是，這種典型美國式，是的，也是保守主義的自立自強想法，在萊特牧師的講道中時常提及。只是我的前牧師也經常不了解，在按照自立自強的計畫走時，同時必須相信這個社會是可以改變的。

42 萊特牧師講道中的最大錯處，不是他談論我們社會中的種族主義。而是在談它時，他把社會當成是靜止的，彷彿它從未進步。他還把這個國家，當作因為受到過去的束縛而無法從事改變。然而這個國家讓他自己的信眾之一有機會競選這片土地上的最高公職，以及建立一個黑與白、拉丁裔與亞裔、老與少的聯盟，而且我們知道，我們也看到，美國是能夠改變的。這才是這個國家真正的天賦。我們的成就讓我們希望——毫無畏懼地希望，我們明天也能做到，且應該做到。

◎ quintessentially American：本質上是美國的。quintessence是指一個東西的精華。

In the white community, the path to a more perfect union means acknowledging that what ails the African-American community does not just exist in the minds of black people; that the legacy of discrimination—and current incidents of discrimination, while less **overt** than in the past—are real and must be addressed. Not just with words, but with deeds—by investing in our schools and our communities; by enforcing our civil rights laws and ensuring fairness in our criminal justice system; by providing this generation with ladders of opportunity that were unavailable for previous generations. It requires all Americans to realize that your dreams do not have to come at the expense of my dreams; that investing in the health, welfare, and education of black and brown and white children will ultimately help all of America prosper.

 In the end, then, what is called for is nothing more, and nothing less, than what all the world's great religions demand—that we do unto others as we would have them do unto us. Let us be our brother's keeper, Scripture tells us. Let us be our sister's keeper. Let us find that common stake we all have in one another, and let our politics reflect that spirit as well.

 For we have a choice in this country. We can accept a politics that breeds division, and conflict, and cynicism. We can tackle race only as spectacle— as we did in the OJ trial—or in the wake of tragedy, as we did in the aftermath of Katrina—or as **fodder** for the nightly news. We can play Reverend Wright's sermons on every channel every day and talk about them from now until the election, and make the only question in this campaign whether or not the American people think that I somehow believe or sympathize with his most offensive words. We can pounce on some gaffe by a Hillary supporter as evidence that she's playing the race card, or we can speculate on whether white men will all flock to John McCain in the general election regardless of his policies.

單 字 解 說

◎ overt（a.）：公然的。與明顯的（obvious）意義略有不同。overt hostility意指公然的敵意，即未經掩飾的。

對白人族群而言，通往更完美聯邦的道路，意謂他們必須承認，困擾黑人族群的問題，並非黑人憑空想像；歧視的傳統以及現今較過去不明顯的歧視事件——是千真萬確的事，必須加以解決。而且不光是說說而已，還須付諸行動，包括對黑人的學校與社區提供投資，執行民權法與確保刑法體系公正，以及提供這個世代他們前幾代沒有的機會階梯。這需要所有美國人一致體認，你的美夢不一定要由我付出代價，而投資黑人、棕色人種、白人兒童的健保、福利、教育，最終將有助於整個美國的繁榮。

因此，最終我們需要的，不多不少，正是世上所有偉大宗教要求的推己及人的精神。讓我們成為我們兄弟的守護者，《聖經》這樣告訴我們。讓我們成為我們姊妹的守護者。讓我們找出共同的利害關係，讓我們的政治也反映出相同的精神。

因為在這個國家，我們是有選擇的。我們可以選擇接受只會製造分裂、衝突、悲觀這樣的一個政治；也可以把種族問題當好戲看，就像我們在看前職業美足傳奇人物辛普森因殺妻疑案接受審判；或者把它當作一場悲劇的事後處理，例如卡崔納風災後；或只把它當作夜間新聞的材料。我們可以在每個頻道播出萊特牧師的講道，日復一日，且從現在直到選舉，一直談這件事，還可以把美國人是否認為我從某個角度，其實是相信或同情萊特那些令人反感至極的話，變成這次選舉的唯一話題。我們可以對另一位參選人希拉蕊・柯林頓支持者的失言窮追猛打，稱它是希拉蕊打種族牌的證據，也可以猜測，無論共和黨總統參選人約翰・麥肯推出什麼政策，這次大選，所有白人男性選民將一致投票給他。

◎ fodder（n.）：牛馬吃的糧秣，或指沒有價值的東西。

We can do that.

 But if we do, I can tell you that in the next election, we'll be talking about some other distraction. And then another one. And then another one. And nothing will change.

 That is one option. Or, at this moment, in this election, we can come together and say, "Not this time." This time we want to talk about the crumbling schools that are stealing the future of black children and white children and Asian children and Hispanic children and Native American children. This time we want to reject the cynicism that tells us that these kids can't learn; that those kids who don't look like us are somebody else's problem. The children of America are not those kids, they are our kids, and we will not let them fall behind in a 21st century economy. Not this time.

 This time we want to talk about how the lines in the Emergency Room are filled with whites and blacks and Hispanics who do not have health care; who don't have the power on their own to overcome the special interests in Washington, but who can take them on if we do it together.

 This time we want to talk about the shuttered mills that once provided a decent life for men and women of every race, and the homes for sale that once belonged to Americans from every religion, every region, **every walk of life**. This time we want to talk about the fact that the real problem is not that someone who doesn't look like you might take your job; it's that the corporation you work for will ship it overseas for nothing more than a profit.

◎ every walk of life：指各行各業。在這裡，walk的用法很特殊，但是卻是習慣用法。

46 我們是可以這樣做。

47 果真如此，我可以告訴你，下次選舉，我們又會討論另一個偏離主題的話題，再下一次再換一個，再下一次又換另一個。然後什麼也未改變。

48 那是一個選擇。或者，此時此刻，就在這次大選，我們可以一起說：「這次不行。」這次我們要談談，破舊的學校是如何搶走黑人、白人、亞裔、西班牙裔、美國原住民兒童的未來。這次我們要拒絕犬儒主義，不讓別人告訴我們，這些孩子學不來，或是那些孩子跟我們看起來不一樣，所以是別人的問題。這些美國的孩子不是那些孩子，他們是我們的孩子，我們不允許他們在二十一世紀的經濟中落在他人後頭。這次不行。

49 這次我們要談談，急診室的排隊行列中，有這麼多沒有健保的白人、黑人、西班牙裔人。這些人無法靠一己之力，對抗華府的特殊利益者，但若我們同心協力，便能與他們一較長短。

50 這次我們要談談，曾讓所有種族的男女過著像樣生活的工廠為何緊閉大門；一度屬於所有宗教、所有地區、各行各業美國人的房屋，為何面臨出售的命運。這次我們要談談真相。真正的問題不在於跟你長相不同的人搶走你的飯碗，而是你任職的企業，把工作運往海外，只為賺取利潤。

This time we want to talk about the men and women of every color and creed who serve together, and fight together, and bleed together under the same proud flag. We want to talk about how to bring them home from a war that never should've been authorized and never should've been waged, and we want to talk about how we'll show our patriotism by caring for them, and their families, and giving them the benefits they have earned.

 I would not be running for President if I didn't believe with all my heart that this is what the vast majority of Americans want for this country. This union may never be perfect, but generation after generation has shown that it can always be perfected. And today, whenever I find myself feeling doubtful or cynical about this possibility, what gives me the most hope is the next generation—the young people whose attitudes and beliefs and openness to change have already made history in this election.

 There is one story in particular that I'd like to leave you with today—a story I told when I had the great honor of speaking on Dr. King's birthday at his home church, Ebenezer Baptist, in Atlanta.

 There is a young, twenty-three year old white woman named Ashley Baia who organized for our campaign in Florence, South Carolina. She had been working to organize a mostly African-American community since the beginning of this campaign, and one day she was at a roundtable discussion where everyone went around telling their story and why they were there.

 And Ashley said that when she was nine years old, her mother got cancer. And because she had to miss days of work, she was let go and lost her health care. They had to file for bankruptcy, and that's when Ashley decided that she had to do something to help her mom.

這次我們要談談各種膚色與信念的男女。他們在同感驕傲的一面旗幟下，一起服役、一起作戰、一起流血。我們要談談如何讓這些軍人，從一場從來不該授權，也從來不該開打的戰爭中返鄉，我們還要談談如何透過關懷他們以及他們的家人，以及給予他們應得的福利，展現我們的愛國心。

 若不是我真心相信，這些是多數美國人希望這個國家能為他們做的，我不會競選總統。這個聯邦可能永遠無法完美，但它世世代代的子民已經說明，聯邦永遠能夠更臻完美。現在，每當我對這種可能感到懷疑與悲觀時，帶給我最大希望的是我們的下一代。這些對改變抱持著想法、信仰、開放態度的年輕人，已在這次的選舉中創造歷史。

 有一個故事，我特別想在今天和大家分享。在我非常榮幸能在馬丁‧路德‧金恩博士冥誕時，到他老家的教堂，亞特蘭大的艾本納澤浸信會演講時，曾說過這個故事。

 一位二十三歲，名叫艾希莉‧拜亞的年輕白人女性，是我們在南卡羅萊納州佛羅倫斯競選活動的組織幹部。選戰一開始，她即參與組織一個非裔美人居多的社區。一天，在一次的圓桌討論中，每人輪流說自己的故事，以及參與這場競選活動的理由。

 艾希莉說，她九歲時，母親罹患癌症，因常請假，因此遭到解僱與失去醫療保險。母親被迫宣告破產，也在那時，她決定為母親做點什麼。

She knew that food was one of their most expensive costs, and so Ashley **convinced** her mother that what she really liked and really wanted to eat more than anything else was **mustard and relish sandwiches**. Because that was the cheapest way to eat.

 She did this for a year until her mom got better, and she told everyone at the roundtable that the reason she joined our campaign was so that she could help the millions of other children in the country who want and need to help their parents too.

 Now Ashley might have made a different choice. Perhaps somebody told her along the way that the source of her mother's problems were blacks who were on welfare and too lazy to work, or Hispanics who were coming into the country **illegally**. But she didn't. She sought out **allies** in her fight against **injustice**.

 Anyway, Ashley finishes her story and then goes around the room and asks everyone else why they're supporting the campaign. They all have different stories and reasons. Many bring up a specific issue. And finally they come to this **elderly** black man who's been sitting there quietly the entire time. And Ashley asks him why he's there. And he does not bring up a specific issue. He does not say health care or the economy. He does not say education or the war. He does not say that he was there because of Barack Obama. He simply says to everyone in the room, "I am here because of Ashley."

◎ convinced（vt.）：說服。
◎ mustard and relish sandwiches：芥末和醬料作成的三明治。relish若當動詞用，是指津津有味地享受某些事物（尤其是食物）。
◎ illegally（ad.）：不法地。

56 她知道食物是最貴的開銷，於是她說服母親，她真正喜歡也最想吃的，莫過於塗了芥末與醬料的三明治。因為這是吃得最便宜的方法。

---

57 她就這樣吃了一年，直到母親病情轉好。她告訴在座的所有人，她加入競選團隊，是因如此一來，她可以幫助這個國家數以百萬計，想要也需要幫助父母的孩子。

---

58 艾希莉可能做出其他的選擇。或許有人告訴她，她母親問題的源頭是領社會救濟、懶惰不肯工作的黑人，或是非法進入這個國家的西班牙裔移民。但是她並未如此。她在對抗不公不義時，選擇尋求共同的夥伴。

---

59 艾希莉說完她的故事後，便開始在房間內走動，詢問每個人支持這場選戰的原因。每人都有不同的故事與理由。許多人是有特定議題的。最後艾希莉問全程默默坐著的一位年長男性加入的原因。他並未說明他的特定理由，既不是為了醫療保健、經濟，也不是為了教育、戰爭，他也未說他會在那裡，是因為巴拉克·歐巴馬。他告訴室內的所有人：「我來這裡是因為艾希莉。」

◎ allies（n.）：夥伴。
◎ injustice（n.）：非正義、不公正。
◎ elderly（ad.）：年長的。

"I'm here because of Ashley." By itself, that single moment of recognition between that young white girl and that old black man is not enough. It is not enough to give health care to the sick, or jobs to the jobless, or education to our children.

But it is where we start. It is where our union grows stronger. And as so many generations have come to realize over the course of the two-hundred and twenty one years since a band of **patriots** signed that document in Philadelphia, that is where the perfection begins.

單 字 解 說

◎ patriot（n.）：愛國者。

「我來這裡是因為艾希莉。」在那一刻，那位年輕白人女性與那位年長黑人男性是相互認同的，但光有這個，仍嫌不夠。它仍不夠將醫療保健提供給病患，將工作提供給失業者，或是將教育提供給我們的孩子。

但是，它可以是我們的起點，聯邦也可從那裡開始茁壯。正如同這許多世代的美國人，在那一群愛國者於費城簽署那份文件後的這兩百二十一年中所體認的，那就是追求完美的開始。

第三部分 🏆 文句解析

◎楊人凱

　　這是歐巴馬於二〇〇八年三月在美國獨立革命的聖地費城發表,有關美國種族問題最有代表性的演說。歐巴馬的習慣,是引用美國歷史上偉大的事蹟、人物與文件,配合演說當地的歷史背景,來談論美國當下所面臨的問題並發表他個人的立場和意見。在這篇文章中,他引用的是美國立國的先聖先賢在制定憲法時所寫下的一段話,這段話是美國中小學生在研讀美國歷史時所耳熟能詳的,所以他只引述了其中最主要的部分。

　　這段話較完整的版本是 "We, the people of the United States, in order to form a more perfect union...do ordain and establish the Constitution of the United States of America.(我們,全美國人民,為了建立更完美的聯邦⋯⋯特此制定美利堅合眾國憲法。)歐巴馬只取了這段文字中We, the people, in order to form a more perfect union." 這幾個關鍵字,並把演說命名為「一個更完美的聯邦」。

　　在此,union是個關鍵字,有聯合、結合、工會(工人的結合)、團體、聯邦的意思,有時甚至可以指男女之間的婚姻。在歐巴馬的演說中,union表面上是指聯邦,實際上它是個雙關語,意指美國的黑人和白人之間也可以存在一種更完美的結合。從這個雙關意義中,歐巴馬把種族問題和美國政治的前景巧妙地結合了起來。尤其他本身就是個黑白混種,對選民來說,他本身就代表了一個既存在的「完美的結合」,因此讓他的演說特別具有說服力。

　　不過,對於勤學英文的讀者來說,不免有一個疑問:「perfect」這個形容詞怎麼可以有比較級和最高級呢?英文老師常教導我們,英文中有兩個形

容詞是不能有比較級的。一個就是perfect（完美），另一個字就是unique（獨一無二的）。因為完美這個字的意思就已經代表好到了極致。既然已經到了極致，哪還有更完美的可能？同理，既然unique已經代表是獨一無二的，在邏輯上就不可能出現more unique（更獨一無二）的情形。基本上，英文老師說的並沒有錯，的確unique這個字沒見過有A is more unique than B的用法，不過，perfect這個字在此卻出現了一個明顯而且非常出名的例外。我們只能說，這是例外而不是常規（an exception rather than a rule）。

　　歐巴馬演說的另一個特色，就是他喜歡運用辯證法（dialectics）；辯證法的精髓就是「正，反，合」。對於歐巴馬來說，媒體對他的攻擊和批評，對手的政策就是「反」，他會提出駁斥，然後提出他本身的立場和觀點，這就是「正」，最後，他會想法把「反」和「正」結合起來，形成一個多數人都認為是合理的，也都能接受的新觀點，這就是「合」。

　　對於美國最敏感的種族問題，歐巴馬在這篇演說中做出了一個整體的回應。他知道他的膚色對若干選民來說是個問題，「有的人認為我太黑了。」「有的人認為我不夠黑。」如他於文中自述，但是他自己從不認為如此。由於他的家庭牧師萊特曾在華盛頓的美國國家記者俱樂部（National Press Club）發表演說時指稱「美國所遭受的九一一恐怖攻擊是導因自美國本身對少數民族的恐怖政策」。這句話和他的一些對美國白人種族主義的指控在媒體上引起軒然大波，使得歐巴馬不得不出來親自滅火。萊特牧師與歐巴馬家族淵源深厚，歐巴馬進教會信教就是萊特牧師帶領的，他結婚時由萊特牧師主持儀式，他的小孩出生時也是由萊特牧師領洗。因此，歐巴馬最終不得不退出萊特牧師所主持的，在芝加哥南區的「三一聯合基督教會」（Trinity United Church of Christ，在此，Trinity是指聖父，聖子，聖靈三者合而為一）。

　　不過，歐巴馬認為萊特牧師對白人種族主義的指控，係出自於牧師本人的親身體驗，有其時代和社會的背景，因此，他並不完全否認（disown）這些指控的真實性。同樣地，對於美國一些中產階級白人認為他們的權益因美國政府對黑人的一些保護政策而受損的看法他也表示尊重。他說，這些看法都執著於美國歷史的過去所發生的一些悲劇，卻完全忽視了美國的偉大在於它不是個一成不變的社會，而是在於它能夠改變的天才性格。他認為，他之所以能夠參選並且在一些白人為多數的州中取得初選壓倒性的勝利，就代表了這種改變的可能性。所以，他說出他的一句名言："The union may never be perfect, but generation after generation has shown that it can always be perfected."「儘管聯邦可能永遠無法是完美的，但是一個世代接著一個世代證明了它是可以被改進的。」

　　最後，歐巴馬引述了一個窮苦的白人女人和一位黑人老先生在南卡羅萊納州歐巴馬選舉後援會相處的感人故事作為這篇演說的結尾。他認為，這就是美國黑白種族問題消弭的開始。

Springfield, Illinois, February 10, 2007

Our Past, Future & Vision for America

—Announcement for President

2007年2月10日於伊利諾州春田市

我們的過去、未來和美國的願景

宣布競選總統

◎ 深度導讀：陸以正（無任所大使）

◎ 單字、文句解析：賴慈芸（國立台灣師範大學翻譯研究所助理教授）

◎ 翻譯：樂慧生（聯合報國際新聞中心編譯組）

◎ 審訂：彭鏡禧（國立臺灣大學外文系及戲劇系特聘教授）

第一部分 ✿ 深度導讀

美國的過去、
未來，與展望

二〇〇七年二月十日在伊利諾州春田市舊州議會大廈前宣布競選總統的演說

◎陸以正（無任所大使）

美國中央政治的常態，是在華盛頓打滾一、二十年後，蓄積了足夠的人際關係，又有把握能募捐到競選所需的以億計算的鉅額費用，才敢問鼎白宮寶座。

唯一的例外是四十二歲當選總統的甘迺迪，因為他父親Joseph P. Kennedy, Sr.家世本就富有，因走私威士忌酒變得更有錢，當年政治捐獻並無限制之時，立下宏願要次子當上總統。再加上第三、四兩子成為政治世家，他人無法模仿。

遇到像歐巴馬這樣沒有耐心的人，這些規矩都變得無足輕重。他兩年多前才選上聯邦參議員，坐席未暖，更無大財團或重量級人物的支持，就想競選全國最高的職位，別人一定會認為他是個瘋子。

但他竟然孤注一擲，敢於大膽希望不可能的奇蹟（見下篇The Audacity of Hope），做到了有志者事竟成。本篇是他藉解放黑奴而不朽的林肯總統（Abraham Lincoln）兩百年誕辰紀念的機會，作他自己政治賭注的資本。至於林肯是共和黨，而他卻是民主黨這一點，對歐巴馬而言，似乎無關緊要。

他也知道別人會笑他迫不及待地覬覦總統職位，未免自不量力。但他說，人

們曾經改變過美國，也會繼續改變它。美國正面臨許多挑戰：包括看不見結束的戰爭，對石油過份倚賴，教育未臻理想，經濟衰退。而聯邦政府因循苟且，不肯也不敢面對問題，才是困難的癥結。

他呼籲美國要重訂施政的優先次序，僅靠金錢或空洞計劃不能救國。每人都要盡責使美國經濟更具競爭力，使社會更加融洽，使教育更普及，使科技更發達，使貧困從美國絕跡。

這篇充滿信心與理想的演說，重點是只要愛美國，即使前途佈滿荊棘，必須勇往直前。每人都須盡責，使國家在數位時代藉投資科技研究而更上層樓。他呼籲這一代美國人要掃除貧窮與疾病，要找到替代石油的能源，要減少排放溫室氣體，要使後續的世代以他們為傲。

任參議員時，反對陷入伊拉克戰爭的無底深淵是一回事；反恐怖分子卻是另一回事。歐巴馬在這篇演說裡提醒他的同胞們：永遠不要忘記六年前的「九一一」事件，美國必須使用軍事、情報，與扼殺財源等方法，追捕蓋達和類似的團體。

這番話出自他口中，當時可能有人懷疑只是討好保守派美國人的競選語言。如今他入主白宮了，從他的發言和行動，媒體與人民才相信那些話出於內心，他是玩真的。

這篇演說既以挑戰布希總統為目的，不能造成錯誤的印象，使人覺得他的思想和布希相似。所以下文立即指責布希一意孤行之不當，誓言要重整與盟國邦誼，向舉世傳播民主自由理念。歐巴馬坦陳：你們都知道我自始就反對伊戰，因為那是個「悲慘的錯誤」，他要把美國的子弟召回國，不願他們戰死他鄉。

本篇結尾那兩段非常有力，表現出他天賦的口才。歐巴馬說：出馬競選並非為他自己，而是為全體國民，為了美國的未來。他用了一連串的話，巧妙地讓聽眾把美國史上最受尊敬的林肯總統，和站在面前的歐巴馬聯在一起。

一般的競選演說，有人會覺得肉麻，有人會責為老生常談；能做到像歐巴馬這樣，不是件容易的事。

第二部分 主文/中譯

主文中譯◎樂慧生（聯合報國際新聞中心編譯組）
單字解說◎賴慈芸（國立台灣師範大學翻譯研究所助理教授）

 Let me begin by saying thanks to all you who've traveled, from far and wide, to brave the cold today.

 We all made this journey for a reason. It's humbling, but in my heart I know you didn't come here just for me, you came here because you believe in what this country can be. In the face of war, you believe there can be peace. In the face of despair, you believe there can be hope. In the face of a politics that's shut you out, that's told you to settle, that's divided us for too long, you believe we can be one people, reaching for what's possible, building that more perfect union.

 That's the journey we're on today. But let me tell you how I came to be here. As most of you know, I am not a native of this great state. I moved to Illinois over two decades ago. I was a young man then, just a year out of college; I knew no one in Chicago, was without money or family connections. But a group of churches had offered me a job as a community organizer for $13,000 a year. And I accepted the job, sight unseen, motivated then by a single, simple, powerful idea—that I might play a small part in building a better America.

首先，容我向冒著寒天，從各地遠道而來的諸位致謝。

 我們全都是有所為而來。這教我愧不敢當，但我心中深知各位來此不僅是因為我，而是因為各位相信這個國家大有可為。面對戰爭，各位相信和平可期；面對失望，各位相信希望不死。面對把各位屏擋在外、要各位安於現狀、讓我們分裂如此之久的黨派政治，各位依然相信我們可以團結成一個民族，追求理想，建構那更完美的聯邦。

 我們今天踏上的就是這樣的旅程。且容我向各位稟報我這一路是怎麼走過來的。誠如各位大都知道的，我並非生長在這個偉大的州，而是20多年前搬來的。當時我是個年輕人，大學畢業才一年，在芝加哥一個人也不認識，既沒錢，也沒有親朋故舊。一些教會給了我一個做社區組織工作的機會，年薪1萬3000美元，我二話不說就接受了，當時我只有一個單純而強大的動機：我可以為建立更好的美國略盡棉薄。

My work took me to some of Chicago's poorest neighborhoods. I joined with **pastors** and **lay-people** to deal with communities that had been **ravaged** by plant closings. I saw that the problems people faced weren't simply local in nature—that the decision to close a steel mill was made by distant **executives**; that the lack of textbooks and computers in schools could be traced to the **skewed** priorities of politicians a thousand miles away; and that when a child turns to violence, there's a hole in his heart no government alone can fill.

 It was in these neighborhoods that I received the best education I ever had, and where I learned the true meaning of my Christian faith.

 After three years of this work, I went to law school, because I wanted to understand how the law should work for those in need. I became a civil rights lawyer, and taught constitutional law, and after a time, I came to understand that our **cherished** rights of liberty and equality depend on the active participation of an awakened **electorate**. It was with these ideas in mind that I arrived in this capital city as a state Senator.

◎ pastor (n.)牧師。這個字本來真的是指牧羊人,因為基督教認為信徒就像羊群一樣,因此常以牧羊比喻傳教。注意pasture(n.)也還是牧草地的意思。
◎ lay-people (n.)沒有聖職的一般信衆,即「平信徒」(這可能是日文翻譯,台灣沿用)。本來是叫做layman或laity,但為了性別正確起見,現在多改稱為lay-people。這個字也常用來指某一專業的門外漢。
◎ ravage(v.)蹂躪、破壞、毀滅。

工作把我帶到芝加哥一些最貧窮的住宅區。我和一些牧師、平信徒共同經營一些深受工廠關閉打擊而處境極其不堪的社區。我發現這些人面對的困境本質上並不只是地區性的問題——關閉鋼廠的決定者是人在遠方的主管;學校缺教科書和電腦,則可歸咎於千哩外政客們對先後緩急看法的偏頗。而當一個孩子訴諸暴力時,他的心裡則有個任何政府都無力獨自填補的洞。

就是在這些住宅區,我得到了我這一生最好的教育,也認識了我基督信仰的真實意義。

如此工作三年之後,我進了法學院,因為我想知道法律該如何為貧乏的人服務。後來我成為民權律師,教憲法,若干時日之後我開始明白,我們所珍視的自由和平等權利,要靠積極參與的覺醒選民來維護。我來到這個州首府擔任州參議員,就是抱著這些想法。

◎ executive(n.) 高層經理。公司總裁CEO則是Chief Executive Officer。
◎ skew (v.) 偏斜。
◎ cherish (v.)珍視、珍愛。這個字是從法文cher (珍愛的、親愛的)而來。
◎ electorate (n.) 選民的總稱。單一的選民是elector。

It was here, in Springfield, where I saw all that is America **converge**—farmers and teachers, businessmen and laborers, all of them with a story to tell, all of them seeking a seat at the table, all of them **clamoring** to be heard. I made lasting friendships here—friends that I see in the audience today.

 It was here we learned to disagree without being disagreeable—that it's possible to **compromise** so long as you know those principles that can never be compromised; and that so long as we're willing to listen to each other, we can assume the best in people instead of the worst.

 That's why we were able to **reform** a death **penalty** system that was broken. That's why we were able to give health insurance to children in need. That's why we made the tax system more fair and just for working families, and that's why we passed **ethics** reforms that the **cynics** said could never, ever be passed.

 It was here, in Springfield, where North, South, East and West come together that I was reminded of the **essential decency** of the American people - where I came to believe that through this decency, we can build a more hopeful America.

◎ converge (v.) 匯集、匯聚。
◎ clamor(v.) 喧嚷、疾呼。
◎ compromise (v.) 妥協、讓步。
◎ reform (v.) 改革、改造。名詞與動詞同形。如同段下文的ethics reforms就是作名詞用。
◎ penalty (n.) 刑罰、處罰。動詞是penalize。

7
在這兒，春田市，我看到美國各行各業人士匯聚：農民和教師，商人和工人，人人都有故事要說，人人都要在桌邊取得一席，人人爭著高聲表達意見。我在這兒交了些摯友，我看到這些朋友今天也在場。

8
是在這兒，我們學會了不同意卻不失風度：妥協是可能的，只要你明白哪些原則絕不容犧牲；只要我們肯相互傾聽，便能以至誠而非至不誠彼此相待。

9
正因如此，我們才能夠改革一個已然破敗的死刑制度。正因如此，我們才能夠把健康保險給予需要的孩子。正因如此，我們才使稅制對勞工家庭更公平合理，也正因如此，我們才通過了憤世嫉俗者宣稱絕不可能通過的道德改革措施。

10
是在這兒，春田市，東西南北交會之所，人們提醒了我美國人民本質上的正派：這兒讓我相信，透過這種正派我們可以建立一個更有希望的美國。

◎ ethics (n.) 道德、倫理。
◎ cynic (n.) 犬儒主義者、憤世嫉俗，對一切都抱持懷疑態度的人。字尾加上 –ism即為犬儒主義。
◎ essential (a.) 根本的、基本的。名詞essence 是要素、本質。也是精華的意思，例如在台灣很風行的雞精就是essence of chicken，essential oil則是指香精油。
◎ decency(n.) 體面、正派、規矩、高雅。形容詞是decent。

And that is why, in the shadow of the Old State Capitol, where Lincoln once called on a divided house to stand together, where common hopes and common dreams still live, I stand before you today to announce my **candidacy** for President of the United States.

 I recognize there is a certain **presumptuousness**–a certain audacity–to this announcement. I know I haven't spent a lot of time learning the ways of Washington. But I've been there long enough to know that the ways of Washington must change.

 The genius of our founders is that they designed a system of government that can be changed. And we should **take heart**, because we've changed this country before. In the face of **tyranny**, a band of patriots brought an Empire to its knees. In the face of **secession**, we unified a nation and set the captives free. In the face of Depression, we put people back to work and lifted millions out of poverty. We welcomed immigrants to our shores, we opened railroads to the west, we landed a man on the moon, and we heard **a King's call** to let justice roll down like water, and righteousness like a mighty stream.

 Each and every time, a new generation has risen up and done what's needed to be done. Today we are called once more–and it is time for our generation to answer that call.

◎ candidacy (n.) 作為候選人的身分。candidate是候選人。
◎ presumptuousness (n.) 自以為是、傲慢。形容詞是presumptuous。
◎ take heart 有信心、勇敢。
◎ tyranny (n.) 暴政、專制。 暴君則是tyrant。

11 也正因如此,在這舊州議會大廈陰影下,林肯曾在這兒呼籲分裂的國家團結起來,共同的希望和理想在這兒仍然生生不息,我今天站在各位面前,宣布我要競選美國總統。

12 我明白這麼宣布有些冒昧,有些大膽。我知道我沒有花很多時間學習華盛頓的那一套。不過我在那兒待得也夠久了,久到知道華盛頓那一套非改不可。

13 我們開國元老高明之處在於,他們設計了一個可以改變的政府制度。我們應該感到鼓舞,因為我們曾經改變過這個國家。在暴政之下,一小群愛國志士竟讓一個帝國屈服了。面對國家的分裂,我們讓國家再歸一統,釋放了所有不自由的人。面對大蕭條,我們讓人們重獲工作,讓數以百萬計的人掙脫貧窮。我們歡迎移民來到我們的海岸,我們開通了西行的鐵路,我們把一個人送上了月球,我們聽見了神的召喚:願公平如大水滾滾,使公義如江河滔滔。

14 每一回,總有一個新的世代興起並完成必須完成的事。今天,又一次,我們受到呼召,到了我們這個世代回應那個呼召的時候了。

◎ secession (n.) 分裂,特別是指美國南北戰爭時期脫離聯邦之事。動詞是secede。2005年中國通過的「反分裂國家法」,官方翻譯就是anti-secession law,表示中國認為台灣的地位就像當初南北戰爭時脫離聯邦的南方州,因此統一有理;台灣則譯為anti-separation law,比較中性。
◎ a King's call:King指耶和華神。引文見聖經阿摩斯書五章24節。

For that is our **unyielding** faith–that in the face of impossible odds, people who love their country can change it.

That's what Abraham Lincoln understood. He had his doubts. He had his defeats. He had his **setbacks**. But through his will and his words, he moved a nation and helped free a people. It is because of the millions who **rallied** to his cause that we are no longer divided, North and South, slave and free. It is because men and women of every race, from every walk of life, continued to march for freedom long after Lincoln was laid to rest, that today we have the chance to face the challenges of this millennium together, as one people–as Americans.

All of us know what those challenges are today–a war with no end, a dependence on oil that **threatens** our future, schools where too many children aren't learning, and families struggling paycheck to paycheck despite working as hard as they can. We know the challenges. We've heard them. We've talked about them for years.

◎ unyielding (a.)不屈從的、堅定不移的。yield (v.) 是順從、放棄、退讓的意思；這個字在捷運上也常聽到,即讓座(please yield your seats to...)
◎ setback (n.) 挫折、阻力。這個字是從片語set back而來,原意是把時鐘的指針往回調,引申為受挫。

⚡15 因為那是我們堅定不拔的信念：在看來毫無勝算的時候，愛國的人能夠
逆轉勝。

⚡16 這是亞伯拉罕・林肯的體悟。他有過他的疑惑。他有過他的失敗。他有
過他的挫折。然而他透過他的意志和話語推動了一個國家，讓一個民族
獲得了自由。正因為有數以百萬計的人起而擁護他的理想，我們今日才
不再分裂：北與南，奴役與自由。正因為遠在林肯已經安息之後，仍有
各種族、各行業的男男女女繼續為自由而前行，我們今日才有機會以同
屬一民族，同為美國人的身分面對這個千年挑戰。

⚡17 我們全都知道今日的挑戰是些什麼：一場不知何時能了的戰爭；對石油
過度仰賴以致前途受到威脅；學校裡太多孩子沒有真正學到東西；一些
家庭任怎麼拚命工作，還是入不敷出。我們知道這些挑戰，我們聽說
過，我們談論這些挑戰也有好些年了。

◎ rally (v.) 團結、聚集、整軍。
◎ threaten(v.) 威脅。

What's stopped us from meeting these challenges is not the absence of sound policies and sensible plans. What's stopped us is the failure of leadership, the smallness of our politics−the ease with which we're **distracted** by the **petty** and trivial, our **chronic** avoidance of tough decisions, our preference for scoring cheap political points instead of rolling up our sleeves and building a working **consensus** to tackle big problems.

 For the last six years we've been told that our **mounting** debts don't matter, we've been told that the anxiety Americans feel about rising health care costs and **stagnant** wages are an illusion, we've been told that climate change is a **hoax**, and that tough talk and an **ill-conceived** war can replace diplomacy, and strategy, and foresight. And when all else fails, when Katrina happens, or the death toll in Iraq mounts, we've been told that our crises are somebody else's fault. We're distracted from our real failures, and told to blame the other party, or gay people, or immigrants.

 And as people have looked away in **disillusionment** and frustration, we know what's filled the void. The cynics, and the **lobbyists**, and the special interests who've turned our government into a game only they can afford to play. They write the checks and you get stuck with the bills, they get the access while you get to write a letter, they think they own this government, but we're here today to take it back. The time for that politics is over. It's time to turn the page.

◎ distract (v.) 使分心、轉移注意。
◎ petty (a.) 微小的、不重要的。此字是從法文petit (小的)而來。
◎ chronic (a.) 長年的、長期的、慢性的（疾病）。如26段的the chronically ill。
◎ consensus (n.) 共識、一致的意見。
◎ mount (v.) 增加、登高。
◎ stagnant (a.) 停滯的、不流動的。動詞是stagnate。

讓我們不能應付這些挑戰的，不是沒有好的政策和合理的方案。而是我們領導者無能，是我們政治格局太小：我們動不動便把注意力轉移到芝麻蒜皮的小事上去，長久以來規避做困難的決定，寧可在政治上輕鬆得分，而不願捲起衣袖去建立務實的共識，以解決重大問題。

19 過去這六年來政府一直告訴我們，我們債台日益高築不打緊。告訴我們，人們覺得健保花費越來越高，薪資卻原地踏步只是不實的幻覺。告訴我們氣候變遷之說是唬人的，說狠話和策畫錯誤的戰爭可以取代外交、戰略和遠見。而當其他種種都失敗時，當卡崔娜颶風來襲，或者死在伊拉克的人數增加時，他們又告訴我們，我們面臨危機是別人的錯。他們使我們把目光從我們真正的失敗轉移，要我們去怪罪另一個黨，或者同性戀者，或外來移民。

20 當人們在幻滅和挫折中別過頭去後，我們知道填補這空洞的是什麼。是那些憤世嫉俗的人，說客，和特殊利益的代表，他們已經把我們的政府運作變成一場只有他們玩得起的遊戲。他們簽下支票，你卻得想辦法埋單，他們登堂入室，你卻只有寫信的分。他們以為政府是他們開的，今天我們來到這兒就是要把它拿回來。那種政治手法已經玩完了，到了翻開新頁的時候了。

◎ hoax(n.) 騙局。
◎ ill-conceived (a.) 設計不良的、規劃不佳的。conceive (v.)是構想、設想的意思。
◎ disillusionment (n.) 幻滅、醒悟。Illusion(n.)是幻覺、假象、錯覺，dis＋illusion(v.)＝幻滅、夢想破滅。
◎ lobbyist (n.)遊說人士、說客。lobby (v.) 即為遊說。旅館的門廳穿堂叫做lobby（n.），但此字是因為英國議會的選民接待廳也叫做lobby，因此就有了「遊說」的字義。

We've made some progress already. I was proud to help lead the fight in Congress that led to the most sweeping ethics reform since Watergate.

 But Washington has a long way to go. And it won't be easy. That's why we'll have to set priorities. We'll have to make hard choices. And although government will play a crucial role in bringing about the changes we need, more money and programs alone will not get us where we need to go. Each of us, in our own lives, will have to accept responsibility—for **instilling** an ethic of achievement in our children, for adapting to a more competitive economy, for strengthening our communities, and sharing some measure of sacrifice. So let us begin. Let us begin this hard work together. Let us transform this nation.

 Let us be the generation that reshapes our economy to compete in the digital age. Let's set high standards for our schools and give them the resources they need to succeed. Let's **recruit** a new army of teachers, and give them better pay and more support in exchange for more **accountability**. Let's make college more affordable, and let's invest in scientific research, and let's lay down broadband lines through the heart of inner cities and rural towns all across America.

◎ instill (v.) 灌輸、滴入。
◎ recruit (v.) 募兵、徵召。
◎ accountability (n.) 問責。

我們已經有了一些成績。我可以自豪地說,由於我帶頭在國會奮鬥,終於促成了自水門案發生以來最徹底的道德改革方案。

 然而華府還有漫漫長路要走,而且前途多艱。也因此我們必須定出輕重緩急。我們必須做些困難的選擇。而雖然要實現我們需要的改變,政府扮演著關鍵性的角色,單單有更多錢和方案卻不能讓我們達成目標。我們每一個人都要在自己的生活中負起一分責任:灌輸給孩子追求成就的觀念;要適應競爭更激烈的經濟,強化我們的社群,而且大家都得做些犧牲。那麼,讓我們開始吧!讓我們一起展開這份辛苦的工作。讓我們改變這個國家。

 讓我們這個世代重塑美國的經濟,讓它能在數位時代競爭。讓我們為我們的學校訂下高標準,並給它們要成功必備的資源。讓我們招募一批教師生力軍,以更好的待遇和更多支援換取他們更負責的任事態度。讓我們使大學學費更便宜,讓我們投資於科研,讓我們在全美各大城市內城(按;指美國城市裡老舊或少數族裔與貧民居住的區域)與鄉間小鎮的中心,都架設寬頻線路。

And as our economy changes, let's be the generation that ensures our nation's workers are sharing in our prosperity. Let's protect the hard-earned benefits their companies have promised. Let's make it possible for hardworking Americans to save for **retirement**. And let's allow our unions and their organizers to lift up this country's middle-class again.

Let's be the generation that ends poverty in America. Every single person willing to work should be able to get job training that leads to a job, and earn a living wage that can pay the bills, and afford child care so their kids have a safe place to go when they work. Let's do this.

Let's be the generation that finally tackles our health care crisis. We can control costs by focusing on prevention, by providing better treatment to the chronically ill, and using technology to cut the **bureaucracy**. Let's be the generation that says right here, right now, that we will have universal health care in America by the end of the next president's first term.

◎ retirement (n.) 退休。但此字的動詞retire意思較廣，除了退休之外，也有離席、休息、就寢的意思。
◎ bureaucracy (n.) 官僚作風。bureau是政府的單位、辦公室，如我們的新聞局就叫做information bureau。此字原是法文的寫字桌。

在我們經濟改變的時候,讓我們這個世代確保我國的勞工能夠分享我們的繁榮。我們要讓他們辛苦賺來、公司承諾要給他們的收入和福利獲得保障。我們要讓努力工作的美國人能夠存錢以應退休生活之需。而且我們要讓我們的工會和工會的組織人員再次振興這個國家的中產階級。

讓我們這個世代終結美國的貧窮。每個願意工作的人都應該有機會接受職業訓練,然後找到工作,賺取一份足夠生活所需的薪水,能夠付帳單,並支應孩子的托育費用。如此一來,他們上班時孩子也有個安全的地方可去。讓我們這麼做。

讓我們成為終於能夠應付健保危機的世代。我們可以經由著重防範、為慢性病提供更好的治療、以及藉科技簡化行政程序等方法控制成本。讓我們這個世代就在此時、此地這麼說:在下一位總統第一任期結束之前,我們便會有全民健保。

Let's be the generation that finally frees America from the tyranny of oil. We can **harness** homegrown, alternative fuels like **ethanol** and **spur** the production of more fuel-efficient cars. We can set up a system for **capping** greenhouse gases. We can turn this crisis of global warming into a moment of opportunity for **innovation**, and job creation, and an **incentive** for businesses that will serve as a model for the world. Let's be the generation that makes future generations proud of what we did here.

Most of all, let's be the generation that never forgets what happened on that September day and confront the **terrorists** with everything we've got. Politics doesn't have to divide us on this anymore—we can work together to keep our country safe. I've worked with Republican Senator Dick Lugar to pass a law that will secure and destroy some of the world's deadliest, **unguarded** weapons. We can work together to track terrorists down with a stronger military, we can tighten the net around their finances, and we can improve our intelligence capabilities. But let us also understand that ultimate victory against our enemies will come only by rebuilding our alliances and exporting those ideals that bring hope and opportunity to millions around the globe.

◎ harness（v.）駕馬、利用。harness本做名詞用，即馬的轡頭。
◎ ethanol (n.) 乙醇、酒精。
◎ spur（v.）催馬。spur做為名詞是馬刺之意，作為動詞則是「用馬刺催馬前行」。
◎ cap (v.) 定限額。

27 讓我們成為終於使美國從石油暴政之下獲得解脫的世代。我們可以取用本土種植的替代燃料，像是乙醇，並鼓勵生產更省燃料的汽車。我們可以設立限制溫室氣體排放的制度。我們可以把這個地球暖化危機變成創新發明、製造新工作機會的契機，以及企業願意作為世界新模範的誘因。讓我們這個世代在此地的所做所為，能令後世引以為榮。

28 最重要的是，我們這個世代絕對不可忘記九月的那一天發生的事，並且全力對抗恐怖分子。在這件事上我們不必再因政治因素而壁壘分明：我們可以合力維護國家的安全。我曾與共和黨籍參議員魯加合作推動通過一件法案，讓我們能取得並銷毀世上一些殺傷力最大，最無敵手的武器。我們可以合作以更強的軍力追蹤恐怖分子，收緊他們的財源網，我們還可以改進我們的情蒐能力。然而我們也得明白，最終要打敗敵人，唯有靠重建我們的聯盟，並把能帶來希望和機會的那些理想送到世界各地，給數以百萬計的人們。

◎ innovation (n.) 創新、革新。動詞為innovate。
◎ incentive (n.) 誘因、動機、獎勵。請注意這個字雖然是 -tive結尾的，但卻是名詞。
◎ terrorist (n.) 恐怖分子。這個字從terror(n.)驚嚇、恐怖而來。恐怖主義是terrorism.
◎ unguarded (a.) 沒有人防備的。即un（沒有）+ guarded（守護的、防備的）。

But all of this cannot come to pass until we bring an end to this war in Iraq. Most of you know I opposed this war from the start. I thought it was a tragic mistake. Today we grieve for the families who have lost loved ones, the hearts that have been broken, and the young lives that could have been. America, it's time to start bringing our troops home. It's time to admit that no amount of American lives can resolve the political disagreement that lies at the heart of someone else's civil war. That's why I have a plan that will bring our combat troops home by March of 2008. Letting the Iraqis know that we will not be there forever is our last, best hope to pressure the Sunni and Shia to come to the table and find peace.

 Finally, there is one other thing that is not too late to get right about this war– and that is the homecoming of the men and women–our **veterans**–who have sacrificed the most. Let us honor their **valor** by providing the care they need and rebuilding the military they love. Let us be the generation that begins this work.

 I know there are those who don't believe we can do all these things. I understand the **skepticism**. After all, every four years, candidates from both parties make similar promises, and I expect this year will be no different. All of us running for president will travel around the country offering ten-point plans and making grand speeches; all of us will **trumpet** those qualities we believe make us uniquely qualified to lead the country. But too many times, after the election is over, and the **confetti** is swept away, all those promises fade from memory, and the lobbyists and the special interests move in, and people turn away, disappointed as before, left to struggle on their own.

◎ veteran(n.) 退伍軍人、榮民。
◎ valor (n.)勇氣、英勇。
◎ skepticism (n.)懷疑論。

29

然而，在我們結束伊拉克戰事之前，這些全都不可能實現。你們大都知道我打一開始就反對這場戰爭。我認為這是個不幸的錯誤。今天，我們為失去心愛家人的家庭，為那些心碎的人，那些英年早逝的人而感到哀痛。美國，到了開始把我們子弟兵撤回來的時候了。現在我們應該承認，犧牲再多美國人，也解決不了橫陳在別國內戰核心裡的政治分歧。正因如此，我有個計畫要在2008年3月之前把我們的戰鬥部隊撤回來。讓伊拉克人知道我們不會永遠待在那兒，是我們迫使遜尼派與什葉派走向談判桌尋求和平的最後、也最可能奏效的一招。

30

最後，有關這場戰爭還有件事我們必須匡正，而且為時猶未為晚。那就是我們的男女子弟兵，那些犧牲最大的退伍軍人歸鄉的問題。讓我們藉由提供他們需要的照護、重建他們所愛的軍隊來表彰他們的英勇。讓我們成為開始這件工作的世代。

31

我知道有些人不相信我們能做到這一切。這種懷疑我能理解。畢竟，每隔四年，兩黨候選人都會提出類似的承諾，我預料今年也不會例外。我們每個總統候選人都會全國走透透，提出十點計畫，發表氣勢恢宏的演講；而我們每一個人也都會大吹法螺，宣揚我們認為使自己獨具資格領導這個國家的那些特質。然而已有太多次，在選舉結束，滿地彩紙清除淨盡之後，那些承諾也全從記憶中逐漸消逝。說客和特殊利益乘虛而入，人們轉頭他去，失望一如既往，只能自求多福。

◎ trumpet (v.)大聲宣告。這個字原指小喇叭（名詞），以及吹小喇叭（動詞），衍伸為大聲宣告。
◎ confetti (n.) 狂歡時灑的五彩碎紙。這個字是外來語，本為義大利文。

That is why this campaign can't only be about me. It must be about us—it must be about what we can do together. This campaign must be the occasion, the vehicle, of your hopes, and your dreams. It will take your time, your energy, and your advice—to push us forward when we're doing right, and to let us know when we're not. This campaign has to be about reclaiming the meaning of citizenship, restoring our sense of common purpose, and realizing that few obstacles can withstand the power of millions of voices calling for change.

 By ourselves, this change will not happen. Divided, we are bound to fail.

 But the life of a tall, **gangly**, self—made Springfield lawyer tells us that a different future is possible.

 He tells us that there is power in words.

 He tells us that there is power in **conviction**.

 That beneath all the differences of race and region, faith and station, we are one people.

 He tells us that there is power in hope.

 As Lincoln organized the forces arrayed against slavery, he was heard to say: "Of strange, **discordant**, and even **hostile** elements, we gathered from the four winds, and formed and fought to battle through."

 單字解說

◎ gangly (a.) 瘦長而難看的，笨拙的。
◎ conviction (n.) 堅信、相信。動詞是convince. 這個字也常用於宗教上的相信。

正因如此,這場選戰不能只是關乎我的選戰,而必須是關乎我們的選戰。必須關乎我們可以一起做的事。這場選戰一定要是能承載你們的希望和夢想的工具和場合。我們需要你們投入時間、精力和建議,在我們做得對時推我們一把,做得不對時提醒我們。我們一定要藉由這次選戰重新伸張做為公民的意義,重新建立同舟一命的共識,並且體認當數以百萬計的人發出要求改變的強大聲音時,其勢沛然莫之能禦。

 光靠我們自己,這個改變不會發生。如果我們分裂,必敗無疑。

 然而,那位自學成功的瘦高律師的生平卻告訴我們,一個不一樣的未來不是夢。

 他告訴我們,話語裡有力量。

 他告訴我們,信念裡有力量。

 而儘管我們在種族、宗教、信仰和身分地位上有諸多不同,我們實屬同一民族。

 他告訴我們,希望裡有力量。

 當林肯組成對抗奴隸制度的部隊時,他說:「我們雖然從四方集合奇怪的、不協調的、甚至彼此敵對的分子,但我們要奮戰到底。」

◎ discordant (a.) 不和諧的、刺耳的。相反詞concordant(a.)則是和諧一致的。
◎ hostile (a.) 有敵意的、敵方的、反對的。

That is our purpose here today.

 That's why I'm in this race.

 Not just to hold an office, but to gather with you to transform a nation.

 I want to win that next battle—for justice and opportunity.

 I want to win that next battle—for better schools, and better jobs, and health care for all.

 I want us to take up the unfinished business of perfecting our union, and building a better America.

 And if you will join me in this **improbable** quest, if you feel destiny calling, and see as I see, a future of endless possibility **stretching** before us; if you sense, as I sense, that the time is now to shake off our **slumber**, and **slough** off our fear, and make good on the debt we owe past and future generations, then I'm ready to take up the cause, and march with you, and work with you. Together, starting today, let us finish the work that needs to be done, and **usher** in a new birth of freedom on this Earth.

 單 字 解 說

◎ improbable (a.)看似不可能，卻是真實的。
◎ stretch (v.) 延伸、展開。
◎ slumber (n.) 睡眠，引申為麻痹狀態。

那就是我們今日的目標。

 那就是我參選的原因。

 不只是要取得一個職位,而是要與你們聚在一起,去轉變一個國家。

 我要打贏那下一場戰役:為了正義和機會。

 我要打贏那下一場戰役:為了更好的學校,更好的工作,也為了全民健保。

 我要接下前人未竟志業:讓我們的聯邦更為完善,建立更好的美國。

 而如果各位願意加入我這看似難以達成的追求,如果你覺得命運在召喚你,而且和我有一樣的看法,一個有無限可能的未來正展現在你我面前;如果你有和我一樣的感受,覺得此刻當從昏沉中甦醒,揮去我們的恐懼,償還我們對過去和未來世代欠下的債,那麼我準備接下這志業,和諸位一起前行,和諸位一起努力。我們一起,就從今天開始,讓我們完成非做不可的工作,為這個地球帶來新生的自由。

◎ slough (v.) (蛇的)蛻皮。引申為擺脫。
◎ usher (v.) 領位、迎賓。

第三部分 🏆 文句解析

◎ 賴慈芸（國立台灣師範大學翻譯研究所助理教授

　　這篇演講是二〇〇七年歐巴馬宣佈競選總統時發表的，地點是在他自己擔任參議員的伊利諾州。他特地選擇了林肯當年宣布競選總統的同一地點，即11段中提到的Old State Capitol（原本是當時的州議會，現在是古蹟），發表此篇演說。

　　1到6段，主要是開場白和自述經歷，以「旅程」作為比喻。從第一段開始，先謝謝遠道而來的聽眾，但從travel轉到第2段的journey，又有比喻之意。到第3段的journey更為明顯，把自己過去半生經歷比喻為一段旅程。第6段的arrive in this capital city作為前面這一大段的高潮：我終於走到這裡了，呼應journey的意象。

　　7到10段連用了三次it was here的句型，承接第六段的arrive。第11段則是前半的高潮：宣佈競選總統。林肯一八五八年就是在這裡宣佈競選總統，並且發表著名的演說：A House Divided。這句話典出聖經新約馬太福音十二章二十五節：「耶穌對他們說：凡一國自相紛爭，就成為荒場；一城一家自相紛爭，必站立不住。」林肯遇刺身亡之後，遺體亦停靈在此供人弔唁。

　　12段是一個較為低調的過場，承認自己政治資歷不深（第一任參議員任期未滿），但重點是已經足以知道華府那一套政治方法必須改變。13段即抓住「改變」一詞，細數前賢功績：脫離英國獨立（brought an Empire to its knees）、解放黑奴（set the captives free）、熬過大蕭條。接受移民、開西部鐵路、登陸月球、馬丁・路德・金恩的民權運動，無一不是求變。馬丁・路德・金恩姓King，因此歐巴馬這裡稱他為King，正好和大英帝國Empire形成

有趣的對照。 "Let justice roll down like water, and righteousness like a mighty stream." 又是聖經典故，出自舊約阿摩司書第五章二十四節：惟願公平如大水滾滾，使公義如江河滔滔（和合本翻譯）。

14段的 "we are called" ， "answer that call" 呼應13段的 "a King's call" ，是整篇演講的主題句：我們這一代的歷史責任。15段又呼應12、13段的change。歷史需要我們，就當勇敢承擔。

16段緬懷林肯，17段則列數當今挑戰。18段痛陳多年弊病皆因美國缺乏高瞻遠矚的領導人，19、20則直接攻擊執政的布希政府，結束在 "It's time to turn the page" ，該換人做做看了，這似乎是全世界所有反對黨候選人的訴求。

21段的Watergate水門事件，至今仍是美國人好談的題材，二〇〇八年又出了一部電影《請問總統先生》（*Frost／Nixon*）。這裡歐巴馬是談到自己的政績，不過就如他自己承認，政治資歷太淺，因此他也沒有在政績上多做著墨，點到為止。

22段的 "has a long way to go" 又呼應開頭的journey意象。這裡也差不多是整篇演講的中間點：1至21段大致以談過往為主，我們如何走到這裡；下面開始談前面還有漫漫長路要走，呼籲大家協力改造國家。

22段以下，出現了重複多次的 "Let us" ，包括整篇演說的最後一個句子。23段開頭的 "Let us be the generation" 一再出現，24段、25段、26段（兩次）、27段（兩次）、28段、30段。因此從23段到30段，基本上就是在描述政見與願景。從26段開始，還有另一種一再重複的句型，就是 "We can" 以及 "We can work together" 。因為這是演說，可以想見當場聽眾受到激勵的情景。

從23－30段的願景說完了，想必掌聲不斷。31段稍微鬆口氣，先說到

聽眾的心態：每隔四年，要選總統的時候，大家都會許下很多政治承諾、希望、夢想。我們怎麼知道你歐巴馬和他們不同？

32段提出他的答案，這才是歐巴馬真正高明之處。願望大家都會許，但歐巴馬說這不只是我的事，還是你們的事，是我們大家的事。 "we can do together" 又跑出來了。這一段重提13段提起的論述： "a calling for change" 。順應天命，追求變革。

33－39都在談林肯。33段只是含蓄用到「divided」這個字，我們就知道他又要提林肯了。果然34段 "a tall, gangly, self-made Springfield lawyer" 就出現了。下面幾段都用He開頭，而且用現在式，彷彿招靈一般，林肯就在眼前，和大家站在一起。39段林肯的名字出現時，達到高潮。這裏引用的就是林肯那篇 "The House Divided" 演說的最後一段。這篇有名的演講，美國人耳熟能詳，更能激起緬懷偉人的心情。

40段以下是結尾的部份，因此有很多鏗鏘有力的短句。43-45段連用三次 "I want" ，展現強烈的企圖心。最後一段的 "make good on the debt we owe past and future generations" ，表明我們對前輩和子孫都有義務，既不能有負前賢，也不能對不起後代，呼應27段的 "make future generations proud of what we did here" ，正是全文的主旨。每個時代有每個時代的天命（林肯的天命就是解放黑奴），我們也該承擔屬於我們時代的天命。

這篇演說結構相當清楚：

1－10段：我為什麼在這裡

11段：所以我要選總統

12－16段：美國歷史上每一代都盡力完成歷史使命

17－21段：但現在政府（小布希）不行

22－30段：所以我們來做這個和那個吧

31－39段：林肯是這樣教我們的

40－46段：我想承擔歷史天命：做總統

　　透過一些關鍵字的連接以及不斷重複的關鍵句型，這篇演說都讓聽眾留下深刻印象。也有許多生動的比喻，如前幾段的journey意象、27段"the tyranny of oil"，把石油比喻做專制暴君；harness 和spur都是騎馬用語，我們可以把「替代能源」安上轡頭，用馬刺催業界「生產更符合能源效益的汽車」。最後一段"slough off our fear"，把恐懼像蛇皮一樣蛻掉，就像蛇蛻了皮，可以獲得新生一樣。由這些例子可見歐巴馬的文學造詣也相當不錯，值得仔細體會。

Boston, Massachusetts, July 27, 2004

The Audacity of Hope

—— Keynote Address at the 2004 Democratic National Convention

2004年7月27日於麻州波士頓

無畏的希望

—— 2004年民主黨全國代表大會主題演講

◎ 深度導讀：陸以正（無任所大使）

◎ 單字、文句解析：賴慈芸（國立台灣師範大學翻譯研究所助理教授）

◎ 翻譯：陳世欽（聯合報國際新聞中心編譯組）

◎ 審訂：彭鏡禧（國立臺灣大學外文系及戲劇系特聘教授）

第一部分 深度導讀

敢於大膽希望
二〇〇四年七月二十七日在麻州波士頓民主黨全國代表大會的主題演說

◎陸以正（無任所大使）

　　這是歐巴馬初試啼聲的第一篇獲得全美人民注意的演講。那時他還只是連任三屆伊利諾州的州參議員，薪俸微薄，無力雇用助理，更別說撰稿人，所以可以確定是他自己的手筆。

　　在民主黨總統提名大會上發表主題演說，是莫大的榮譽。雖然NBC、CBS和ABC三大電視網看不起這位在全國政治舞台上還不怎麼有名的黑人，因而未做現場轉播，但公共電視（PBS）、CNN、MSNBC、福斯（Fox News）和專轉播而不報新聞的C-SPAN頻道，都從頭到底播出，統計觀眾達九百一十萬人，使歐巴馬得以嶄露頭角。

　　本篇中最使人動容的警句，是他說：「沒有一個所謂自由派的美國，也沒有一個保守派的美國；只有美利堅合眾國。」那年，四十一歲的歐巴馬決心競選聯邦參議員，能夠被邀在全國代表大會演說，無異給他最好的曝光機會。

　　伊利諾州的傳統是民主黨比共和黨強。歐巴馬演講之前，共和黨籍聯邦參議員候選人賴恩（Jack Ryan）就因估量難以勝選，自動退出競爭。到八月，才有凱斯（Alan Keyes）出來和歐巴馬競爭。二〇〇四年十一月開票結果，凱斯只得到27％選票，歐氏獲得70％，從此遷到華盛頓，進入全國注目的政治舞台。

民主黨固然有濃厚的自由主義傳統,但在總統提名大會上,請個黑人來發表主題演說,還是歷史上第一次。歐巴馬了解台下三四千位全美地方黨部代表的心理,因而選擇用最直接的方法面對膚色的疑慮。

開門見山,他就說:「讓我們面對現實,今天我能站在台上,好像是不大可能的事。」他仔細敘述家世:從肯亞來美留學的父親小時放羊,祖父是替人煮飯的僕役。他母親來自肯薩斯州,由外祖母撫養成人。他很技巧地沒直說母親是白人,只用「不可能的愛情故事」形容,聽眾自然了解他的涵意。

他引用美國獨立宣言起首第一句,強調人人生而平等,不著形跡地批評了種族歧視。美國人可以愛怎麼想就怎麼想,愛說什麼就說什麼,那就是「美國的奇蹟」。種種「小小的奇蹟」累積起來,就是生活的自由。

他列舉在伊利諾州小城小鎮遇到的平凡老百姓的困擾:製造洗衣機廠的工人失業了,因為工廠要搬到墨西哥;喪失了工會的福利補助,因而付不起兒子的醫藥費;或成績優異的女高中生,因為繳不起學費,進不了大學。

他說,請別誤會:人民並不期望政府替他們解決所有的問題,他們會自求解決之道。話鋒一轉,他說人民只不願意繳納的稅款,被福利機構或國防部浪費掉。此時幾乎可以保證,台下會有如雷掌聲。

歐巴馬能感動聽眾,套句范仲淹的話,因為他「以天下為己任」。他舉許多小事:貧民區的孩童不識字,老人負擔不起藥費,乃至阿拉伯裔家庭被非法拘留,都是他的事,他都要管。

他說,美國不屬於黑人、白人、拉丁裔人或亞裔人,美國就是美國,我們都是一家人。歸根究底,他問美國人:你要二〇〇四年的總統選舉,成為落入貪腐的舊式政治競爭呢?還是帶來新希望的一場選舉?

儘管有歐巴馬的滔滔雄辯,民主黨代表大會選出的總統候選人、麻州聯邦參議員凱利(John Kerry),還是輸給了尋求連任的布希總統。反而是那篇演說給了歐巴馬信心,兩年後決定競選全國最高的職位,改寫了美國歷史。

第二部分 主文/中譯

主文中譯◎陳世欽（聯合報國際新聞中心編譯組）
單字解說◎賴慈芸（國立台灣師範大學翻譯研究所助理教授）

 On behalf of the great state of Illinois, crossroads of a nation, land of Lincoln, let me express my deep gratitude for the **privilege** of addressing this convention. Tonight is a particular honor for me because, let's face it, my presence on this stage is pretty unlikely. My father was a foreign student, born and raised in a small village in Kenya. He grew up herding goats, went to school in a tin-roof shack. His father, my grandfather, was a cook, a domestic servant.

 But my grandfather had larger dreams for his son. Through hard work and **perseverance** my father got a scholarship to study in a magical place: America, which stood as a **beacon** of freedom and opportunity to so many who had come before. While studying here, my father met my mother. She was born in a town on the other side of the world, in Kansas. Her father worked on **oil rigs** and farms through most of the Depression. The day after Pearl Harbor he signed up for duty, joined Patton's army and marched across Europe. Back home, my grandmother raised their baby and went to work on a bomber assembly line. After the war, they studied on the GI Bill, bought a house through FHA, and moved west in search of opportunity.

 單字解說

◎ audacity（n.）大膽、無畏、魯莽、放肆。形容詞是audacious，此字正反意涵都有，可以是正面的大膽、突破，也可以是負面的冒失、放肆。

◎ keynote address（n.）主題演講。keynote原來是音樂用語，指主音，譬如C大調的主音是C。大會或研討會常會請keynote speaker演講，為整場活動「定音」，就叫做keynote address或是keynote speech。

謹代表一個國家的中心,林肯的土地,偉大的伊利諾州,容我對有幸在
這次大會中發表演說,表達誠摯的謝意。對我而言,今晚是特殊的榮
耀,因為各位可以看出來,我原本不太可能站在台上。我父親是在肯亞
一個小村落出生、成長的外國學生。他幼年放牧山羊,在簡陋的鐵皮屋
上學。他父親,也就是我祖父,是個廚子,一個家庭幫傭。

 儘管如此,祖父對他兒子懷有更大的夢想。憑著勤奮與毅力,家父拿到
獎學金,可以前往神奇國度美國深造。對無數曾來美國的男女,美國是
自由與機會的明燈。他在美深造期間認識我母親。她生於世界另一邊,
堪薩斯州一個小鎮。大蕭條多數時間,她父親在鑽油平台與農場工作。
珍珠港事變後次日,他志願從軍,加入巴頓將軍麾下的部隊,行遍歐
洲。我外婆在家撫養女兒,並在轟炸機生產線工作。戰後,他們靠著退
伍軍人權利法案的補助進修,透過聯邦房屋管理局買一棟房子,此後向
西遷移,尋找機會。

◎ privilege（n.）特權、榮幸
◎ perseverance（n.）毅力、堅持不懈。動詞
　是persevere。

◎ beacon（n.）燈塔。
◎ oil rigs（n.）石油鑽油井。

And they, too, had big dreams for their daughter, a common dream, born of two continents. My parents shared not only an **improbable** love; they shared an **abiding** faith in the possibilities of this nation. They would give me an African name, Barack, or "blessed," believing that in a tolerant America your name is no barrier to success. They imagined me going to the best schools in the land, even though they weren't rich, because in a generous America you don't have to be rich to achieve your potential. They are both passed away now. Yet, I know that, on this night, they look down on me with pride.

 I stand here today, grateful for the **diversity** of my **heritage**, aware that my parents' dreams live on in my precious daughters. I stand here knowing that my story is part of the larger American story, that I owe a debt to all of those who came before me, and that, in no other country on earth, is my story even possible. Tonight, we gather to **affirm** the greatness of our nation, not because of the height of our skyscrapers, or the power of our military, or the size of our economy. Our pride is based on a very simple **premise**, summed up in a declaration made over two hundred years ago, "We hold these truths to be self-evident, that all men are created equal. That they are **endowed** by their Creator with certain **inalienable** rights. That among these are life, liberty and the pursuit of happiness."

 That is the true genius of America, a faith in the simple dreams of its people, the insistence on small miracles. That we can tuck in our children at night and know they are fed and clothed and safe from harm. That we can say what we think, write what we think, without hearing a sudden knock on the door. That we can have an idea and start our own business without paying a bribe or hiring somebody's son. That we can participate in the political process without fear of **retribution**, and that our votes will he counted–or at least, most of the time.

◎ improbable（a.）不太可能的。是在probable（可能的）前面加上否定字首im- 所造的字。
◎ abiding（a.）持久的、不變的。動詞abide是繼續下去、維持的意思。
◎ diversity（n.）多元、多樣。這個字近年很紅，尤其是biodiversity（生物多樣性）。
◎ heritage（n.）遺產、傳統。
◎ affirm（v.）確認、證實。下文第6段的reaffirm就是再次確認。

他們也對自己的女兒懷有很高的期望，這是一種源自兩個大陸的共同夢想。我父母親不僅共享不太可能的愛情，更同樣堅信這個國家的可能性。他們為我取了個非洲名字，巴拉克，意指「受到祝福的」。他們認為，在這個具有包容性的美國，名字不會阻礙你邁向成功。即使並不富裕，他們仍指望我有朝一日能進入美國頂尖學校就讀，因為在寬宏大量的美國，不必非得富有才能發揮潛力。如今他們皆已離開人間。不過我知道，今晚他們無比自豪的俯看我。

今天，我站在這裡，對我繼承的多元傳統滿懷感激，因為我深知，父母親的夢想仍活在我寶貝女兒身上。我站在這裡，心知我的故事只是更多美國人故事的一部分，是國家的先賢造就了我。除了這個國家，世上再也沒有其他國家可能實現我的故事。今晚，我們相聚一堂，為了確認我們國家的偉大，並不是因為我們摩天大樓的高度、軍力或經濟規模。我們的驕傲奠基於一個非常簡單的前提上，兩百多年前以一項宣言總結：「我等之見解為，下述真理不證自明：凡人生而平等，秉造物者之賜，擁諸無可轉讓之權利，包含生命權、自由權、與追尋幸福之權。」

那就是美國的真正天賦，相信人民簡單的夢想，和堅持創造小小的奇蹟。我們夜裡可以為孩子蓋好被子，知道他們衣食無缺，而且不會受到傷害。我們可以暢所欲言，寫下心聲，而不會聽到突如其來的敲門聲。我們可以規畫並開創自己的事業，無須行賄或雇用某人的兒子。我們可以參與政治，不必擔心受到報復。我們的選票一定算數──至少大多數時候都算。

◎ premise（n.）前提。先決條件。
◎ endow（v.）給予、賦予。be endowed by the Creator就是造物者（上帝）給的。
◎ inalienable（a.）不能讓與的、不可剝奪的。alien（v.）在法律上是「轉讓」，因此 alienable（a.）是可轉讓的，加了否定字首 in+就變成「不可轉讓的」。
◎ retribution（n.）懲罰、報復、報應。

This year, in this election, we are called to reaffirm our values and commitments, to hold them against a hard reality and see how we are **measuring up**, to the **legacy** of our **forebears**, and the promise of future generations. And fellow Americans–Democrats, Republicans, Independents–I say to you tonight: we have more work to do. More to do for the workers I met in Galesburg, Illinois, who are losing their union jobs at the Maytag plant that's moving to Mexico, and now are having to compete with their own children for jobs that pay seven bucks an hour. More to do for the father I met who was losing his job and choking back tears, wondering how he would pay $4,500 a month for the drugs his son needs without the health benefits he counted on. More to do for the young woman in East St. Louis, and thousands more like her, who has the grades, has the drive, has the will, but doesn't have the money to go to college.

Don't get me wrong. The people I meet in small towns and big cities, in diners and office parks, they don't expect government to solve all their problems. They know they have to work hard to get ahead and they want to. Go into the collar counties around Chicago, and people will tell you they don't want their tax money wasted by a welfare agency or the Pentagon. Go into any inner city neighborhood, and folks will tell you that government alone can't teach kids to learn. They know that parents have to parent, that children can't achieve unless we raise their expectations and turn off the television sets and **eradicate** the **slander** that says a black youth with a book is acting white. No, people don't expect government to solve all their problems. But they sense, deep in their bones, that with just a change in priorities, we can make sure that every child in America has a decent shot at life, and that the doors of opportunity remain open to all. They know we can do better. And they want that choice.

◎ measure up to達到……標準、符合……要求。measure（v）是測量。

◎ legacy（n.）遺產、遺贈。
◎ forebear（n.）祖先，通常用複數形。

今年，在這次大選中，我們的天命就是重申我們的價值觀與承諾，並在艱困中堅持下去，無愧前人遺澤，並謹守對後代子子孫孫的承諾。美國同胞們，不管是共和黨人、民主黨人或獨立派人士，今晚，我要告訴各位：我們仍有未竟之業，必須全力以赴。我在伊利諾州蓋爾斯堡遇見的勞工需要我們。他們因為美泰克家電廠遷往墨西哥而失業，現在必須和自己的子女搶時薪七美元的工作。我遇見的一位父親需要我們；他剛失業，強忍淚水，不知道沒有保險以後該如何支應兒子每月四千五百美元的醫藥費。東聖路易的年輕女子及成千上萬像她的同胞也需要我們。她有優良的成績，有幹勁，有意願，但沒有錢進入大學就讀。

但別誤解我。我在小鎮大城、餐館、辦公大樓遇見的人，從不指望政府為他們解決所有問題。他們知道必須努力工作，才能出人頭地，他們也想這麼做。芝加哥周遭各郡的人會告訴你，他們不希望自己交的稅被某個福利機關或五角大廈白白浪費。各地貧民區的居民會告訴你，不能單單指望政府教導孩子如何學習。他們知道，為人父母者必須善盡教養子女的職責。我們必須提高孩子們的期望，關掉電視，不能讓手中拿著書本的黑人孩子被別人恥笑是在學白人，否則孩子終將一事無成。不，人們不指望政府解決他們所有的問題。不過他們打從內心深處意識到，只要改變輕重緩急的優先順序，我們就可以確信，每個美國孩子都能擁有生命中適當的機會，機會之門永遠為所有人敞開。他們知道，我們可以做更好。他們想擁有這種選擇的機會。

◎ eradicate（v.）根除、消滅。拉丁文radix是根的意思，e則是否定的字首。radical當名詞用時是指「詞根」，也可以指中文的「部首」。
◎ slander（n.）毀謗、詆毀。

In this election, we offer that choice. Our party has chosen a man to lead us who **embodies** the best this country has to offer. That man is John Kerry. John Kerry understands the ideals of community, faith, and sacrifice, because they've defined his life. From his heroic service in Vietnam to his years as **prosecutor** and lieutenant governor, through two decades in the United States Senate, he has devoted himself to this country. Again and again, we've seen him make tough choices when easier ones were available. His values and his record affirm what is best in us.

 John Kerry believes in an America where hard work is rewarded. So instead of offering tax breaks to companies shipping jobs overseas, he'll offer them to companies creating jobs here at home. John Kerry believes in an America where all Americans can afford the same health coverage our politicians in Washington have for themselves. John Kerry believes in energy independence, so we aren't held **hostage** to the profits of oil companies or the **sabotage** of foreign oil fields. John Kerry believes in the constitutional freedoms that have made our country the envy of the world, and he will never sacrifice our basic liberties nor use faith as a **wedge** to divide us. And John Kerry believes that in a dangerous world, war must be an option, but it should never he the first option.

◎ embody（v.）使具體化、體現。
◎ prosecutor（n.）檢察官。
◎ hostage（n.）人質。

在這次大選中,我們提供了這種機會。民主黨已經推出一位領導者,可以象徵這個國家最佳的選擇。這個人就是約翰·柯瑞。他非常清楚社群、信心與犧牲的理想,因為他的生命就是如此。他曾在越南英勇作戰,擔任多年檢察官和副州長,在美國聯邦參議院服務二十年,把自己獻給這個國家。我們一再看著他在有比較容易的選擇時,往往走上比較艱難的路。他的價值觀與紀錄足以印證我們的最佳特質。

- -

柯瑞認為,在美國,勤奮會得到回報。他不主張為那些將工作機會移往海外的企業寬減稅負,而主張為在國內創造就業機會的企業減稅。柯瑞認為,在美國,人人均應負擔得起華府政治人物享有的醫療保險。柯瑞相信,美國應力求能源自給自足,才不會受制於石油公司的利潤或外國油田遭到破壞的要脅。柯瑞並認為,美國憲法明文保障的自由使美國成為全球各國欣羨的對象,他絕不可能犧牲我們的基本自由,更不可能利用信念離間我們。柯瑞深信,在一個危機四伏的世界,我們必須將戰爭列為選項之一,但它永遠不應該是頭號選項。

◎ sabotage（n.）陰謀、蓄意破壞。sabot是荷蘭人穿的木鞋,此字據說是工廠或鐵路罷工時,工人用木鞋卡住機器或放在鐵軌上而來。
◎ wedge（n.）門擋、楔形物。比喻為導致分裂的東西。

A while back, I met a young man named Shamus at the VFW Hall in East Moline, Illinois. He was a good-looking kid, six-two or six-three, clear-eyed, with an easy smile. He told me he'd joined the **Marines** and was heading to Iraq the following week. As I listened to him explain why he'd **enlisted**, his absolute faith in our country and its leaders, his devotion to duty and service, I thought this young man was all any of us might hope for in a child. But then I asked myself: Are we serving Shamus as well as he was serving us? I thought of more than 900 service men and women, sons and daughters, husbands and wives, friends and neighbors, who will not be returning to their hometowns. I thought of families I had met who were struggling to get by without a loved one's full income, or whose loved ones had returned with a limb missing or with nerves shattered, but who still lacked long-term health benefits because they were **reservists**. When we send our young men and women into harm's way, we have a **solemn** obligation not to **fudge** the numbers or shade the truth about why they're going, to care for their families while they're gone, to tend to the soldiers upon their return, and to never ever go to war without enough **troops** to win the war, secure the peace, and earn the respect of the world.

 Now let me be clear. We have real enemies in the world. These enemies must be found. They must be pursued and they must be defeated. John Kerry knows this. And just as Lieutenant Kerry did not hesitate to risk his life to protect the men who served with him in Vietnam, President Kerry will not hesitate one moment to use our **military might** to keep America safe and secure. John Kerry believes in America. And he knows it's not enough for just some of us to **prosper**. For alongside our famous individualism, there's another ingredient in the American **saga**.

◎ marine（n.）海軍陸戰隊。此字小寫時為形容詞，意思為與海洋有關的。例如marine biology是海洋生物學。
◎ enlist（v.）入伍。
◎ reservist（n.）後備軍人。此字是從reserve（保留、儲備）而來。
◎ solemn（a.）嚴肅的、莊重的、神聖的。這個字帶有宗教意味，天主教修士修女入會時發的大願就是solemn vow。

不久前，我在伊利諾州東莫林的海外作戰退伍軍人協會遇見一個名叫夏穆斯的年輕人。他儀表堂堂，身高約六呎二寸或六呎三寸（約188至190公分），兩眼炯炯有神，笑容可掬。他告訴我，他是陸戰隊員，下星期就要前往伊拉克。他向我解釋從軍的原因，他如何全心信任國家及領袖，如何投入職責與服務時，我心想，這個年輕人真是我們每一個人所夢想的孩子。但我接著自問：我們為夏穆斯所做的，是否對得起他為我們所做的？我想到九百多位男女官兵，他們都是為人子女、為人夫、為人妻、為人友、為人鄰居。這些人再也不會回到家鄉。我想到我遇見的一些家庭。他們必須在家人退伍後全無收入或肢殘，或精神失常的情況下，吃力張羅一家生活所需。這些人因為是後備軍人，無法享有長期醫療健保福利。我們在把年輕男女送入險境時，我們揹負神聖的義務，不捏造數字，或掩飾他們出兵的真相，在他們離家時，代為照顧眷屬，在官兵返國後照顧他們，在沒有確保勝利、鞏固和平、贏得全球尊敬的足夠兵源時絕不作戰。

但容我澄清。在這個世界，我們有真正的敵人，必須找出他們。我們必須找到他們的行蹤，擊敗他們。柯瑞明白這個道理。在越南戰場上，柯瑞中尉為保護同袍而甘冒生命危險。柯瑞總統將毫不遲疑的以我們的軍力捍衛國家安全。柯瑞對美國懷有無比堅定的信心。他知道，一部分人繁榮昌盛還不夠，因為除了我們知名的個人主義之外，美國傳奇另有一種要素。

◎ fudge（v.）捏造、竄改。
◎ troops（n.）軍隊（複數型）。也可用來形容一群（小孩），a troop of（children）。
◎ might（n.）力量、威力。形容詞mighty是有力的，強大的。基督教常說神是almighty，即全能的（all＋mighty）。注意此字與may的過去式同形異義。
◎ prosper（v.）成功、興旺、繁榮。
◎ saga（n.）英雄傳奇、史詩。原義是指中世紀北歐的英雄傳奇故事。

A belief that we are connected as one people. If there's a child on the south side of Chicago who can't read, that matters to me, even if it's not my child. If there's a senior citizen somewhere who can't pay for her **prescription** and has to choose between medicine and the rent, that makes my life poorer, even if it's not my grandmother. If there's an Arab American family being rounded up without benefit of an **attorney** or due process, that threatens my civil liberties. It's that fundamental belief–I am my brother's keeper, I am my sister's keeper –that makes this country work. It's what allows us to pursue our individual dreams, yet still come together as a single American family. "E pluribus unum." Out of many, one.

 Yet even as we speak, there are those who are preparing to divide us, the spin masters and negative ad **peddlers** who embrace the politics of anything goes. Well, I say to them tonight, there's not a liberal America and a conservative America–there's the United States of America. There's not a black America and white America and Latino America and Asian America; there's the United States of America. The **pundits** like to **slice–and–dice** our country into Red States and Blue States; Red States for Republicans, Blue States for Democrats. But I've got news for them, too. We worship an awesome God in the Blue States, and we don't like federal agents poking around our libraries in the Red States. We coach Little League in the Blue States and have gay friends in the Red States. There are patriots who opposed the war in Iraq and patriots who supported it. We are one people, all of us **pledging allegiance** to the stars and stripes, all of us defending the United States of America.

◎ prescription（n.）處方。此處文中prescription是prescription drug（處方藥）的簡稱。動詞prescribe 除了醫囑、開藥的意思之外，也是規定的意思。
◎ attorney（n.）律師。
◎ peddler（n.）兜售者、傳播者、小販。動詞peddle本作沿街叫賣，引申為傳播、宣揚（流言）。
◎ pundit（n.）專家、大師、權威人士。

這個要素就是，我們相信我們是一體的。如果芝加哥南區有某個孩子無法閱讀，這就是我的事情，即使他不是我的孩子。如果某個地方有一位老人家，付不起處方藥的費用，必須在用藥與付房租之間擇一，我會覺得自己太窮，即使她不是我的祖母。如果某個阿拉伯裔美國家庭被捕，卻請不起律師或缺少適當法律程序，我的民權也受到威脅。就是因為這種基本信念：我要守護我的兄弟姊妹，美國才能運作如恆。它使我們得以放手追求個人的夢想，同時又使我們成為一個美國大家庭。「合眾為一」。

然而就在我們正在演說的此刻，部分有心人士隨時準備分化我們。他們擅長捏造，經常散播負面消息，為了政治什麼都可以說。今晚我要對他們說，沒有所謂的自由美國與保守美國，只有美利堅合眾國。沒有什麼黑人美國、白人美國、拉丁裔美國、亞裔美國，只有美利堅合眾國。自命權威者喜歡把我們的美國切割成紅色美國與藍色美國；紅色代表共和黨，藍色代表民主黨。不過我也有話要告訴他們。藍州和紅州崇敬同一個上帝；紅州和藍州一樣也不喜歡在圖書館四處窺伺的聯邦幹員。藍州也打少棒，紅州也有同志朋友。到處都有反對伊拉克戰爭的愛國人士，也有支持戰爭的愛國之士。我們共同構成一個國家，全都效忠星條旗，捍衛美利堅合眾國。

◎ slice-and-dice（v.）Slice和dice都是廚房用語，slice是切片，dice是切丁。但現在也常用在統計上，表示可以把同一份資料用不同的角度做出各項數據。
◎ pledge（v.）發誓、保證。也可做名詞用，即誓言。
◎ allegiance（n.）忠誠、效忠。

In the end, that's what this election is about. Do we participate in a politics of **cynicism** or a politics of hope? John Kerry calls on us to hope. John Edwards calls on us to hope. I'm not talking about blind **optimism** here–the almost willful ignorance that thinks unemployment will go away if we just don't talk about it, or the health care crisis will solve itself if we just ignore it. No, I'm talking about something more **substantial**. It's the hope of slaves sitting around a fire singing freedom songs; the hope of **immigrants** setting out for distant shores; the hope of a young naval lieutenant bravely **patrolling** the **Mekong Delta**; the hope of a millworker's son who dares to **defy** the odds; the hope of a skinny kid with a funny name who believes that America has a place for him, too. The audacity of hope!

In the end, that is God's greatest gift to us, the **bedrock** of this nation; the belief in things not seen; the belief that there are better days ahead. I believe we can give our middle class relief and provide working families with a road to opportunity. I believe we can provide jobs to the jobless, homes to the homeless, and **reclaim** young people in cities across America from violence and despair. I believe that as we stand on the crossroads of history, we can make the right choices, and meet the challenges that face us. America!

Tonight, if you feel the same energy I do, the same urgency I do, the same passion I do, the same hopefulness I do–if we do what we must do, then I have no doubt that all across the country, from Florida to Oregon, from Washington to Maine, the people will rise up in November, and John Kerry will be **sworn in** as president, and John Edwards will be sworn in as vice president, and this country will reclaim its promise, and out of this long political darkness a brighter day will come. Thank you and God bless you.

◎ cynicism（n.）懷疑主義、犬儒主義。此字希臘字根cyno就是狗，據說該哲學學派認為像狗一樣不穿衣服、拋棄家庭和世俗眼光才是幸福。形容詞cynical是憤世嫉俗的、好挖苦的。
◎ optimism（a.） 樂觀主義的。此字的拉丁文字根optimus是「最好」之意，optimize是「最大化」。
◎ substantial（a.）重大的、實在的、基本的。名詞substance有實質、本質之意。
◎ immigrant（n.）移民。Im-是向……內移動，migrate（v.）是遷徙，因此immigrate（v.）就是im+migrate向……境內遷徙，即移民。

歸根究柢,這就是這次大選的重點。我們參與的是犬儒的政治,還是希望的政治?柯瑞號召我們迎向希望。約翰・愛德華茲號召我們迎向希望。我在這裡說的不是盲目樂觀;那種一廂情願,以為只要我們絕口不提,失業問題自會迎刃而解;只要我們視若無睹,醫療健保危機就會自動消失。不,我談的是更重大的課題。它是圍火而坐的奴隸唱著自由之歌時的希望,是移民前往遙遠國度時的希望,是一名年輕的海軍中尉英勇巡弋湄公河三角洲時的希望,是一名工廠工人的兒子不畏逆境的希望,是一個瘦小孩的希望,他相信儘管自己有個古怪的名字,美國還是有他容身之處。無畏的希望!

歸根究柢,這是上帝給我們的最大恩賜,國家的磐石;就是相信還沒有發生的事情,相信未來會更好。我相信,我們一定可以協助我們的中產階級鬆一口氣,為勞動家庭提供一條機會之路。我相信,我們能提供失業者工作,提供無家可歸者房子,並協助美國各地的城市年輕人脫離暴力與絕望的深淵。我相信,在我們站在歷史十字路口的此時此刻,我們絕對可以正確選擇,迎接當前的挑戰。美國!

今晚,如果各位感受到與我相同的活力,與我相同的緊迫感,與我相同的熱忱,與我相同的希望;如果我們為所當為,那麼我相信,美國各地,從佛羅里達州到奧勒崗州,從華盛頓州到緬因州的同胞將於十一月奮起,柯瑞將宣誓就任總統,愛德華茲將宣誓就任副總統,這個國家將重拾承諾;歷經漫長的政治黑暗後,光明的日子將會到來。謝謝各位;上帝保佑你們。

◎ patrol(v.)巡邏、巡查。
◎ Mekong Delta(n.)湄公河三角洲,越戰的戰場之一。
◎ defy(v.)違抗、藐視、反抗。
◎ bedrock(n.)基石、基岩。
◎ reclaim(v.)領回、改過。reclaim…from的話,就是改掉暴力、邪惡等。
◎ be sworn in宣誓就職。sworn是swear(v.)發誓的過去分詞。結拜兄弟就是sworn brother。

第三部分 🏆 文句解析

◎賴慈芸（國立台灣師範大學翻譯研究所助理教授）

這場著名的演講讓歐巴馬聲名鵲起，一夕成為全國知名的政治明星。他當時還只是個芝加哥的民權律師，才在競選參議員。二〇〇四年年底他才第一次選上伊利諾州聯邦參議員。講題「敢於希望」出自芝加哥黑人牧師Jeremiah Wright的一篇佈道詞，但歐巴馬這場演講太過轟動，因此二〇〇六年歐巴馬出版自傳時，仍採用了《敢於大膽希望》作為書名。（繁體字版書名為《勇往直前》〔商周〕，簡體字版則譯為《無畏的希望》〔法律〕，較接近原題目）。Audacity一字本有些微負面意涵，有點膽大包天、莽撞、不顧身分、放肆等意味；但歐巴馬巧妙運用，意思是以前我們黑人不敢做的夢，不敢希冀的夢想，現在都要大聲說出來。與二〇〇〇年雪梨奧運的主題曲"Dare to Dream"〈敢於夢想〉頗有異曲同工之妙。「黑人也可以當美國總統？」這個百年前黑人想都不敢想的奢望，今天還真的成了事實。

第1段有兩個說法都與伊利諾州有關。Crossroads of a nation（全國的十字路口）是指芝加哥，因為芝加哥是全美鐵路樞紐；另一個說法是Land of Lincoln（林肯故鄉）。由於林肯擔任過伊利諾州的州議員和聯邦眾議員，伊利諾州的車牌至今還有Land of Lincoln字樣。歐巴馬常常提及林肯，兩人頗有相似之處：都是律師出身，都先擔任伊利諾州的公職，後來也都當上了美國總統。

第1段後半到第3段，都是歐巴馬自述家世。第3段有不少提到美國歷史的專有名詞，像是The Depression（一次大戰後的大蕭條）、Pearl Harbor（二次大戰的珍珠港事件）、Patton（二次大戰的美國名將巴頓將軍）、GI Bill

（退伍軍人法案，一九四四年通過，補助退伍軍人及家屬受大學教育）、FHA（Federal Housing Administration聯邦房屋署），頗有喚起共同記憶的效果，提醒大家他也是「正港美國人」之後。第四段更引用一七七六年的美國獨立宣言（United States Declaration of Independence）中的名言，提醒聽眾美國偉大的歷史。第五段則是細數民主的好處：人人可以自由發表意見、參政、投票，不必擔心文字獄或祕密警察夜半來敲門，也不必行賄。最後一句是提到二〇〇〇年布希與高爾的票數爭議，所以說「大多數時候都算數」。

第6段進入正題：二〇〇四年美國總統大選。這場大會本是為民主黨的候選人造勢，不過到第八段才出現候選人John Kerry的名字。第6段裡用了政治演說中常見的排比手法：先說we have work to do之後，運用了三次more to do for...。第7段也有些與美國相關的說法，如collar counties是指圍繞芝加哥（像領圈一樣）的五個郡；Pentagon是五角大廈（美國國防部所在地）；inner city是指貧困的內城區，因為美國的中產階級大都住在郊區，內城區開發較早、貧民多、治安差。

第8段細數凱瑞的經歷：越戰英雄、檢察官、副州長、參議員。第九段連用五個John Kerry believes...開頭的句子，慷慨激昂地陳述Kerry的政見。第10段則談對軍人的照顧問題，ＶＦＷ是Veterans of Foreign War的縮寫。其中提到九百多位官兵是當年（二〇〇四年）在伊拉克傷亡的美軍人數。自二〇〇三年美伊戰爭爆發至今，美軍死亡人數已經超過四千人，而伊拉克死傷人數更達十幾萬。

請注意11段結尾與12段開頭是要連在一起看的。11段結尾說，美國以個人主義著名，但美國傳奇中還有另外一個成分：就是12段第一句的A belief that we are connected as one people。接下來幾個「人飢己飢，人溺己溺」的例子都相當能感動人心。本段中I am my brother's keeper典出舊約聖經創世紀：

亞當的長子該隱殺了次子亞伯，耶和華問該隱，你的兄弟亞伯在哪裡？該隱就說，「我豈是看守我兄弟的嗎？」（Am I my brother' s keeper?）後來該隱就受到耶和華詛咒，因為耶和華認為手足應該互相照應。但只講兄弟未免有些性別不正確，因此又講了一句I am my sister' s keeper。近年有一本暢銷書就叫做My sister' s keeper（中譯本書名為《姊姊的守護者》）。E pluribus unum這句拉丁文意為「合眾為一」，印在美國國徽正面那隻鷹嘴上叼的綬帶上，也出現在美國硬幣上，代表美國精神。

12段慷慨激昂地宣示「合眾為一」，13段則抨擊分裂國人的名嘴spin masters、打負面選戰的negative ad peddlers。台灣分藍綠陣營，美國則分藍紅陣營。這段的liberal America、Blue States是指民主黨，conservative America、Red States是指共和黨。但歐巴馬否認這種簡單的二分。一般認為共和黨比較多傳統基督教徒，因此他強調「民主黨州一樣崇敬上帝」；一般認為民主黨比較捍衛個人隱私，他就強調「共和黨州一樣討厭國安局人員刺探隱私」；共和黨的小布希打過少棒聯盟，但「民主黨州一樣支持少棒」；民主黨較支持同性戀，「共和黨也有同性戀的友人」。最後the stars and stripes就是美國國旗「星條旗」，左上角是五十顆星，代表五十州，十三條紅白相間的條紋則代表最初建國時的十三州。

14段開始準備結尾。呼應講題「希望」，這一段出現了九次「希望」，務必確保候選人的名字能引起「希望」的聯想。這段又回溯了歷史：黑奴的希望（林肯的形象又呼之欲出）、移民前來美國時的希望、越戰英雄（John Kerry）、紡織廠工人之子（John Edwards）的希望，最後以自己（有奇怪非洲名字的瘦小孩）作結，再高呼希望無畏。

15段又重提believe是美國最大的資產，一共連用五次believe。最後一段則呼籲大家投票。If you feel the same energy I do這句裡的do即feel。如果你也

跟我一樣，那麼請投民主黨一票，帶國家走出黑暗，步向光明。

全文有奇特的個人傳奇故事（混血背景）、有深厚的美國歷史記憶（林肯、大蕭條、二戰、伊拉克戰爭、奴隸、移民、少棒）、有平民的小故事（軍人、失業的工人與父親、付不起醫藥費的老太太、讀不起大學的女學生）、有呼籲（希望、相信、合眾為一），巧妙交織成動人有力的演說。

國家圖書館預行編目資料

敢於大膽希望：歐巴馬七篇關鍵演說／聯合
報策劃. 編譯 -- 初版. -- 臺北市：寶瓶文化,
2009.04
　　　面；　公分. --（catcher；28）
中英對照
ISBN 978-986-6745-66-9（平裝附光碟片）
1. 英語　2. 讀本
805.18　　　　　　　　　　　　98004525

catcher 028

敢於大膽希望——歐巴馬七篇關鍵演說（附VCD）

策劃・編譯／聯合報
取材自 President Barack Obama In His Own Words，並感謝美國在台協會協助提供文稿

發行人／張寶琴
社長兼總編輯／朱亞君
主編／張純玲・簡伊玲
編輯／施怡年
美術主編／林慧雯
校對／張純玲・陳佩伶・余素維
企劃副理／蘇靜玲
業務經理／盧金城
財務主任／歐素琪　業務助理／林裕翔
出版者／寶瓶文化事業有限公司
地址／台北市110信義區基隆路一段180號8樓
電話／(02) 27463955　傳真／(02) 27495072
郵政劃撥／19446403　寶瓶文化事業有限公司
印刷廠／世和印製企業有限公司
總經銷／大和書報圖書股份有限公司　電話／(02) 89902588
地址／台北縣五股工業區五工五路2號　傳真／(02) 22997900
E-mail／aquarius@udngroup.com
版權所有・翻印必究
法律顧問／理律法律事務所陳長文律師、蔣大中律師
如有破損或裝訂錯誤，請寄回本公司更換
著作完成日期／二〇〇九年二月
初版一刷日期／二〇〇九年四月三日
初版十七刷日期／二〇〇九年四月十七日
ISBN／978-986-6745-66-9
定價／三五〇元

Copyright©2009 by UNITED DAILY NEWS
Published by Aquarius Publishing Co., Ltd.
All Rights Reserved
Printed in Taiwan.

愛書人卡

感謝您熱心的為我們填寫，
對您的意見，我們會認真的加以參考，
希望寶瓶文化推出的每一本書，都能得到您的肯定與永遠的支持。

系列：C028 書名：敢於大膽希望——歐巴馬七篇關鍵演說（附ＶＣＤ）

1. 姓名：＿＿＿＿＿＿＿＿＿＿ 性別：□男 □女

2. 生日：＿＿＿＿年＿＿＿＿月＿＿＿日

3. 教育程度：□大學以上 □大學 □專科 □高中、高職 □高中職以下

4. 職業：＿＿＿＿＿＿＿＿＿

5. 聯絡地址：＿＿＿＿＿＿＿＿＿＿＿＿＿＿＿＿＿＿＿＿＿＿＿＿＿
　　聯絡電話：(日)＿＿＿＿＿＿＿＿＿＿ (夜)＿＿＿＿＿＿＿＿＿＿
　　　　　　(手機)＿＿＿＿＿＿＿＿＿＿

6. E-mail信箱：＿＿＿＿＿＿＿＿＿＿＿＿＿＿＿＿＿＿＿

7. 購買日期：＿＿＿年＿＿月＿＿日

8. 您得知本書的管道：□報紙／雜誌 □電視／電台 □親友介紹 □逛書店 □網路
　　□傳單／海報 □廣告 □其他

9. 您在哪裡買到本書：□書店，店名＿＿＿＿＿＿＿ □劃撥 □現場活動 □贈書
　　□網路購書，網站名稱：＿＿＿＿＿＿＿ □其他＿＿＿＿＿＿

10. 對本書的建議：(請填代號 1. 滿意 2. 尚可 3. 再改進，請提供意見)
　　內容：＿＿＿＿＿＿＿＿＿＿＿＿＿＿＿＿＿
　　封面：＿＿＿＿＿＿＿＿＿＿＿＿＿＿＿＿＿
　　編排：＿＿＿＿＿＿＿＿＿＿＿＿＿＿＿＿＿
　　其他：＿＿＿＿＿＿＿＿＿＿＿＿＿＿＿＿＿
　　綜合意見：＿＿＿＿＿＿＿＿＿＿＿＿＿＿＿＿＿＿＿＿＿＿＿

11. 希望我們未來出版哪一類的書籍：＿＿＿＿＿＿＿＿＿＿＿＿＿＿＿＿

讓文字與書寫的聲音大鳴大放
寶瓶文化事業有限公司

（請沿此虛線剪下）

寶瓶文化事業有限公司　收

110 台北市信義區基隆路一段 180 號 8 樓

8F,180 KEELUNG RD.,SEC.1,

TAIPEI,(110)TAIWAN R.O.C.

（請沿虛線對折後寄回，謝謝）